"A swoony, heartfelt romance that's as delicious as chocolate. You'll fall in love with Whitney, Thierry, and Paris in Stringfield's debut and want to book your own trip to the City of Light." —**Ashley Woodfolk,** *New York Times* bestselling author

"*Love Requires Chocolate* is a sweet, swoony escape with a lot of depth. I loved getting lost in this delightful, affirming romance." —**Elise Bryant,** author of *Happily Ever Afters*

"Infectiously fun and deliciously sweet. *Love Requires Chocolate* is a whirlwind journey of confidence, friendship, and romance that'll leave you charmed, hungry, and racing to book your own trip to Paris!" —**Elle Gonzalez Rose,** author of *Caught in a Bad Fauxmance*

Love REQUIRES CHOCOLATE

A LOVE IN TRANSLATION NOVEL

RAVYNN K. STRINGFIELD

joy revolution

Text copyright © 2024 by Electric Postcard Entertainment, Inc.
Jacket art copyright © 2024 by Bex Glendining

All rights reserved. Published in the United States by Joy Revolution,
an imprint of Random House Children's Books,
a division of Penguin Random House LLC, New York.

Joy Revolution and the colophon are trademarks of Penguin Random House LLC.

In association with

GetUnderlined.com

Educators and librarians, for a variety of teaching tools,
visit us at RHTeachersLibrarians.com

Library of Congress Cataloging-in-Publication Data is available upon request.
ISBN 978-0-593-57154-5 (trade pbk.) — ISBN 978-0-593-57155-2 (lib. bdg.)
ISBN 978-0-593-57156-9 (ebook)

The text of this book is set in 12-point Calluna.
Interior design by Ken Crossland

Printed in the United States of America
10 9 8 7 6 5 4 3 2 1
First Edition

Pour les résidents de la Maison Française
à l'Université de Virginie (2013–2016)
et Professeur Blatt. Merci mille fois.

7 Things I Thought Were True About Paris Before I Arrived in Paris

1. Everyone wears black because they're effortlessly cool. (Note: Add more black to fall wardrobe. Red feels too flashy for Paris. This is unfortunate since my wardrobe has more shades of red than a Sherwin-Williams paint store.)
2. The streets are paved with cheese and wine and chocolate—or at least the shops lining them have all those things—which is perfect since I am absolutely <u>craving</u> some French chocolate!
3. Sexy people with sexy accents are everywhere.
4. Everybody is always kissing. Always. (Except me, obviously. I am here to <u>work.</u> Gotta make Josephine Baker proud of me with this one-woman show, or may my ancestors haunt me forever.)
5. Paris is for culture lovers: lovers of art, lovers of food, lovers of history, lovers of music . . . Anything you could ever want is waiting for you in Paris.

6. French boys <u>invented</u> romance—longing stares and wistful sighs, tasteful compliments and easy flirting. (Again, maybe I don't have time for an epic Parisian love story, with all my sightseeing and writing, but who knows what other kind of stories the city will inspire?)

7. As Nana says, "Paris always holds the promise of a great love story."

SCENE ONE

SOME PEOPLE DON'T APPRECIATE
THE VALUE OF A GOOD LIST!

"Mademoiselle!"

An out-of-breath man's face crowds my phone screen as I slowly turn, capturing the bustling street outside Gare du Nord. The sound of the city is at a reasonable volume, so I can hear myself think. Though, admittedly, all the French landing on my ears is super jarring. I feel like a fish dropped into a huge new tank. Every voice jolts me, because even though I know the language, I can't make my brain translate words fast enough to keep up yet.

The man's face wobbles on the screen as my hand trembles with excitement. *I'm here!*

"Uh, hi!" I say, lowering my phone, then lifting my cat's-eye sunglasses. "Or bonjour! You're kind of in my shot." I point to my phone with what I hope is a charming smile. The man's cheeks are red from the heat, and his expression tells me he is uninterested in my shot.

"Are you Whitney Curry?" His thick accent nearly swallows my name.

"Yes! That's me! The one and only!" I say, my stage smile turning into a real one. I finally notice that he's holding a letter-sized piece of cardstock that has LYCÉE INTERNATIONAL DES ARTS À PARIS (LIA)—**WHITNEY CURRY** printed across it. My name is bolded, and I'm impressed by the fancy school insignia embossed at the top. I wonder if he'll let me have the sign for my memory book.

"I am Monsieur Guillaume Polignac, your ambassador from Lycée International des Arts, Paris, here to escort you to the dormitories." He mops his brow with a handkerchief, and I immediately stick my hand out.

"Enchantée—" I start, but Monsieur Guillaume Polignac cuts me off.

"This way." I try not to bristle at the fact that he ignored my attempt at French. My nose wrinkles at the rudeness anyway, but since he *is* my ride to my new home, I try to keep pace as I follow him up the sidewalk. When we stop at a tiny blue car, he struggles to lift my monogrammed trunk with the letters "W.C." in spiraling white type on the front, and my brown leather valise, mumbling and probably cursing to himself in French.

"What do you have in here—a whole person?"

"Oh, just the essentials," I tell him brightly. "Costumes, accessories, special lights. You know . . . everything a girl needs to thrive. There's no such thing as being overprepared!"

Monsieur Guillaume Polignac raises his eyebrows at me before giving the trunk one last shove to pack it inside. "Such strange luggage."

"It's vintage. Very rare." I climb into the passenger seat and buckle myself in, making sure to pull my braids out from under the seat belt. My heart is thudding against my rib cage, and I do my best to remain still. I want to do my "I'm excited" dance, but a quick glance at my stone-faced driver curbs the impulse.

Monsieur Polignac does not ask any questions, nor does music come on when he starts the car, which is just as well, as it would only interrupt my daydreaming. Before we've even started moving, my mind is buzzing. I am envisioning myself renting a car and driving out to Château des Milandes, the old estate where Josephine Baker spent much of her life with her children, on the weekends I have off from my rigorous Parisian art school schedule. I need to stand where she stood. I need to breathe the same air she did. I need to soak it all up so that one day I might be as iconic as she was.

I'm trying to manifest greatness, but my phone is vibrating in my pocket incessantly, making a grating noise against the car door. Texts flood in from my mom, asking a thousand questions about the flight and reminding me to turn on my location sharing. Another deep inhale and exhale before I dig my phone out and turn it on do not disturb.

Not right now, Mom. I'm drinking in Paris. I try not to think about my mom's anxiety about me traveling alone for the first time and all the fights I had with her that led to this moment. I feel a little guilty that I do consider texting Nana instead, wanting to share this momentous occasion with at least one of them, but I ultimately decide that updating them both will have to wait. I sit back in the seat and think, *I'm soaking up my new life far, far away from Mom's fussing.*

Monsieur Polignac inches through traffic down a picturesque street. You know, like the ones on postcards, with beautiful gardens enclosed by iron lace and cream-colored buildings that could double as elaborate cakes. We pass gorgeous glass storefronts spilling over with perfumes and scarves and purses. Beautiful people window-shop or clutch fresh flowers and baguettes. I even think I catch a glimpse of a chocolate shop. Bicyclists navigate the paths. It all feels like something out of a guidebook of Paris rather than the real thing. Excitement runs like lightning through my body, but I feel a small pit forming in my stomach. There's so much to see. How will one semester be enough time?

"First visit to Paris?" Monsieur Polignac asks.

"Oh, oui," I reply, slowly peeling myself away from the window. "I've wanted to come here my whole life. It's my nana's favorite city. She used to live here." I rattle off Nana's entire artistic career as a relatively well-known performer, singing and dancing throughout Europe and often in New York City in her twenties. But it's not enough to just be the granddaughter of the incomparable Diana Curie. I've got to make a name for myself.

The *legendary* Whitney Curry.

Monsieur Polignac's bushy eyebrows move up and down, and I know I've probably lost him at some point in my speech as we wind down another narrow street. But then his eyes have an unexpected mischievous sparkle, and he makes a turn.

"Well, it's out of the way, but everyone should see it

4

as soon as they arrive . . . ," Monsieur Polignac mutters to himself. After several minutes in thick traffic, the buildings begin to fall away, and I can see the river, the Seine, with boats drifting down it, toting tourists taking photos. This is the river of songs and poems, the one that couples in romance movies walk along together. My heart is so full after these first few minutes in this city, and I'm suddenly sure I know what those lovers in all the classic Parisian-set stories feel.

On the street, people walk, bike, drive, and ride scooters around this busy area, making use of the many bridges to cross to the Left Bank. I have an urgent need to hear the chatter of the boulevards, to be out wandering the streets. I'm here to study, but I'm ready to be among them, getting to know the city as well as I know my audition materials. I consider leaving the window up so as to appear a little bit saner, but one only arrives in Paris for the first time once—and it's imperative to do it right. I roll down the window and let the wind blow across my face as I take pictures with the Polaroid I stuck in my purse. The pit in my stomach starts to shrink, and I imagine it spiraling away like a ribbon in the wind. It's replaced with a molten excitement that electrifies every vein in my body.

We arrive at a bridge with huge winged horses stationed on pedestals on either side, looking infinitely statelier than any of the numerous statues I've seen thus far. All of Paris looks elaborate, elegant, but these lions are positively ornate, and my eyes greedily drink them in.

"C'est le Pont Alexandre III," Monsieur Polignac informs me as we join the line to make a turn to cross the bridge. I lean farther out the window, trying to snap a photo of the sculptures before they are no longer in view. Monsieur Polignac clears his throat. "You will want film for this. . . ." He points ahead and a little to the right.

My mouth drops open.

There, right in front of me, is the Eiffel Tower. Its base is partially obscured by trees and buildings, but the iron structure is unmistakable. It's *tall,* towering above the landscape, sunlight glinting off it. Years of dreaming of this moment, and here I am, zipping across the Seine in a car on the most beautiful bridge in the world, looking at one of the most iconic monuments ever. And with the window down, all I hear is snatches of French—and maybe bits of other languages I can't discern. Folks around the world want to be where I am right now. Before I know it, my throat is tight, and my eyes are itchy as they fill with tears.

I know Monsieur Polignac is looking at me with concern, but I can't hold it in. Tears are streaming down my face, and I hiccup like a baby. I'm overwhelmed in the best way.

"Ça va aller, mademoiselle?" he asks, peeking at me from the corner of his eye.

"Oui, ça va," I reply. "I just want to remember this moment."

And even though the picture I'm about to capture will never tell the full story about how I feel in this moment, I lift my camera to my face to capture it anyway.

"The school is just ahead, near la Sorbonne. We are in le Quartier Latin. You will be but a short walk from the

6

Seine," Monsieur Polignac says after a while. We've passed the Eiffel Tower, where I got a few more pictures and cleaned my face with a handkerchief, courtesy of my guide, who continues weaving us through the city. I get the sense that he's not taking the most efficient route, instead allowing me to see a few more sights, including the edge of the Luxembourg Gardens. We arrive in the fifth arrondissement, and I see lots of school campuses and cafés. Young people who I assume are students sit in front of the cafés, smoking and laughing with their friends, textbooks likely shoved into bags under the tables and forgotten.

There's so much to see, and the prospect is thrilling, but I can already feel anxiety swelling in my chest as I think about navigating these streets on my own. When I first started driving, Mom always joked that I'd get lost going to school. She wasn't wrong. . . .

But that's a Tomorrow Whitney problem. Today Whitney is still experiencing her first Parisian car ride through intense Parisian traffic. The views are definitely worth focusing on.

I pluck my paper map from my bag and trace my short—but tastefully nude-colored—manicure over the different neighborhoods, which coil around each other like a snail shell. I colored in each one and annotated places I wanted to see. "Well, I can check 'experience the Eiffel Tower for the first time' off my list!" And after placing the annotated map on my knees, putting my journal on top of that, and steadying my hand, I do.

"Is that how you will be seeing Paris?" Monsieur Polignac chuckles. "By list?"

"Lists have never failed me. There's nothing wrong

with writing things down and checking them off. Gives me a happy feeling." I wave my list gently in his direction.

"What do you have on there?"

I clear my throat and poke out my chest. I've been researching all summer. Whitney Curry's Epic Parisian Bucket List has been vetted and obsessed over. Ironclad. Thrice approved, by three generations—Nana, Mom, and moi.

I start to read:

"First was see the Eiffel Tower. Then, have a luxurious picnic under it, with cheese and . . ." I cough to cover up the word *wine.*

He laughs.

"Second, visit all the museums, especially the Louvre, of course."

"Bien sûr," he replies.

"Third, spend an entire month investigating all the churches. Notre-Dame, Sacré-Cœur, Sainte-Chapelle, et cetera . . ."

"Et cetera . . ." His eyebrow lifts. "Don't forget that our beloved Notre-Dame is still under construction from the fire. It is not yet open to the public again."

"Oh, right. I will just have to pay my respects from afar. I have every major church marked." I point at the elaborate map, a supplement to the list currently spread out on my lap. "I have to see the Moulin Rouge and learn to make macarons and éclairs. But I'm still investigating the best pastry workshop to attend. Then I'll need to stroll down the Champs-Élysées and stop at all of these shops." I tap my route. "I need to experiment with perfume and make my own and get out to Versailles, and I *have* to visit

8

a chocolatier . . ." My mouth can barely keep up with my list, causing me to nearly stumble over that last item. One of my greatest loves in life—after vintage dresses and midtwentieth-century theater—is *chocolate.* I almost don't want to taste it here; it'll probably ruin chocolate for me for the rest of my life.

"You've got a lot of things you want to do," he says, giving me a look that's somewhere between bemusement and amusement. Either way, I can tell he's done hearing about my list even though I'm not halfway through.

I am nothing if not prepared to have the best semester of my life, starting with checking off everything on my Parisian bucket list. Most of it is for research purposes (that just happen to be lifelong dreams), which will inform the writing and execution of a fantastic one-woman senior thesis show, something my nana would be proud of.

He glances over at me before turning left down a dead-end street. The shrubbery falls away for a moment, and I can see a soccer field filled with boys about my age chasing a black-and-white ball. One boy sneakily cuts across the group and kicks the ball in the opposite direction, causing the rest to yell in protest. The boy's focused face is disrupted by the barest grin, which causes me to smile.

Monsieur Polignac notices me watching and finishes his thought: "You will discover more if you wander. This is the type of city where magic can be found in the most unlikely places. People miss it when they run around the city with their guidebooks and websites."

I nod and smile. Whatever.

He's not a believer in the power of lists.

And he's missing out.

I could never leave my study-abroad experience up to chance. Magic is made, not discovered.

He points. "Et voilà!"

At the end of the cobblestone road is a massive building the color of cream, with bright shutters, iron balconies, and rose-colored window boxes spilling over with flowers. A gingerbread house. That's the first thing that pops into my head. Something out of a fairy tale.

"Welcome to the Lycée International des Arts!"

I look up. The warm light from the window washes over us.

"Welcome home, Whitney Curry," I whisper to myself. I take a steadying breath and open the car door.

SCENE TWO

LESS INNER MONOLOGUE, MORE VERBAL FILTER

There's so much more to see on my way to my room. I stop in my tracks every few feet, admiring the view from a window, a glorious painting of the French countryside hanging on the wall, the room we pass filled from floor to ceiling with books. I am imagining myself walking these halls with a stack of plays tucked under my arm and chatting with friends when the most elegant double staircase I have ever seen in my life makes me pause to catch my breath. Monsieur Polignac doesn't see me stop and stumbles over my trunk. *Whoops.* He grumbles, and I turn back to give him an apologetic smile.

"Sorry, this is just so *decadent*," I say. I lose myself in a new daydream of dressing up in a beautiful vintage dress with a full skirt, a fascinator, and a pair of lacy gloves, twirling and dancing between the stairs. There's a swarm of photographers clamoring for my photo as I go, of course.

I'm making a mental note to make a real note about my

idea when a grunt to my left breaks the reverie as Monsieur Polignac hefts my trunk and starts for the left set of stairs.

"Okay," he grunts. "Allons-y."

"Huh?" Again, my brain hasn't switched to French yet.

"Come along, Mademoiselle Curry." Monsieur Polignac has already nearly reached the top of the first set of stairs. "Let us get you to your room."

It turns out that my room is on the sixth floor—a fact I regret as I watch Monsieur Polignac blow out a huge breath, dropping my trunk outside room 5A. I wince, hoping my lights are still intact.

Not what matters most, Whitney, I remind myself.

"Here you are," Monsieur Polignac says, dabbing at his forehead with his handkerchief. "I will leave you to settle in."

He drops a key in my hand and gives me a kinder, though still a bit hesitant, look before lumbering back down the hall—albeit massaging his lower back as he goes.

I glance at the door to my room, which has three names—Nora Belaïdi, Sophie Bernard, and Whitney Curry—written on slips of paper and taped to it underneath the little painted "5A." A wave of anticipation and excitement washes over my body.

Before I can reach for the doorknob, the door swings open. There's a tall, willowy white girl with feathery, long blond hair in the doorway, and behind her I can see another girl sitting on a twin bed near a window with light brown skin and curly dark hair pulled back into a ponytail.

"Hi!" I say, giving the two a megawatt smile. "Or should I say, salut! You must be my roommates!"

The girls exchange quick glances.

"Hello, I am Nora," the blond says, her French accent thick and throaty. She has striking blue eyes. "I am in the dance program, and I am from Belgium." *Good,* I think. If this girl were in the theater track, she would have directors fawning all over her. I notice that, almost immediately, Nora has dropped herself back into her desk chair to continue video chatting with a very pretty Black girl she must have been talking to before I popped in.

I see the girl on the screen cut her eyes at me, and though they are speaking French, I understand the essence: *Who is she?*

"This is our roommate, Fatima, since you decided to leave us at the last minute," Nora tells her in English—on purpose, I assume, to make sure I understand.

Got it, I think. *I'm not supposed to be here. I am not a first-choice roommate.* I'm struck by the intensity of the moment, but I decide to push it away. I can't let this get to me. So I turn my attention to the other girl in the room and revive my smile as Nora and the girl on the screen—Fatima—finish their quick, whispered conversation in French.

"I'm Sophie," the girl on the bed offers more or less indifferently. "Switzerland. Composing." She's also very pretty but shorter, with light brown skin and hair that curls out from under the headphones she's wearing around her neck.

"Well, amazing! I'm Whitney Curry, theater track, United States." I want to keep introducing myself, but the urge to dissect the cold welcome I just got from Nora is warring with my desire to document the entry into my new life. "Hang on."

I pull my trunk and valise into the room by the only

bed that hasn't been made up yet, in the far corner by the closet and another window. Then I fish my lavender Polaroid camera out of my satchel purse, fastening the metal clasp at the top when I'm done.

I snap a shot of the room at large, the beds by the windows, the desks next to them. There's nothing on the floor or on the walls yet—just a few unopened suitcases. Nora and Sophie must have gotten here right before me.

"I know we'll be busy with school, but I have *so* much I want to do. Do you think it's too ambitious to try every chocolate shop in the city?" I point the camera at the name tags on the door and snap another shot.

Sophie and Nora are quiet; Fatima, I notice, is still on Nora's computer screen, and she's watching me, too. My eyes flit over to them, and my inherent and inconvenient need to fill silence kicks in, so I continue. "I might see if I can find this shop near here—I made a list of all the cafés and pâtisseries walkable from the school." I dive into my satchel again for my colorful map of Paris so that I can show it to them. A couple of my emergency tea lights fall onto the floor with the map. A nervous chuckle escapes me, but still, the girls are giving me *nothing* to work with. I might as well be talking to marble statues. The thought makes me a little itchy.

"But first I *have* to change," I say, gesturing to my general state of disarray while giggling. To my horror, I can't stop. "Nothing worse than keeping on an airplane outfit. I literally have no idea how people make 'travel chic' work." I start shimmying out of my pants. Nora's and Sophie's brows furrow—finally some kind of response—and that does make me crack a tiny grin. One thing about theater kids: we aren't precious about changing in front of people.

I have to do a little dance to get my clean shorts over my butt. They're figure flattering, but the waist doesn't quite accommodate my ample backside, which makes getting them on a tiny hassle. The things I do for beauty.

At this point, I see Nora whisper a quick goodbye to Fatima and shut her laptop. The gesture makes me start talking again before I have a chance to overthink how I might have come across to the should've-been-roommate.

"Is there a mirror?" I ask, but before either of my roommates can respond, I notice a full-length mirror on the inside of one of the closet doors. "Parfait!" I turn to check myself out from a few different angles, trying to surreptitiously steal a few glances at my roommates in the glass. My hands find my braids and twist them into a low bun, just for something to do.

There are two large windows in the room. The one between Nora's and Sophie's beds looks out to the side of the school, and the one near my bed and the closets looks over the courtyard. I peer out of it as I do my hair. There's a beautiful manicured lawn with neatly planted flowers and hedges, populated by an actual birdbath and some adorable park benches—the kind with iron spirals for arms.

"It's like we're living in the house from *Madeline*," I say, half to myself. Then I spin back to my roommates. "So! Chocolate, anyone?"

My smile wilts a little when I realize that Nora and Sophie are glancing at each other, Nora's expression a slightly deeper frown than Sophie's. I bite my lower lip. I could sense that I was doing too much, and yet their reaction still makes my stomach drop. Sophie stands slowly from the bed and walks over to Nora as if trying not to startle me, fearing that any sudden movements might kick me into overdrive again.

Yikes, I think. *Nice one, Curry. Really gotta find that off switch.*

"We . . . need to go check something with Monsieur Polignac," Sophie says. Her accent is less pronounced than Nora's, but I still admire the way *Polignac* sounds as it rolls off her tongue. I never could get that "gn" sound right in class—another thing to add to my Things I Want to Improve On list. "See you later."

Sophie takes Nora by the hand, but the blond doesn't need much encouragement. She follows Sophie out of the room, closing the door with a light click.

"Okay . . . ," I sigh, my shoulders dropping. "That went well."

I shake it off. Literally. A full-body shimmy to rid myself of any nervous energy that lingers from my awkward first encounter with my new roommates, accompanied by a huge breath. Nana says a good deep breath will always do the trick. So far in my life, she's been right: her advice has cured me of stage fright, given me the confidence I needed to propose this trip to my parents, even helped me drift off to sleep on nights when my mind won't stop spinning. So now, a good deep breath will help me get a handle on my nerves. It was always the plan to go to Paris, but getting unbearably overwhelmed and freaking out my roommates, who clearly did not have a talkative American girl in mind to round out their trio, was not. In fact, they were planning on someone else entirely.

Perspective, I think, drawing my shoulders back and lifting my chin. So what if today wasn't the grande entrée I had in mind? It's okay that even the best things, like actually living my dream life, come with more than a few big feelings in practice. I think it's okay that I don't know how to process it all just yet. I just got here. It's okay to give myself a minute.

And yeah, I know I can be a little . . . *much.* But ultimately, everyone comes around and sees me for the absolutely *delightful* ray of sunshine I am.

Eventually.

I settle at my desk, pulling my satchel over from my bed to start placing some of my dearest treasures along the small shelf over it. A photo of Nana performing at a Parisian cabaret in the seventies. The lavender Polaroid camera. My already-stuffed leather journal, into which I slip my boarding passes for this trip.

Satisfied with my little display, I look up and out the window on my side of the room. Night is falling, and the sky is on fire with bright reds and oranges near the horizon, blossoming into blue above. I can see a star or two beginning to shine, competing with the setting sun for the spotlight.

I correct myself. They're not competing. Their luminance is unique, and their shines are for different times. They share the stage and make each other more beautiful.

As I think this, a new light catches my attention. My phone's lit up with another text flurry from my mom. I rattle off a quick message to let her know that I got to my new school—LIA—safely and that I'll call once I've unpacked and settled in a bit more.

After receiving a thumbs-up emoji from my mom, my phone calms down, and I swipe over to another text thread.

It's from Archi, my best friend, who is already preparing for her own study-abroad experience next semester in Rajasthan, India. Our high school in DC prioritizes semester- and year-long study-abroad trips that align with our specific research projects. I was supremely lucky to get into the theater track in this elite Parisian art exchange program. My theater cohort is only five high schoolers from around the world, though the whole program comprises dance, visual art, composing, and musical performance cohorts as well.

Archi was accepted into a program focused on art history and museum curation. Knowing her, she's already packing, even though her trip is still a few months away. She's sent a quick selfie with pieces from a new scrapbook she's working on, her grin taking up the entire screen.

Archi: Wish I was there with you!

I smile.

Whitney: No, you're right where you're supposed to be. Let's video chat soon!

Yup, she's right where she's supposed to be, and so I am. Whitney Curry, an American in Paris.

". . . And if you can, take a crossbody purse and kind of pull it to the front of your body so that pickpockets have a harder time grabbing it."

I'm in the library on the first floor, surrounded by shelves of hardback books with gilded edges. It's old but cozy, made brighter by handcrafted rugs on the floor and long couches that might have been in style around the turn of the twentieth century. The couches are gorgeous but also fairly uncomfortable, so I've tucked my legs under my butt as I sit on the end of one of them and lean my upper body against the hard arm of it to talk to my mother on video chat.

"Sure," I say absentmindedly, adjusting an earbud and shifting a little so the light from the lamp I'm sitting next to falls more on my face. "Although I kind of think that if a pickpocket wants to steal your stuff, you're just out of luck."

There's silence on the phone. I can only see the top of Mom's ponytail as she rummages in her chest of drawers for an exercise top, but I can almost hear her face stretch into an expression of the utmost disapproval. Guilt immediately tugs at my stomach.

"Whitney," Mom begins firmly once she's back in the frame. Even though it's just after working hours for her back in DC and any sane person would be getting ready to stretch out on the couch and binge some TV shows, enjoying the silence of a teenager-free house, my mother is about to go running.

Who does that?

"This was part of the agreement," she continues as she quickly changes out of her DC-litigations-lawyer work clothes—a navy suit and cream blouse today—and slips into her exercise wear. "I let you go to Paris, and you do everything you can to be safe."

"Mom, I know," I sigh, letting my head fall back against the couch, which has carved wood detailing along the top, making for a harder bump than I was prepared for. "But the *constant* stream of cautions is making me more nervous than just being here. I get it, you want me back in one piece. *I* want me back in one piece, too! But you're gonna fry my nerves before I even get a chance to go anywhere or do anything."

I don't mention how her anxieties on top of my own are too much for my body to take. I try to make my voice level and smooth, no judgment, which I know Mom appreciates. My efforts have succeeded when she sniffs sharply, the nostrils on her brown face flaring.

"I understand," she says, pulling off the severe-looking black-rimmed rectangular glasses she only ever wears for work.

I wait, because once I've given my side, I always let Mom take some time to give hers. Sometimes we can meet in the middle, often we don't, but at least most of the time we try to understand where the other person is coming from.

"Baby, I know your nana goes anywhere and does anything she wants because God made her without a desire to use the good sense He gave her." Being caught in the middle of Nana and Mom's bickering is one of my life's biggest trials, but this time I let the dig at Nana slide without comment. It's worth it, because when she continues, her voice has softened. "Your nana takes lots of risks that I'm just not built to understand or take for myself. And you might be a lot like me, but you're also a lot like her. Brave.

Adventurous. Willing to explore the world. I'm fine right where I am. Your travel bug? I don't have it, so you gotta be patient with me while I figure out how best to support you now." I know Mom would never stop me from doing something I really want to do, but her fear might have held her back for a while. I can forgive her an overprotective streak; she's doing her best. And so am I.

I get it. And she's right. I inherited my mom's hips and thighs, her grin and long hair; if I can trust genetics, I'll still be a knockout when I'm in my forties. And there's nothing we both love more than a trip to a stationery store for our list-making needs. To date, she and I have never been late for an engagement, save for church one time when I was fifteen—and that was only because before the divorce, Dad had actually been home that weekend and in less than twenty-four hours had managed to misplace his favorite ties.

But for the quirk that Mom didn't get, my love of vintage fashion and the glamour of the stage, Nana is always there to pick up the slack. Nana is the one who took me to buy my own stage makeup during my first high school play in the ninth grade, when all the theater department had was crusty junk that only matched the white kids' skin tones. She's the one who took me to see Alvin Ailey for the first time for my thirteenth birthday; we got dressed to the nines and strolled into the Kennedy Center like we owned the place. And when Mom hesitated to let me do this study-abroad trip, Nana's the one who bought my plane ticket and emailed the details to my mother so she wouldn't have an excuse to stop me.

I got the best of both of them, but Nana's traveling spirit propelled me across the Atlantic.

"I want you to have the best time," she says finally as she walks down the stairs in our house toward the front door, ready to start her run. I feel a pang of something that can't be homesickness because I just got here. My mom smiles at me. "And remember to be safe."

And I promise her that I, the queen of multitasking, can absolutely do both.

After I hang up with my mother, go upstairs for a quick shower, and do a round of speed unpacking, I tuck myself into my bed, wondering if this is really my life. I feel the urge to talk to someone about it, but Nora and Sophie were already asleep by the time I made it to our room, and judging by how our meeting went earlier in the day, I don't think waking them up mid-REM sleep will do me any favors. I sigh and turn onto my side.

If I wiggle to the edge of the bed, I can see out the window. On the ground, quaint lamps cast the garden in a soft glow, and in the sky, the stars have taken over for the sun. Maybe I'm imagining it, but it feels like I can see more of them here than I ever could at home. More stars, more wishes, right?

As I stargaze, I create a new list for my journal.

Promises to Myself I Have to Keep

1. I will have a first day for the history books.
2. I will be grateful for every step of this adventure.
3. I will never take this view for granted.

22

SCENE THREE

ENTER MONSIEUR GRUMPY THIERRY

The sun is assaulting me when I wake up groggily the next morning. I mean, it's blazing right into my face. I make a mental note to pull down the blinds before I go to sleep tonight. It'll help dial down the morning rage. I bury my face in my pillow to block out the light.

Wait. . . . The sun shouldn't be this aggressive at seven a.m.

I grab my phone and huff. It's well past eight a.m. on my first day of classes, and I had a whole plan to be up with the Parisian sunrise.

I blink away the prickling feeling of sleep in my eyes. *Small setback, Whitney,* I think. *There's still plenty of time to turn this day around.* Even though it's later than I planned, I still have a full hour to get ready, swing by registration, and grab some breakfast before my first class.

I sit up in bed, throwing my covers away from me. Nora's and Sophie's beds are empty, the spreads pulled up neatly, their bags gone from their desks. I groan when I realize they didn't bother to wake me up. Granted . . . they *were* asleep when I got back last night. Even though my rational brain has kicked in when I eventually get out of bed, I'm still fuming a little when I make it to the shower down the hall. After a quick wash-up and skin-care routine, I hustle back to my room. The room, which felt small when Sophie, Nora, and I were in here together last night, suddenly threatens to swallow me whole. It takes a moment of searching my mind before I find the silver lining, but it's there: the good news is I can put on my Édith Piaf playlist at maximum volume and waltz around my room as I get ready, with no side glances. I smile as the opening notes of "La Vie en Rose" waft lightly through the room. The music makes the room feel cozy and enfolds me in memories of Mom, Nana, and me perched on Nana's wraparound porch at her house just outside DC.

I've been thinking about my outfit for my first full day in Paris for weeks. It's a lucky thrift store find from earlier in the summer: a white halter-top dress with wide lapels, a full skirt that blooms into swirls around my calves when I walk, and a matching belt that cinches my waist. I slip it on, then arm myself with jewelry: a pair of understated gold hoops Nana gifted me a few Christmases ago, a locket with a photo of my parents together a couple of years before I was born, and a thin watch with a square face and leather band. I tug on a pair of white kitten heels, sweep half of my braids up into a knot behind my head, and throw my journal, camera, and phone into my satchel. A few swipes of mascara, a pair of carefully drawn winged lines on my eyelids, and a dab of deep red lipstick later, I'm ready to go.

It's a gorgeous Parisian day when I set off down the path lined with tiny smooth stones that leads across the courtyard to the administrative building, which is my first stop. I'm supposed to get a physical copy of the information I was emailed a few weeks ago, with new details added. My schedule has already been built, full to the brim with every drama, music, and literature class LIA has to offer—okay, as many as I could realistically fit in—but classroom numbers and locations may have changed.

The sun is just barely hidden behind billowy white clouds, and birds chirp and chase each other overhead. I do a tiny skip-hop number, thinking this must be how Belle felt walking through her town in *Beauty and the Beast.*

Though I have no intention of falling in love with a beast. Or falling in love at all. I am laser focused on what I came here to do. My two main goals: one, complete every activity on my Parisian bucket list, and two, put on the best one-woman show known to man for my senior thesis. In that order. There is no show without a solid amount of firsthand research, right?

Easy.

I reach the administrative building, fully ready to collect my final schedule and do some serious game planning. I swing open the door, calling "Bonjour!" as the rusted door handle comes off in my fist.

I freeze, horrified to have broken a literal antique on my supposed-to-be-perfect first day at school, and then look from the handle to the man sitting behind the desk in the lobby. His head, which is covered in light dustings of fluffy gray and white hair, is cocked curiously, lines appearing on his tan forehead as he appraises me.

My eyes widen, and I cover my mouth with my free hand. "Oh, I—" I try, then switch to broken, hesitant French. "Désolée! Je . . . n'ai pas . . . intendée—" I try not to get flustered as my French—which, admittedly, isn't the best on a good day and in a less stressful context— completely crumbles in my mouth. I know it isn't the right phrasing but my brain isn't helping me fix the situation, so I'm left standing there, searching for a phrase, letting my mouth open and close as I start and stop sentences.

The man stands and comes around the desk, letting out a light chuckle. "Je n'ai pas fais exprès . . . is the right way to say this, but it is okay," he says, his voice scratchy but warm like a wool cardigan. "This is old. It falls off every day." He reaches for the handle, which I gladly part with. "Are you a new student?"

"Yes," I offer eagerly, feeling relief at actually being able to communicate with him. "I'm an exchange student from America—Virginia, just outside Washington, DC. It's my first day."

He nods gently, and I feel his warmth and calm in my chest. I love people like this, people who can make you feel right at home no matter where you are.

"You will want Cécile," the man says, pointing to a door down the hall and to the right. He returns to his seat, setting the handle on the desk.

"Thank you." I beam at him, getting a twinkle of dark eyes in response. "I mean, merci."

I start off toward the door the man pointed out but turn back quickly. "Oh, wait, what's your name, sir?"

"I am Henri," he replies. "Just Henri."

"Enchanté," I reply, dipping into a slight curtsy. "I'm Whitney. Whitney Curry."

Henri bows his head. "Good luck, Whitney Curry."

I give him a little wave and finish the short walk to the head administrator's office. After my door handle incident I'm less inclined to go for another dramatic entrance, but I gather myself and step brightly and deliberately into the room.

Tapping away at a computer is a blond woman with her hair cut into a severe bob and wiry glasses perched on the tip of her nose.

I open my mouth to speak, but the phone rings. A millisecond later, she's snatched it up. "Allô?"

Then she sees me and holds up one finger. She replies to whoever is on the other end of the call with a long string of fast French that I can't decipher, pauses for a moment, then says, "Okay. Merci. À demain." Then she resets the phone on its docking station.

"Hi," I say as soon as she looks my way again. "I'm Whitney Curry. I'm an exchange student this semester at LIA, and I'm here to check in."

Cécile seems like the kind of person who stays even-keeled and unflappable. She barely gives me a second glance as she pulls a green folder from a stack next to her desktop and hands it to me.

"Fill these out," she says quickly. "Ensure everything we have listed for you—contact information, emergency numbers—is correct. Return the top three sheets to me, and the rest you may keep. Your class schedule is on the second page in your welcome packet. Each exchange student is assigned a French language tutor, and your tutor's information may be found on page five. A map of the campus is on the left side of your folder."

"'Kay, got it," I say, nodding briskly. I respect her efficiency, a woman after my own heart. Cécile grabs a pen out of the cup on her desk and offers it to me, but I'm already pulling my purple fountain pen from my satchel. I find that fountain pens are better than regular ballpoint ones for important documents—to-do lists, script ideas, and filling out essential paperwork.

I uncap the pen and write "W" on the line beside "nom" on the first form, giving it a stylish flourish to set the right tone, when something very solid jostles me. My jaw drops as I register the damage: a huge line across the paper from where the "h" starts.

"Are you kidding me?" I huff. "It's ruined!"

There's a small snort from behind me. "That is a bit dramatic, no? It is hardly ruined."

Dramatic? Me? I may shine onstage, but in real life, that is *not* a word I appreciate. How is it that we can use such a precious word, born in theater and art, and turn it into a sexist insult?

I whirl around, anger flooding my head like it's about to burst into flames, and find myself nearly face to face with a frowning, dark-skinned Black boy about my age. Well, face to throat, as he's got a good six inches on me. It almost unsettles me, but I gather myself.

"Listen," I begin, taking a tiny step forward with the intent to make him cede ground, but the boy squares his broad shoulders and folds his arms over his chest, standing firmly rooted, full lips still pulled down in a grimace.

Cécile's typing doesn't slow, but I can feel her gaze on my back, watching the storm forming in her office. "I've been here less than a day, and I already alienated my roommates and I really don't know why. Then I broke a building I'm pretty sure is a Parisian landmark."

"You broke a—?"

"Not finished," I say. He raises his eyebrows but falls silent. "Now, you may not respect the sanctity of a first day, but in my world, first days set the tone—and this one is not just for my first week or month, no, but for my whole semester. If things go well here, this trip could *change my life*. This is an auspicious occasion, and you, sir, are ruining it!"

The boy doesn't respond. I fold my arms over my chest, matching his stance and returning his challenging look. He doesn't move, and I give him a once-over—not enough to get a good sense of him but enough to know that he is *very* cute, and he has some great shoes.

His mouth—previously pursed in a line—twitches like he wants to laugh, and I narrow my eyes again, daring him to.

Finally, he clears his throat and rubs a hand across the back of his head, which is covered with short, neatly formed twists. "Well, I think perhaps you may have bigger problems if your day can be ruined by one tiny mishap," the boy says. He rolls his dark brown eyes. The glare I shoot him should have him shaking in his boots, but he's peering around me at Cécile, who, to her credit, has not changed her expression throughout this whole exchange.

Then he says something in French that I don't understand. When I stare at him blankly, he shoots back a look of mild disdain. My nose wrinkles in reaction to the patronizing response I'm getting for not having great French language skills—yet.

"Et elle ne parle pas français—c'est génial," he adds, before switching to English. "I am only here to get my last tutoring assignment, and then I will be out of your way."

"Well, good timing," Cécile says with the barest hint of a smile on her face. "Thierry Magnon, meet Whitney Curry—your tutoring assignment."

I blink rapidly, stunned. The boy's frown deepens. Cécile has a touch of humor in her eyes, which irritates me. I have to stop myself from wishing her deeper frown lines.

Then I collect myself. I hear *You've got good sense, Whitney; act like it* in my mom's voice echoing in my head—a reprimand I hate, so I plaster a smile on my face and will it to stop.

"Where are my manners?" I chirp. "It's lovely to meet you." Now is a perfect opportunity to try out some French mannerisms, so I lean forward and try to air-kiss near both of his cheeks. But the motion startles him, so he backs up quickly, tripping over his feet and toppling into the chair behind him, knocking his head against the wall with a dull thud.

"Oh, my gosh!" I say, panicked. "Are you concussed?" I turn to Cécile. "Will I get kicked out of study abroad for accidentally concussing my tutor?"

Cécile makes a noncommittal shrug, only half glancing over her screen to see if my injured tutor is okay. I turn back to him, only to find him grimacing and rubbing the back of his head.

"Are all Americans so dangerous?" he asks. "Or is it just you?"

Great! This day just keeps getting better and better.

4 Things I (Already) Hate About Thierry Magnon

1. He's rude! I didn't actually believe the whole "French people are rude" thing until Thierry proved that it is, indeed, factual. This is totally antithetical to the "French boys _invented_ romance" thing; there is _nothing_ romantic about this grouchy smart-ass.
2. He doesn't respect universal truths about the sacredness of first days—or penmanship, apparently!
3. He thinks he can go around calling girls "dramatic." What he's actually doing is belittling my feelings and trying to make me believe that my emotions aren't valid. News flash: they are. Men are always trying to convince women that they're hysterical—I paid attention when we read "The Yellow Wallpaper" in English last year.
4. He's smug! He thinks just because he's got the nicest pair of sneakers I've seen so far on this side of the Atlantic, he can do/say whatever he wants. I accidentally concuss him _once,_ and he thinks he's so much better than me. But I don't care what Thierry Magnon thinks of me. If he looks at me like that again, I'm gonna scuff his shoes.

SCENE FOUR

BREAKFAST AT THIERRY'S

The boy—Thierry—finishes massaging his head and glowers. "I suppose you cannot switch assignments?" He glances at me skeptically as he rises from the chair and wipes a hand down the front of his hoodie.

"Hey!" I say indignantly. "What are *you* mad about? *I'm* the one who should be mad and asking for a switch!" I turn to Cécile. "I will need an immediate transfer to another tutor, s'il vous plaît and merci."

"You made me trip. I could have gotten hurt."

"You should've just held still!" I say impatiently. "I was doing the thing! Faisant la bise!"

"How was I to know that?"

"Seriously? You're French!"

Cécile's head swivels back and forth between us and sighs. "No switching. You will come to an agreement . . . outside."

She goes back to her desktop and immediately begins

tapping away as if the two of us never interrupted her to start with.

"Okay, I guess that means we're dismissed," I say, but I turn to find I'm speaking to no one. Thierry's evaporated.

I snatch my folder off the counter and leave the office, ready to scour the grounds for Thierry, but when I glance to my left he's sitting on a bench muttering to himself and bouncing his leg. He's doing it so fast, it's giving me mild motion sickness, though I get that he's upset.

Now that we're not in a heated exchange or trying to figure out if we need to take him to the hospital, I can get a good look at Thierry. He's got dark brown skin that is well moisturized, by the way it catches the fluorescent light in the hallway, and perfect twists—fresh, too, judging by the tightness of them. His outfit is understated: he's got on a black hoodie pulled over a white T-shirt and a pair of black joggers. Respectable. The shoes are what sets it off: a red pair of Air Force 1s. Spotless. I take a deep breath to apologize, but before I can, he speaks up.

"I do not even *want* to do this," he spits. I do a quick sweep to see who he's talking to, but he's alone in the hall. *Anger management, much?* "And of course, I am paired with an American princess."

I jolt. *Who's he calling a princess?*

"Um, one, not a princess," I interrupt. "Two, enough with the sexist insults, thanks. And three, hello, I'm right here!"

He peers at me out of the corner of his eye and groans, clutching his head between his hands like he's got a headache. At least the leg bouncing has momentarily ceased.

"My voice cannot be that grating," I say, rolling my eyes. "I've been told I sound like young Marilyn Monroe."

Thierry rolls his eyes in return. "Explain to me how you are not a princess?"

"Well, you aren't exactly Prince Charming, are you?" I shoot back. "Do you make a habit of going around ruining nice girls' days?"

"Are you always so loud?"

"Are you always so rude?"

We enter into a glaring contest, which I win when he inhales sharply and breaks his gaze. And of course as soon as I turn away, I notice my missing roommates walking together down the hallway, watching me and Thierry with what I might call conspiratorial interest.

"I did not *ask* to be a tutor," he retorts bitingly, pulling me back to the scene. The words deflate him as they come out of his mouth, and he slumps back against the wall. Thoughts of Nora and Sophie are long gone as I wait for him to continue.

His head hangs a bit, and then after a moment, he softens, his jaw unclenching, donning an expression that makes him appear younger than he probably is. I tap my toe against the hardwood floor as I weigh my options. On the one hand, this boy has made a mess of my morning. On the other . . . he does look really sad.

I straighten up before going around him and perching myself on the other end of the bench. I will myself to find a crumb of patience for this boy because I know my mother would insist that if I am nothing else in this world, I must do my best to be kind.

"Fine, I'll bite," I say. With the haze of anger gone, I can fully appreciate what a stately profile he has as I study him. "If you don't want to be a tutor, why are you here?"

Thierry glances at me and huffs out a short laugh.

"And you are nosy, too? Wonderful," he says.

I sigh. "You know what, forget it. This was a mistake. I'm going to see if I can't find the café for breakfast." I get up and head toward the front door.

I don't slow down even though I can hear his footsteps following me.

I wave to Henri as I march out. He looks up from his cup of coffee to give a small smile.

I take a few more determined strides, until I land in the gravel path again, and then stop in my tracks. I don't give Thierry enough warning, and he runs into me. Again.

"You've apparently got a lack of coordination skills to match your attitude," I say.

Thierry rubs his eyes with one hand, not even trying to mask his frustration. "Okay, I'm leaving."

"No, wait." I grit my teeth. "I don't actually know where the café is."

He squints, trying to keep the morning sun out of his eyes. Then, without a word, he sets off across the court-yard diagonally from the administrative office toward a smaller one-story building the same cream color as the school.

Thierry turns back. "Are you coming?"

With a sigh, I follow.

The Lycée International des Arts café is more like your typical American dining hall than I was expecting, filled with long tables and a buffet-style line, but my disappointment is chased away before it can settle by the aroma of warm, buttery bread and coffee. Thierry leads me through a maze of tables and chairs toward a case filled with a modest assortment of breads and breakfast pastries.

My stomach rumbles as I appraise the choices: golden brown baguettes stand tall in their lined basket next to the case, little brioche buns line the bottom of the display, and a few fruit-filled spirals and turnovers take over the top. In the middle is a selection of the most delectable croissants I have ever seen.

This is no prepackaged business like we get in the United States. The croissants I know from grocery stores at home often look wilted, soft, and a little chewy. But these? These are so exquisitely honey brown, the color must only exist in France, and they look plump yet delicate. The whole row is a tiny battalion of buttery perfection compared to the misshapen things I'm used to.

I stop salivating long enough to see Thierry staring at me. *Why is he looking at me like that . . . ?* But then I realize I've got my hands pressed to the glass case with my nose no more than an inch away.

I remove my hands and clasp them behind me. He gives me another one of those odd looks. I've only known him for about fifteen minutes, so I can't be sure, but I don't think that's a face reserved for people he likes. Especially since he hasn't shown me a smile or any gesture of friendliness even *once* since we met. It feels like I'm getting off on the wrong foot with everyone here. Maybe I'm not everyone's cup of tea, but I've always at least been *someone's*!

"It's not the best breakfast in Paris, but Mathilde makes

very good coffee," Thierry tells me, breaking me out of my little musing.

"Who?" I ask, but no sooner does the word leave my mouth than a short young woman with light brown skin, bright gray eyes, and thick, dark curly hair trapped in a hairnet barrels through the swinging door behind the counter. She's balancing two huge bags of coffee beans and is wearing a black apron adorned with two floury handprints.

"Mathilde!" Thierry greets the girl warmly.

"Thierry!" Mathilde says. She drops the beans next to the register, then props herself up on the counter so she can lean over and air-kiss Thierry's cheeks. I don't even have time to make a smart remark about how *she* gets a proper greeting before they're speaking to each other warmly in rapid French.

Mathilde moves like lightning. She pulls levers on the espresso machine, and a second later she is at the case, grabbing a pain au chocolat. After she hands Thierry the pastry on a small dish, she notices me.

She says something quietly to Thierry without taking her eyes off me. Thierry scowls briefly, then fixes his face.

"Mathilde, this is Whitney," he says. "Whitney, Mathilde."

"N'est-elle pas mignonne, Thierry?" Mathilde interjects. When I smile apologetically, she tries again in English, "You are so cute. American?"

"Thank you, and yes, I am," I say with a little smile that has more warmth to it this time. Mathilde moves and speaks quickly, like a little tornado, but I decide I like her. "Thierry says you make good coffee. I would love to try it."

Mathilde puffs up like a proud little peacock. "I do. You want food?"

"Oui," I say enthusiastically, ignoring the way Thierry is doing nothing to hide his smirk. "I'd like a croissant, s'il vous plaît."

Mathilde nods and is off again, pulling levers and grabbing plates.

Now Thierry's outright laughing. First time I've seen this boy smile, and he's laughing at me?

"What?" I ask, defensive.

"Why do you say 'croissant' like you are choking?" Thierry says. He imitates me.

"I do not sound like that," I insist, inching away from him and inspecting the pastry case again. "My accent is perfect." *I mean, it is, isn't it?*

He's almost doubled over with laughter now and has to catch himself on the case.

"I would like to know the name of the person who has been lying to you about your accent," Thierry replies.

Mathilde is back at the counter and is passing me my coffee and croissant, which I take gratefully so I have an excuse to avert my attention from my companion.

"Is he always so mean?" I ask her, getting ready to find my debit card in my satchel.

"Thierry?" Mathilde asks, feigning surprise. "Mais non, c'est un ange." She chuckles when I suck my teeth. Beside me, Thierry drops a few coins into Mathilde's hand.

"If I am so mean, why am I paying for your breakfast?" he asks. I don't have time to protest or even act shocked, since Thierry has already waved goodbye to Mathilde and started moving toward the tables by the time I put away my wallet.

"Merci." I offer Mathilde a quick smile, which she responds to with a wink, and follow Thierry.

"Just so this doesn't come up later, thanks for breakfast," I say quickly as I slide into the seat facing Thierry. He's chosen a spot right by one of the huge windows at the front of the café. I can see a few students milling around in the courtyard. "But you should know I'm not in the habit of letting strange, rude boys pay for my food."

I wait for him to respond, but Thierry only raises his eyebrows and gives me an insolent, impassive expression. He's got really bright eyes and long lashes, I observe, but I look away, then wonder why I'm noticing his eyelashes anyway. He likely doesn't even appreciate them.

"Bien sûr," Thierry says finally. "I only did not want to be accused of 'ruining' your day later."

I'm about to huff, but I turn it into a deep breathing moment. Then I roll back my shoulders and take a bite of my croissant. Suddenly, I am no longer worried about Thierry Magnon and his level-ten sarcasm. My only concern is how I have lived seventeen years of my life without having had a fresh French croissant. I lean forward so that the plate catches the little flaky bits that don't quite make it into my mouth. My hand covers my mouth as I chew.

"Oh, my goodness," I moan, too consumed with the pastry that's melting in my mouth to care that I've just moaned over food in the presence of my new enemy.

When I open my eyes again, Thierry's shaking his head.

"You Americans," he says dryly. "You all think everything is magical when you come here. It is just breakfast."

I wrinkle my nose at him. This boy is determined to be unlikeable. I take another bite before I answer. "I think it

39

is. Magic. And the fact that you don't believe that means you're missing out."

He falls quiet. His long fingers absentmindedly pick at a corner of his own pastry. I decide that I like Sarcastic Thierry better than Brooding Thierry—but not by much. So I do what I do best: I keep talking.

"I guess if we've gotta do this tutoring thing, you should probably give me your number," I suggest, sliding my phone across the table toward him. He considers me briefly before picking it up and tapping in his contact information. I sip my delicious coffee while I wait.

He slides it back without looking at me, like we're passing classified information or something. I want to giggle, but I think better of it.

"I texted myself so I will have yours," Thierry says gruffly before occupying himself by gazing out the window again.

"Great, thanks," I reply slowly, dropping my phone back into my satchel. *Guess that part of the conversation is over. . . .* I notice that the big clock on the wall across from me reads almost nine a.m. "Well, as pleasant as this has been, I've gotta figure out how to get to class before I'm late."

"I will walk with you," Thierry tells me as I push myself up from my chair. I try not to respond the way I want to: *No, thanks. I'd rather miss all of my first day's classes than have you walk me there and be further in your debt.*

Instead, I ask, "Don't you have class?"

"Not right now," he replies. "I go to school on the next block, and I don't have a class this morning."

"I'm confused. Why are you tutoring at LIA, then?"

"It's an international school," Thierry says with a shrug.

"There aren't enough French-speaking students there to serve as tutors, so they ask students from other schools to help, and my older sister went here."

"Ah."

"Should I show you to class?"

"Sure. I'm going to Drama Fundamentals."

"Are you sure?" he asks.

I take out my schedule and flap it in his face. "It says so right here."

"I figured you'd already mastered that class," he replies, a smile tucking itself into the corner of his mouth.

I roll my eyes and try to be annoyed at his attempt at a joke but struggle to hide a small grin.

We leave the café and walk across the courtyard back toward LIA in an awkward silence that doesn't seem to bother him but I can't stand.

"The classrooms are on the first two floors of the building. The theater is in the annex, through here. That is where your first class should be." Thierry pulls the front door and props it open with his foot as he waits for me to walk in. Once I do, he walks around me and down the hall to the right. I have to move quickly to keep pace with him. He's got long legs, which makes for a fast gait.

There are students slowly making their way into various classrooms, and we pass a few loitering in the hallways. I follow Thierry through another set of doors and into a smaller building behind the main school and dormitory. When he finally slows to a stop in front of the theater, we linger, Thierry tapping his fingers against his thighs and me biting my lower lip as I study the small potted plants on either side of the entrance.

"Well . . . thanks," I say suddenly. "I'm just gonna . . . go in now." I make a move to go inside but end up tripping and stumbling a bit. My face warms, but I only straighten and lift my chin. Maybe he'll think I meant to do that.

Thierry's making that face again—the smirky one. I'm about to tell him if he doesn't stop doing that, I'm going to trip him the next time, but before I have a chance to speak, he gives me a lazy two-finger salute and says, "I will be in touch about tutoring." Then he spins on his heel and strides away.

I exhale heavily—half glad to be rid of him and half annoyed at the lack of a formal goodbye—and successfully enter the theater, this time without injuring any doorframes. None of the three seats in the front row is occupied yet, so I swing myself into the one closest to the aisle and scan the room. Three minutes isn't a lot of time to make a new friend, but I've certainly made do with less before.

There's only four other students in here—my new theater cohortmates—and all of them have their faces buried in their phones. I put on my best smile and try to catch someone's—anyone's—eye. Near me, a girl with deep brown skin and curly hair chopped at her earlobes is wearing a leather jacket and drumming a pen on the table. Behind her, a stocky pale white boy with startlingly blue eyes and nearly buzzed blond hair, like it's recently started growing out, is bobbing his head to whatever's coming out of his earbuds. To his right, I see a lanky boy with curly black hair that obscures his eyes, thus putting me out of his line of vision. When I realize everyone is either attached to their phones or engaged in whispered conversations with the person sitting next to them, my smile droops.

A perfect opportunity to meet a new best friend wasted by modern technology. I drum my fingers on my leg and bob my head, but within seconds, I am also on my phone. If you can't beat 'em, join 'em, and I tap around on the phone until I find myself swiping through some old photos of me and Nana that pop up in the corner of my screen.

Nana has always told me I have a personality that could draw people to me like bees to honey. I feel less like honey right now, though, and more like . . . well, dog poo.

Maybe, just maybe, having the perfect semester abroad in Paris isn't going to be as easy as I thought. *Magic is made, Whitney,* I reassure myself, *not discovered.*

Our teacher, a small, light brown woman with voluminous sand-colored hair, strides into the room just as the clock on the right-hand wall switches from 8:59 to 9:00.

I straighten in my seat as the woman pushes up the sleeves of her navy blazer and adjusts the scarf around her neck, the rich green and white of it mirroring the Algerian flag. "Bonjour, tout le monde," she says, her voice filling the space. "I am Madame Hassan, and I look forward to meeting each of you.

"In this class, we will study the fundamentals of performance. We will work on diction, projection, improvisation, and movement. We will study scripts and learn to interpret language and blocking. We will investigate mood and history."

Madame Hassan regards each of us with a sharp eye.

"Perhaps you think you have a natural gift for theater"—Madame Hassan's eye seems to linger on me as she explores the room—"but here, we are dedicated to the *practice* of our craft. You. Will. Work."

Her words might scare someone else, but I settle into my resolve.

"You have all come here with specific projects to work on over the course of the semester. Who would like to share a bit about their work?"

My hand flies into the air. Madame Hassan's gaze is intense, but she nods at me, giving me permission to speak.

"Hi, I'm Whitney Curry! I'm working on a project about Josephine—" I start, excitement bubbling into my voice, but Madame Hassan makes a sharp noise that cuts me off.

"En français, s'il vous plaît," my teacher says curtly.

I swallow but manage to stumble through a little elevator pitch about my one-woman show highlighting the loves of my idol, Josephine Baker, which will hopefully include both musical numbers and monologues.

"I'm sure you will find the inspiration you need to make this project compelling," Madame Hassan says in a tone that tells me what she really thinks: *Uninspired.* I wilt a little in my seat but try to stay positive.

Maybe I've just got to try a little harder to discover my magic.

SCENE FIVE

LOST IN TRANSLATION

I've walked so much today that even though it's a mild early-September afternoon in Paris, I'm concerned that my braids are going to be a frazzled mess at the roots—or worse, that I'll drip sweat all over my journal. Coffee stains might be an artistic aesthetic, but I'm pretty sure sweat stains are not.

I'm in a small grassy area, admiring the buildings that give the city a neat, uniform look as they line wide boulevards. The simple beauty makes my breath catch in my chest. I've been here a week, and Paris still feels as exciting and new as it did the moment I stepped out of Gare du Nord.

I break away from the small pack of LIA students on this Black American History in Paris tour with me and shade my eyes from the sunshine with my hand to get a better view of a statue of Alexandre Dumas. The school has a number of extracurricular activities you can sign up for each weekend. This tour seemed like a good way to explore the city until I feel more comfortable going out on my own.

I'm surprised to see that Nora and Sophie are on the trip. They stand off to the side, chatting. When they see me, they stop, and I feel a little self-conscious once again. We've been skirting each other for the past week, in part because I made myself a little more preoccupied with my script for my thesis than I might have ordinarily.

Which reminds me: I'm on this tour to get some inspiration. I won't let my roommates distract me.

Yikes, that lasted .5 seconds, I think when I realize that the two of them have wandered closer. I would assume it was unintentional, but they're staring straight at me.

"Uh, hi," Nora begins.

"Hi . . . ?" I say, my hesitation stretching out the one-syllable word and my pitch rising at the end.

"I just—We just wanted to apologize for getting off on the wrong foot," Nora says, gesturing to herself and Sophie. "Our reaction was unkind. My reaction in particular was unkind; you were only trying to be friendly."

There's a moment when I mentally question why Nora and Sophie suddenly want to be on good terms, but it's overshadowed by the realization that if we make up now, I won't go through my entire semester here friendless. And yet, I have to ask.

"So, what gives?" I prod Nora. I don't want to scare her off, but I want to know more about Fatima, the girl whose place I apparently took. "I get I wasn't your first choice for a roommate. What happened?"

"Oh." Nora chews her bottom lip thoughtfully. "A small

drama. Our friend Fatima was supposed to live with us this year. You saw her on-screen when you came in."

"That much I've gathered," I tell her. "Where is she?"

Nora and Sophie definitely exchange glances, but I decide not to call them out. "She and her boyfriend had a bit of a fight, and she decided she needed some space. Last month, she left to go on a study-abroad trip in Senegal when a spot opened."

Geez, imagine taking an entire continent of space when you break up with your high school boyfriend, I think, but mercifully do not say out loud. What I actually say: "Oh. She left you high and dry, then?"

"High and dry?" Sophie interjects curiously. I didn't think she was paying much attention to the conversation.

"I guess that's an American expression," I tell her with a shrug. "Anyway, I get it. You wanted to room with your friend, you were hurt by her leaving and overwhelmed by me. I know I come off kind of strong. My excitement was a little over the top, and it sometimes results in Hurricane Whitney."

"Should we start over?" Nora asks, laughing. Again, the tiniest of doubts eats at the back of my mind. I push it away, motivated largely by the prospect of finally having friends here. I'm willing to overlook what might just be anxiety on everyone's end.

"Sure," I say, extending a hand, which Nora promptly ignores, going for bisous instead. Sophie and I nod at each other. Nora is a bit of a mystery, but Sophie is fairly "what you see is what you get," from what I can tell.

We turn our attention back to the statue of Alexandre Dumas.

"I didn't know he was Black," Sophie says quietly.

Our tour guide, a tall, thin Black man in his midthirties from the visual arts department at LIA, nods. "Indeed, Dumas was of Haitian descent—"

"And did you know he had a son who was a playwright and novelist?" I ask her, pointing to another side of the statue. I snap a quick picture with my Polaroid camera.

"Really?"

"Mhm." I nod vigorously. "Everyone forgets about him because his dad was such a literary badass—" I catch myself. Somehow, I know my mother has heard me cuss in front of an authority figure from across the Atlantic and is going to berate me seconds after I get off my plane in December. Fortunately, Sophie smiles at me conspiratorially, and I feel a little less self-conscious.

"Yes, I was getting to that," the guide says, saving me from further embarrassment. He sniffs a little, and I nod at him to indicate he should keep going. I can tell he's growing a bit miffed, but a small part of me finds the exchange amusing.

Our professor/tour guide continues his speech, and I take a million and a half longhand notes. I've already filled eight journal pages, and I know I'm missing things. I try to write down all the details that come to mind as we ride in our bus to the next hotspot location. Once we arrive, I'm reminded that my multitasking abilities do not include walking and writing well at the same time.

I pull my annotated map from the back of my journal and cross-check it with the tour's itinerary for the third time.

My hand shoots into the air.

"Yes?" the tour guide asks, tightness in his voice.

"Are there any other monuments to Black dramatists in the area?"

"None that are on our route," he says. He opens his mouth to continue his script, but I have another question.

"Are there any museums dedicated to Black history in the city?"

"Oui, but none that are on our route," the guide repeats. Despite the walking-heavy parts of the tour, this guy doesn't seem to have broken a sweat except in the last few minutes. He begins to pat his pockets as if to look for his phone. "Does anyone have the time?"

"It's two o'clock," I contribute helpfully. "That's why I was asking about monuments! This tour's almost over, and I still have so many questions about what I've been seeing and—"

"Perhaps you should consider booking a private tour, where we would be able to cater to your needs a little more specifically," the guide interrupts me, pushing his glasses up on his nose.

"Oh, that's a great idea!" I say enthusiastically, jotting that down, too. "Do you have any recommendations for tour companies?"

The guide makes a strangled sound before muttering, "You may find some on the school website." He clears his throat and addresses the whole student group, saying loudly, "Bon, let's head to Montmartre."

A few minutes later, our group nosily disembarks the bus in a neighborhood at the base of a hill. The guide leads us to a set of stairs that seems to go on forever, but after a few steps, I notice a small chalk drawing: a pink Disney castle with the words "Sacré-Cœur" written in white underneath. My heart swells in my chest—how apt that this moment feels like a fairy tale. I capture a picture before scurrying up behind my group.

Finally, I'm able to stop focusing so much on all the stairs that I'm climbing and see that they open up onto a plaza packed full of people. Atop even more stairs is the biggest, most impressive hundred-some-year-old Roman Catholic church I have ever seen.

Sacré-Cœur is an eggshell-white basilica with one huge dome in the middle whose top comes to a point and two smaller ones on either side, in front of a pure blue cloudless sky. I assume that the sky is this clear because of the altitude—I'm so high up, if I even whispered right now, I'm sure God would tell me to pipe down. And when I look out, every corner of Paris is spread below me as far as the eye can see. It seems very appropriate that a church is this high up.

A stroke of inspiration hits me, and I perch on a step, fish out my journal, and write enough to fill a couple of pages. I wish Archi was sitting beside me with her well-curated scrapbook.

I'm yanked from my daydreams and back into reality by a juggling clown wiggling his hat at me and asking for money. I don't have any loose euros, so I only shrug apologetically at him.

The clown frowns at me through his painted red grin and walks away.

I look left and right and realize that I can't see my guide among all the happy tourists taking pictures in the plaza at the bottom of the steps. I walk over to the steps and go up a few, trying to survey the crowd. But my group is no-where to be found.

They're probably in the church, I think quickly, my heart starting to thump in my ears. I scramble up faster than I might under other circumstances, taking the steps two at a time. Another quick scan shows me that my group isn't here, either. A squeak of distress escapes me. You would assume a big group of foreign teenagers would be easy to spot, but unfortunately, everyone is a visitor here. I hear tons of languages in addition to French.

I take a moment to pause and gather myself. This is no time to lose my head. They couldn't have gotten that far. I curse myself for taking that moment to write; I have to strike a balance between capturing the moment and *staying safe.* The list of attractions the tour promised we would hit is shaking in my hands; I read it and realize that there's a garden close by that we're supposed to be seeing next.

Okay, head there, Whitney. But as I review my map, I don't have a good sense of how to get from where I am right now to that garden. Everything starts to blur as my eyes fill with water. Even if I could see, pretty much any-thing that's not in a straight line is a no-go for me. . . .

I hear my mom's gentle ribbing about my abhorrent sense of direction in the back of my head, and I am furi-ous that I've managed to prove her right in less than two weeks. A tear born of panic and anger at myself escapes the corner of my eye.

I make my way back down the endless stairs to the street, where there are more people rolling carts of grocery bags behind them than wearing cameras around their necks. An older gentleman with a newspaper under his arm and his face partially shaded by a cap seems friendly enough.

"Excusez-moi," I say, waving to get his attention. The man slows but doesn't stop. "Est-ce que vous savez comment . . . ?" My throat tightens when I realize I'm translating word for word, rather than using common phrases, and the man won't quite understand what I'm asking.

I try a different tactic. I flash my map and point to a green area not far from Sacré-Cœur. "Quelle direction?"

"Ah, okay," the man says, to which I almost sigh in relief, but then he immediately begins speaking in rapid-fire French with a few hand motions that I can't grasp the meaning of. Still, his tone is so genuine that I say, "Merci mille fois," in spite of having understood nothing. I smile, yet as he walks away, I feel the expression crack and strain. I'm well past panic and into unfamiliar territory.

I walk a little farther and try to wave down a middle-aged woman toting a bag of groceries, but she looks straight ahead as if doing so will make me disappear. After that a young couple walks by, but I decide not to try them as they ignore me, too.

It's unnerving, and my body fills with hot pinpricks as the tears come. I move down the street. By the time I stop again, I can barely see the top of Sacré-Cœur anymore.

"Okay, Whitney," I say, trying to talk myself down, though my voice shakes as hard as my hands. I pull out my phone. "It's the twenty-first century, not the Stone Age. Use your phone."

It takes me a few minutes, but I manage to order a ride-share back to school. The wait time says three minutes, and I feel the tightness in my chest loosen for two and half, before my phone rings.

Who is calling me from a French number?

I answer it with a swipe of my finger. "Hello?"

A brusque voice answers me in French. It takes a few tries, but I discern that the driver can't find me and is asking for my location. The map in the app can't place me accurately on the street, and I don't have enough data overseas to make the GPS work properly.

There are no restaurants or grocery stores or anything identifying around—it's all beige immeubles in narrow streets that are common in the city center. I can tell by the clotheslines overhead and on the balconies that I've stumbled into a new neighborhood, but I'm too far down the street to see the signs. I wouldn't be able to tell north from west with a compass, so I couldn't give the driver directions if I wanted to.

I struggle through the conversation, trying to describe my surroundings in broken French, but after a minute, the driver simply disconnects. I feel like I could scream—and what's worse, the tears won't stop. What is the point of all this high-tech mumbo-jumbo and super military-level surveillance if I can't even get a driver to find me?

I keep walking, passing all manner of Parisians. It would be a thrilling opportunity to people-watch if I weren't preoccupied with the all-consuming fear of never making it back to my school and dying alone on the streets of Paris. This was *not* on my list.

Eventually, my wandering leads me to a small, enclosed area of greenery that I think is the garden I was hoping to find ages ago. But the place is deserted, and if my tour group has been here, they are obviously long gone.

The good news is that it's shaded here, and I spot a small bench along the fence that I immediately fall down on. I shake my foot out of one of the tan ballet flats I've got on and bring it up to my lap to massage it. Of all my footwear options, the flats seemed the most sensible for an all-day walking tour, but I might as well have been wearing high heels for six hours. In addition to being scared out of my mind, my feet are swollen, and my formerly cute white blouse with embroidered cherries all over it and red cigarette pants are drenched in sweat and covered with dirt.

This is the end of Whitney Curry, an American in Paris. Lost, alone, disgusting, and unable to communicate. I sigh ruefully, my breath hitching in my chest, wishing that my French were better. *I guess I could have used the tutoring after all, not that Thierry would have been a willing participant—*

My internal monologue screeches to a halt.

Thierry.

My mouth screws up at the thought, but I currently don't have any other options, and I don't know anyone else to call; even though Nora, Sophie, and I are good now, I haven't exchanged numbers with them yet. Considering he hates me, it's a long shot, but . . .

I'm messaging him before I have a chance to talk myself out of it.

> **Whitney:** Hi, Thierry, it's Whitney Curry, from tutoring. I wouldn't bother you, but I'm sort of lost in the city and can't find my way back to the dorms. Can you help me?

To my surprise, three dots start dancing on the left side of my screen moments after "Delivered" pops up under my own text.

Thierry: Where are you?

I glance around, trying to figure out how to give him a good sense of my location. Again, I'm too far away from any street signs, and getting up to find out is not happening—I am rooted to this bench.

Whitney: Um, I'm not sure. I think I'm still in the Montmartre area, and I can't be far from Sacré-Cœur.

I'm sitting in front of this little fenced-in garden. I can send you a pin of my location.

Thierry: 👍

I interpret his reply as an invitation to share my location. It takes another minute or two, but he messages back.

Thierry: I am not far. I will come get you. Stay there.

I'm about to breathe a sigh of relief when I remember that my knight in shining armor is Thierry Magnon, and he is undoubtedly going to be an asshole about this.

SCENE SIX

IN WHICH I, WHITNEY CURRY, MAKE A DEAL WITH A CHOCOLATE-COVERED DEVIL

When Thierry shows up about ten minutes later with his signature focused facial expression on, he's less knight in shining armor and more . . . covered in flour?

"You are not having a good start to your semester, are you?" he inquires, smirking when he gets close. I'm slumped on the bench with my eyes half closed, dying of exhaustion, so I can only manage a tiny sneer at his comment even though I originally intended to thank him. He folds his arms over his chest and raises his eyebrows at me.

"Thanks." The word has a little more bite to it than I want, so I smooth out the next bit. "Thank you for coming."

There's a pause, not uncomfortable, but it's long. "Bon, allons-y," Thierry announces after several moments, pointedly ignoring my olive branch. "There is a métro stop nearby. We will get you back to the dorms."

"We're not walking the whole way?" I ask, perking up as

I decide to simply follow his lead both in these directions home and in how the rest of this interaction is going to go.

"We can—"

"No, no!" I cut him off quickly, gathering my purse and hopping up from the bench. "Trains are good. Great, even. Let's go."

Thierry gives me a skeptical look but starts off, and I follow. I'm quiet for a minute as we walk, the street starting to open up a little bit. He takes me on a route I don't recognize from the bus tour, and judging by the way his body reacts to dips in the road and ill-positioned waste receptacles, I take it he walks this way often. I want to pay attention to where I'm going so that if I end up here again, I won't get lost, but I'm very distracted by the fact that in addition to a bunch of flour on his shirt, Thierry's got a few smudges of something dark and brown on his arm. And when I quicken my steps to edge closer to him, there's a light, pleasant, sweet scent coming off him.

"You smell like sugar," I say after a while. Thierry's brow furrows as he glances down at me. Frowning, always frowning with him. He's going to have permanent worry lines by age thirty if he keeps this up. "You're also covered in chocolate. Did you lose a fight with a Hershey bar or something?"

It seems like he's not going to answer—quelle surprise— but eventually Thierry's mouth puckers, and he gives in.

"I was finishing up at work when I received your message," he tells me. I think he might say more, but he falls silent again.

"Where do you work?"

"My stepfather owns a chocolate shop—"

"Oh, my gosh," I gush before I can stop myself. "Visiting a real chocolatier is *very* high on my Parisian bucket list. I'm going to come by one day. What's it called?"

Thierry cuts his eyes at me. Fair, I did just invite myself to his family's chocolate shop.

"Chocolat Doré." His French has a lilt, a melody, to it that his voice lacks when he's speaking English. His usual brusqueness momentarily dissipates. It's like there are these different Thierrys—one sarcastic, one brooding, now this one that might be soft—and I wonder which is the real one.

"That sounds lovely," I say, not able to keep a tiny sigh from escaping me. "Do you work there every day? Or just on weekends?"

"Every day that I am not tutoring," Thierry says shortly. And there's the grumpiness again. I realize there's a pattern to his thorny responses, and I decide to try to gently ease around it.

"You sound awfully put out about it," I say innocently. He doesn't give in, just keeps walking with his hands in his pockets. I press on. "I mean, if *I* got to work in a *decadent*-smelling shop, surrounded by an endless array of chocolates, I would assume that I'd died and gone to heaven."

Again, Thierry eyes me suspiciously, as if he doesn't quite trust me, but he still doesn't say anything. The grumpiness is *so* unbecoming. I have a sudden desire to rub the furrow between his brows with my thumb to erase it.

"Listen, either you tell me what the deal is, *or* I'll talk the entire way back to the dorms. It's totally up to you," I say, shrugging.

While I wait for him to decide, I keep scoping out the area. Montmartre is super cute, and it would be my favorite part of Paris so far if there weren't *so many stairs.* Hills are definitely the real enemy in this situation. But I love the colorful storefronts with their elegant signage. We pass a couple of gardening stores with flowers and plants packed so tightly that they practically spill out the front doors. I see a toy store and a hair salon—and even a record store on the opposite side of the street that I'm already plotting to get Thierry to stop at.

"*Pffff,* when you put it that way," Thierry says with a very French-sounding sigh. Then a tiny mischievous glint appears in his eyes. "You have a list of things you want to do in Paris?"

"One: Yes, doesn't everybody? Two: We are way past that point of the conversation. Three: Based on the way you asked that, you're making me regret messaging you." As we walk, I'm hit with the overpowering smell of cooked meat and roasted vegetables, accompanied by the faint sizzle of a slab of beef hitting a hot surface. The hunger that nudged me when I noticed the sugar-and-butter aroma on Thierry comes back full force. Up ahead, I see a kebob stand with a line at least ten people deep. The more people, the better the food, I always figure. "Can we stop to eat? I'm starving."

Thierry clearly wants to smile, but the upward curve of his mouth disappears quickly. He nods, then rubs the back of his neck with one hand as he glances away, a storminess returning to his face. The motions remind me of the way he was bouncing his leg when I found him outside Cécile's office earlier in the week. He must get fidgety when he's annoyed. When we've joined the line, I turn back to him, expectant.

"You have good taste. Everyone around here loves these kebobs," Thierry tells me. I give him a light poke in the arm, and he sighs. "I only began to work in the shop a few weeks ago," he says after a very long pause.

"Why did you just start working at the shop? Feels like there's a story," I say.

"It's part of my punishment."

"Punishment?" I ask.

"I was in a fight at one of my football matches. . . ."

"Why were you fighting?" *God, he is exhausting,* I think. *Just get to the good stuff!*

He exhales sharply. "*Eh, some* of the spectators called me a name I'd rather not repeat when I was on the field. J'sais pas . . . it was like something came over me, and then my teammates were pulling me out of the stands."

While Thierry's talking, I'm once again struck by his skin. It's dark and looks soft, but it also glistens in the late-afternoon sun. Even with the lines that have formed on his forehead, his complexion is smooth and clear.

"Got it . . . ," I say. We move up a few paces. "And you were the one who got in trouble?"

"Yeah . . . ," he says bluntly and without changing his vaguely bored countenance.

Thierry is saved from having to say more as we make it to the front of the kebob line. The guy at the cash register is about our age, tall and lanky with floppy black hair under a kufi and morose-looking eyes. Thierry greets him warmly, and they carry on for a bit in French before I subtly clear my throat.

"Amir, this is Whitney Curry. She is a student at Lycée International des Arts," Thierry tells him. I wave and smile brightly. "Whitney, this is Amir. We play football together. Our team practices at LIA. The art school has the best field somehow."

"A football player and chef!" I say, ignoring Thierry's dig at my art school. Nana always says a little bit of flattery will get you a long way.

Though maybe not with Amir, whose expression doesn't really change.

I pucker my lips in embarrassment and busy myself with checking the tiny chalkboard hanging from the top half of the window counter, then order a couple of beef kebobs. When I'm done dropping a few euros into Amir's outstretched hand, Thierry does the same. A different man with a carefully coiffed and oiled beard hands us our meal in two thick pieces of butcher paper, and we step away from the counter to take a few bites, waving good-bye to Amir.

The meat is well seasoned and comes away from the stick easily when I bite into it. The veggies are cooked just enough to retain their crunch. There's a container of sauce, but I'm content to eat the kebobs just like this. We tear into our food in grateful silence.

As I finish up, I realize I can still see the record store from here, painted bright yellow and inviting. I drop my empty skewer in the nearest trash can.

"Do you like music?" I ask Thierry. Without waiting for an answer, I look both ways, then dash across the street.

I hear him calling me, but I don't stop. He'll catch up.

The shop door opens with a tinny tinkle from a bell

over the entryway. You can't tell from the outside, but the spot is spacious and well-lit. A person I presume is the owner sits on a stool in a corner behind the counter, clicking away at something on a computer. I murmur "Bonjour" and receive a quiet greeting in return, then start to peruse. A few rows of wooden boxes contain all sorts of records, and without looking for anything in particular, I flip through a few of them just to see the album covers.

I'm admiring some of the records on the shelves along the wall when I hear the bell sound again. Thierry enters the shop, his mouth tight. I think he might be a little angry, but something about the music playing in the background softens his face. It's a jazzy number I don't recognize, to my surprise.

"When I see a record shop, I just have to check it out, you know?" I say as he comes to stand next to me.

"No, I don't know," Thierry replies, his face straight. I roll my eyes but mostly ignore him and twirl to the boxes on the other side of the row. This section is marked "Jazz," and I tap the tips of my fingers together in delight as I comb through them. Nothing is particularly striking except a Louis Armstrong album that I end up buying. Thierry waits near the door as I pay.

"For my nana," I tell him, patting the bag swinging on my arm as we leave.

"Are you ready to go back now?" Thierry asks, and it sounds like *he's* not ready for our impromptu adventure to be over. He glances at my new accessory and exhales a little puff of air that I think might be irritation, but he's not looking at me like that's true. I expected him to be annoyed at all my pit stops, but he only seems a tiny bit amused. Interested, even.

How self-involved of me, I think, *to assume that the first French boy I meet is secretly crushing on me. Plus, that* cannot *be. For a number of very good reasons. I'll have to list them later.*

"Yeah, I guess," I say, sighing. "I like Montmartre, though. This area has a lot of character. When you're not lost, that is."

"You will have to come back sometime," Thierry says, and we set off once again for the métro stop. This time I only mentally make note of cute things I want to check out instead of actually stopping. I am especially tempted by a flea market pop-up with tables full of jewelry and crystals, which I ogle as best as I can while still moving forward, but I feel like I've already tempted fate—or, rather, Thierry's temper—enough for one day.

I notice that up ahead, there's a spot where people are disappearing underground, presumably walking down into a métro station. That must be where Thierry is taking us.

The stop eventually comes into view. As Thierry heads underground I slow down, admiring the art nouveau sign made of intricate iron. He plucks his wallet from his back pocket and searches inside for something. A small piece of plastic that looks like a credit card—a Navigo pass. As we approach the turnstiles, I realize I don't have one.

When Thierry looks back at me from halfway down the flight of stairs, I say quickly, "I don't have a métro pass."

"You can buy one here," Thierry tells me, pointing to a small machine, where he's already tapping on the touch screen. "You will want a monthly pass. It's good for trains and buses."

I nod as he continues tapping, even though I have no real desire to teach myself how to use the bus system, which is infinitely more confusing than the trains. Thierry shows me how much it'll cost, and I insert my debit card, surprised when the pass drops right down into the slot below. I grab it, and moments later, we've tapped our passes to the turnstiles and made it onto a platform.

The next train isn't coming for eight minutes, so Thierry passes the time by leading me to a map on the wall and explaining how to navigate the trains. I end up watching him, how he gestures with his hands and pauses in his sentences as he thinks of how to explain it to me, rather than trying to remember it all. I know how to use the maps in theory—how to determine which way I'm going and all that—from using the trains around DC, but in practice, I still have to make an "L" with my forefinger and thumb to remember which direction left is. Super inconvenient when your director is calling out your blocking.

After he finishes and falls silent again, the cloud of moodiness settles back over his face. I leave him to his solitude for about twelve seconds before I realize I'm bursting with more questions, and I want to see how much Thierry might let me push against his facade.

"I'm still thinking about what you said earlier," I begin. "About those guys at your match . . . they said something racist, didn't they?"

Thierry gives a short, wry laugh. "You Americans think you have a monopoly on racism. It exists everywhere, even in France."

He's dismissing me, but he's also dismissing the intensity of what happened. I feel myself growing warmer, and it's not because of the hot, late-summer air blowing around the station. Indignation is rising in my body. It's an uncomfortable pressure pushing at my insides, threatening to come out. He continues, "Sometimes we experience it on social media—the comments, the trolls—but a lot of times, it is the fans at the stadium. They yell all sorts of things. Harass us—me and the other African guys on the team. But it has never been that bad before."

"It seems . . . so American, you know?" I say. "The sort of stuff I see and hear everywhere I go in the States. France isn't supposed to be like that. I mean, how could it be, when so many Black Americans have found homes here? It's supposed to be a haven."

"How do you mean?" Thierry asks, and I almost smile at the question. His English is so perfect that the phrasing here makes him feel a little more real.

"It's like my senior thesis project," I say, and I see him lean forward slightly—possibly out of interest, possibly to hear me better over the scream of the train on the rails on the other side of the quai. "I'm doing a project on Black Americans who fled to Paris. Mostly artists. Well, it's really about Josephine Baker in particular, but there were others who came, too. People like James Baldwin and Richard Wright and a bunch of jazz musicians who became expatriates. But Josephine is the one who stands out to me. I wanna see what she saw . . . know what she knew. She came here for a reason. Those artists—Josephine—they felt free here. And I want to know why."

"A place can be a haven and not be perfect," Thierry

muses. Then he adds, "You are an artist, Whitney Curry?" I feel a sliver of the iciness between us melt when he says my name. I feel warm, but it might just be the non-air-conditioned space we're in.

"I'm an actress. Like my nana," I announce proudly, tossing my braids over my shoulder. "And also a playwright."

"I should have guessed," he says, and the cloud over his face splits for a second so I can see this glimpse of something when the corner of his mouth almost—but not quite—tugs up in a smile. It's a softer expression than what I have come to be used to with him, and I like it better than Grouchy Monsieur Thierry.

Maybe he's not totally hopeless.

"I do not know why they would want to come here," Thierry adds after a moment. "At least you can talk about it there. In France, they try to make us believe that everyone is French first. Liberté, égalité, fraternité." He looks down at me. "Here, they believe so deeply that we are all equal that they will not see the trouble they have made colonizing African countries. Trouble that made my grandmère come here from Mali. The French have a very selective memory."

"The French aren't the only ones," I say with a dry laugh. "Maybe I shouldn't have built up Paris to be so perfect in my mind."

"Perhaps not perfect," Thierry replies quietly, almost as if he is thinking to himself rather than speaking aloud, "But Paris is home. And it *is* beautiful and ugly all at once."

We're quiet for a while, and after a few minutes, I hear rumbling in the distance as train lights begin to flash in the depths of the tunnel; then, out of nowhere, a huge metal body bursts out in front of us, attempting to screech to a halt. I move to get in front of a set of doors, but Thierry holds out a hand.

"Let them pass," he murmurs.

The doors open, and a few people file out: a mother pushing a giggling child in a stroller, an elderly couple holding hands so they don't get separated, a small group of teens my age pushing each other and jumping to hit the signs hanging from the wall. As soon as the last teen exits the car, we board.

I immediately sit on the seat closest to the door I entered, my feet still protesting after the day's events. Thierry opts to stand in front of me, leaning against a pole with his arms folded over his chest. I can see the mess he's made of his clothes more clearly from this angle, the chocolate streaks on his forearms and on the bit of his biceps visible under his black T-shirt sleeve. He appears strong, angular, and powerful. I wonder how I didn't realize he was an athlete before.

"Whitney?" I hear a voice stir me out of my reverie. Thierry's staring down at me with a frown on his face, though at least this time it seems more out of concern than irritation. I'll take it, I guess.

"Oh, what, was I totally gone?" I ask. The doors have closed, and a muffled voice is speaking over the PA system. A second later, the train jolts and begins moving along the tracks.

"You do that often?" Thierry asks. He doesn't even move when the train does. It's like he's learned to surf the mechanical currents of the métro.

"Um, yeah," I say, wrinkling my nose a bit. "I was just thinking."

He raises his eyebrows. "What were you thinking about?"

Your arms, I think, but remind myself that that's not really a suitable conversation topic for a grumpy boy you just met. Especially one who called you "dramatic" and a "princess" only days ago.

Jeez, get a grip, Whitney Curry.

I clear my throat and try to recall where our conversation went before we boarded the train. I can't come up with anything, so I grin sheepishly and let us fall into another comfortable silence until we reach our stop. The train stutters to a halt, and Thierry moves toward the automatic doors. He leads the way out onto a mostly empty platform and up a set of steps to our left. When we emerge from underground, the sun has begun to set, and it looks like the sky is on fire. Thierry starts down a boulevard I recognize that LIA sits on the end of, and I admire the glow the sun gives the city at twilight as we walk. I begin to see the barest hint of a cream-colored building as we reach the fence that marks the start of LIA's campus. Our soccer field comes into view.

"So, when can you play soccer again?" I ask finally.

"Football. And when I am done with my punishment," Thierry tells me. "I must work in the shop when I am not tutoring. You are my last assignment." He shoots me a quick glance. "If I receive a good review from you, the coaches will end my suspension early, and I can return to the team before the season is over. The rest of my assignments spoke highly of me. But I do not suppose you will have anything nice to say about me."

We're almost in front of the building, but I stop in my tracks.

"Whitney?" he asks, turning when he realizes I'm not beside him.

"Shh, I'm thinking," I hush him, closing my eyes and holding up my hand. Then I open them and take him in again: Thierry, standing in the métro car as it jerks along and not budging an inch. How he navigates the streets of Paris so easily, explains everything so well.

I open my eyes.

"Okay, Thierry Magnon, I have a proposal for you," I say finally, putting my hands on my hips and lifting my chin.

"Whatever it is, I feel I will regret saying yes," Thierry counters sarcastically. I ignore him. I'm getting pretty good at that.

"I will write you a good tutoring review so that you can go back to playing soccer—"

"Football."

"Whatever. I will write you the most glowing tutoring review you have ever received . . . *if* you promise to help me find all the places I need to go to in Paris for research on my play project." I purse my lips so that I won't keep talking and possibly deter him from saying yes. But at that moment I notice a bit of chocolate on his cheek, almost on his jawline, illuminated under the glow of the streetlight that's just flickered on. Before I can stop myself, I step forward and swipe the smudge off with my thumb.

"Chocolate," I explain. Curiosity grips me, and I bring my thumb to my mouth to taste it. I think it might be dark

69

chocolate, the way it's rich but almost bitter, but the bitterness passes after a moment, and I'm left with something bold but delicately sweet. I've waited my whole life to try real Parisian chocolate, and my first taste came unexpectedly. I want to dedicate the moment to memory, the depth of the flavor, not so light and sweet as American chocolate, and smooth on the tongue. "You taste good."

Thierry's eyes widen a smidge in surprise, and I worry that once again, I have done too much, but then the corners of his mouth turn up in a *real* smile at last! I'm reveling in my victory when the hint of dimples appears in his dark brown cheeks, and in that moment, I just know Thierry Magnon means trouble for me.

"I have some questions," he says.

"Shoot," I reply. He cocks his head in curiosity. "I mean, ask your questions."

"What if I don't like the places on your list?"

I gawk at him, shocked. "What do you *mean* what if you don't like the places on my list? Are *you* performing a one-woman show based on your original research?"

Thierry makes a throaty sound that I assume is one of agreement. "What if I have suggestions?" he asks. As we start to walk again, the back of his hand grazes mine.

I jolt. And every rational thought flies out of my mind. "Suggestions for what?"

"Places to visit for your research."

I have to gather myself before I die of embarrassment. Where is my mind?!

"Okay, well, I will have to vet your suggestions, obviously, but I'll consider them."

"Last question: If we do this . . . am I in danger of you tasting my face again?"

This time I take a beat to consider before I answer. "I make no such promises."

"Okay, Whitney Curry," he says finally, a glimmer of mischief dancing in his dark eyes, "I accept your proposal."

<u>Terms of Agreement Between Whitney Curry</u>
<u>and Thierry Magnon</u>

It is hereby understood that Whitney Curry
and Thierry Magnon are bound by the terms
of this agreement. Curry will provide
Magnon with a good review on his tutoring,
contingent on his commitment to serving as
research and travel guide to Curry.

The following conditions supplement this
agreement:
1. Curry will agree to perform her best in
   tutoring sessions. (This will enable her to
   conduct solo research trips in the event
   that Magnon is unavailable to assist.
   Magnon will provide Curry with at least 24
   hours' notice for a change of plan.)
2. Magnon may at any time be subjected to any
   of the following research assistant duties:
   photography, cinematography, translation,

and making his métro seat available should
no others be open for Curry.
3. Curry and Magnon will keep all
   communication, both in person and
   digitally delivered, civil.
4. Curry and Magnon will stay focused on the
   tasks, with no unnecessary distractions.

We hereby agree to these conditions, with
acknowledgment that they may be amended at
any time if both parties are in agreement.

Whitney Curry
Signature

Thierry Magnon
Signature

SCENE SEVEN

I REGRET EVERYTHING

It's been less than forty-eight hours since Thierry and I worked up and signed our agreement, and I'm already plotting how to make an amendment. I didn't think I needed to sign a legally binding document to ensure I don't kill him, but we're twenty-three minutes into a tutoring session, and if I don't propose it now, he may not live to see tomorrow.

As much as that would please me, I'm sure he has family who would object.

"Non," Thierry snips. "Encore une fois, c'est pas 'j'ai allé,' c'est 'je suis allée.'"

On second thought, I might be doing them a favor.

We've decided on a neutral location for our lessons: the corner of the cafeteria where we sat on my first day. In between making espresso drinks, Mathilde sends some glances our way, not bothering to hide her smirk. I'm glad *someone* finds this amusing.

While I didn't think we'd be immediate friends after he saved me in Montmartre, this reaction is jarring, especially considering I—mortifyingly—licked a bit of chocolate straight off his face, and then made a joke about it! I spent all of that night, the next day, and even a good portion of class time this morning going back and forth on whether I should still be embarrassed for such a blatant display of—relatively—innocent thirstiness. In Montmartre, he smiled. I saw some dimple! Now he's acting like I kicked his dog. If he even *has* a dog. I wonder what his problem is. Thierry is objectively good-looking, but not nearly so handsome that I'll allow him to distract me from my work only to deal with inexplicable mood swings.

I just need to focus.

"Whitney," Thierry snaps, bringing my internal monologue to a crashing halt. His dark skin is next to faultless, except for the lines between his eyebrows and the frown that's decided to make an encore appearance. "You know this."

I'm trying to refocus on the open book in front of me, from which Thierry is attempting to tutor me in choosing between "avoir" and "être" when I need to conjugate verbs in le passé composé.

But Thierry is also impatiently tapping his middle finger on the table, causing the muscles in his forearm to jump.

Even though I know he isn't going to soccer practice, he's dressed in casual athletic wear—a new pair of joggers, sneakers, and a fitted graphic T-shirt. I follow his finger tapping up his arm to his bicep. This is a problem. . . .

"Oh, my gosh, could you *please*—" I start exasperatedly,

and I reach over and put my hand over his to stop the tapping.

He glances down at our hands, then up at me, and I pull my hand back so fast you'd think I'd been electrocuted, cradling it in the other against my chest. "Sorry. My bad."

Great, not only am I sweating over a boy, I'm going to fail my French language class. I don't understand how he expects me to concentrate in these conditions!

"This is silly," I say finally, taking a finger and lazily shutting my book.

"Maybe to you," Thierry says, grimacing a little. "But we have an agreement. I help you with this and you help me get back to football. You're supposed to focus."

"Yes, but, Thierry, we're in *Paris*!"

"C'est pas vrai?" He doesn't roll his dark eyes, but I can tell it's taking every ounce of his strength not to. Nora and Sophie walk in at that moment, likely in search of coffee, and they pause when they see me. I notice their eyes move and linger on Thierry. I wonder if I might be missing something, but I wave anyway. Sophie waves back immediately, but Nora takes a second. When she does wave, though, it's warm. I mouth, *Help me!*

"Hi, Whitney," Sophie calls. "Do you want to go on a walk with us after we get a coffee?"

Even though I did, in fact, ask for help, I feel resigned. Thankful to my roommates, though, for the short reprieve. It would be inconsiderate to leave Thierry here when he's supposed to be helping me, so I heave a sigh.

"I wish I could. . . ." I gesture to all the books spread on the table in front of me.

Both girls smile and shrug, continuing on their way,

Nora shooting me one more curious glance over her shoulder. When my eyes snap back to Thierry, he's watching me with a straight face and a raised eyebrow.

I toss my braids back over my shoulder haughtily. "I only mean, why teach me French out of a book in a cafeteria on school grounds when we're literally in Paris? Don't you think this is a case when I should get out into the world and practice? Learn by doing?"

"Perhaps," Thierry concedes grudgingly, "but you barely know a handful of phrases now. How do you plan to talk to anyone?"

"C'est vrai," Mathilde agrees as she leans over the table with a new espresso for me. "Les Français . . . the French, we are precious about our language. A little French is better than none, but . . ." She lets her statement hang, and I pout.

"My French *cannot* be that bad!" I protest.

"Oh, ma chérie," Mathilde says, clucking her tongue with a sympathetic grimace. My mouth falls open.

"Et tu, Brute?" I ask her.

"And what will you do with Latin in Paris?" she scoffs, before opening my book back up and tapping a page at random. "Non, you will study and learn. Tout va bien se passer. Thierry is a good teacher."

Thierry stares at me with a straight face like he's on a workplace sitcom. I tighten my mouth so I don't laugh, but I can't stop myself from shaking my head.

"Bon . . . ," Mathilde says. "Amusez-vous."

And with that she zips back toward her counter, then disappears behind the swinging door.

"How do you know Mathilde, again?" I ask in an attempt

to deflect from learning at all costs. And maybe I am a *little* curious about how he is so familiar with this really pretty older girl. . . .

"She is friends with my older sister, Célestine," Thierry grumbles. "And she worked at our family's shop while she was in high school."

"You have sisters?" I prod.

"Yes. Célestine is twenty, and Lucie is ten."

Even though Thierry is still a grump, something about his face softens a fraction when he mentions his sisters. I want to press further and learn more about his family, and I'm also curious about this chocolate shop that he says very little about.

"When can I try some chocolate from your family's store?" I ask, but Thierry's already glaring at me again.

"No more distractions," he says seriously. "Let's try again."

I groan.

At 2:55 p.m. the next day, Monsieur Laurent is speaking animatedly in front of the blackboard, but I'm not hearing any of it through the brain fog settling on me. It's a shame, because his French theater history class—one of my only sessions taught in an actual classroom with chalkboards and desks, as I have vocal and contemporary dance in studio classrooms in the theater annex and drama fundamentals in the theater itself—has quickly become one of my favorites.

Monsieur Laurent is young, probably in his late

twenties—even saying thirty is pushing it—and is enthusiastic about everything. When he started our first class by passing out sheets of paper with a few poems by Léopold Senghor on them with such gusto that he nearly knocked his wiry glasses off his face, I grinned. Before he gets really started on a good lecture, he ties back his tightly coiled hair so that it doesn't fall in his face, leaving his hands free to gesticulate wildly.

Today he's teaching with the windows open, his sleeves rolled up to his elbows and his tweed jacket draped across the back of the chair. It's warm for a September day in France, and of course, there's no air-conditioning. Sweat beads collect on his deep brown forehead.

Between the heat, my lack of comprehension skills when it comes to spoken French, and my focus on how I'm going to introduce myself to Monsieur Laurent after class and ask him to cochair my thesis project without being late to meet Thierry at 3:15, I'm missing what I know must be a great (but slightly off-topic) lecture on the French education system. The form that Monsieur Laurent has to fill out is peeking out from underneath my journal, and I mentally rehearse my script: *Hi, Monsieur Laurent! As you know, exchange students have to have a professor at LIA oversee their senior projects while in Paris. My advisor in DC has already done most of the work to get me started, so I just need someone to look at drafts and grade the final. . . .*

I urge myself to concentrate better, but by the time I do that, Monsieur Laurent is wrapping up, closing this week's script—Voltaire's *Candide*—with a *pop* and yelling out the reading for next class over the sounds of a dozen international students sliding books and notebooks off their desks, shoving them into bags, and fleeing into the late-afternoon sunshine.

It's 3:01. I quickly push myself out of my seat and stand in front of Monsieur Laurent's desk. He's shuffling together some loose papers, but he sees me pretty quickly and straightens up as he flashes me a smile.

"Ah, bonjour, Whitney!" Monsieur Laurent says brightly.

"Bonjour!" I reply with equal enthusiasm, then falter. "Je voudrais . . . me présenter?" Even though I'm pretty sure that's right, my statement comes out as more of a question.

Monsieur Laurent gives me an understanding look before he continues in English. "It can take a little while to adjust to so much French," he says. He speaks perfect English (of course). "I know we are to use French in class, but how is English, just for today?"

"Thanks," I say, a grateful exhale escaping me before I think to trap it. I can mostly follow when being spoken to in a classroom setting, but speaking stresses me out. "You're bilingual! That's so cool."

"Yes." Monsieur Laurent grins. "I earned my PhD at Yale, and I visit Connecticut once a year to see friends there. But learning languages takes time. You'll get it." He perches on the edge of the desk and leans forward so his forearms rest on his leg. "Did you have a question about the assignment?"

"Not exactly," I start. Then I fish a stack of papers that I stapled together this morning out of my messenger bag and hand it to him. "Part of why I wanted to come to Paris to study is to do research for my senior project at this amazing art school—I almost couldn't believe it when

I got in. And . . . well, I wanted to know if you would be willing to be a cochair."

His dark brown eyes brighten a bit as he flips through my research proposal with interest. I try not to speak as he glances at my summary of the project, which is starting to take the shape of a vaudeville-inspired performance featuring Josephine's songs, some original dances, and monologues about her life. My outlines, my plan, and a small list of potential sources I want to start with are in the portfolio as well. When he gets to the end, I'm barely holding in my desire to blurt out *What do you think?*

"Whitney, this is impressive," Monsieur Laurent says, holding up the proposal. "Ambitious."

My face falls a little. "Do you think I can't do it?" I've learned the hard way that when my teachers tell me my ideas are ambitious, it's usually because I'm trying to do a few years' worth of work in a paper that's due in two weeks. Or more recently—i.e., in Madame Hassan's class— "ambitious" has come to mean *your actual performance and how you believe you are performing are not matching.* My ego is still smarting from that one, if I'm honest.

"Oh, no! No, no! I really meant it is ambitious," he replies. "Perhaps you need to focus a little more, narrow your questions down, but you can do this. But, Whitney, are you sure you would like me to be your cochair? Maybe Madame Hassan is a better fit for you? She teaches . . . more of the performance and creative work." Monsieur Laurent gently waves *Candide* in front of me. "I simply teach the words and context."

I consider his question. He looks earnest, like he's really trying to do what's in my best interest, not just passing me off on another teacher. I can't ask Madame Hassan; frankly, she scares me a little with her intensity, which is saying something because nobody out-intensifies me. And even though I'm thinking it, I don't want to say, "I really want a Black professor to be my cochair on this project." I love that Ms. Skinner, the theater teacher from home who encouraged me to pursue this, helped me get started and has been serving as my American cochair, but I want to make sure I have more than just white folks giving me feedback on this particular subject.

"I'm sure," I say firmly. "I think you're the right person for the job. Theater is theater, and the classics influence the new classics."

Monsieur Laurent smiles again. "Mm . . . bon, c'est vrai. D'accord . . . I will need a chance to read your proposal more thoroughly, but perhaps then we can schedule a time to meet next week?"

I'm positively beaming. "That sounds great!" I'm ready to launch into a monologue of gratitude, but then I check the time. It's 3:20, and I'm officially late meeting Thierry.

"I've gotta run," I say, "but we'll talk soon!"

"À plus tard, Whitney," Monsieur Laurent says, tipping his curly head toward me. I take the gesture as being excused, so I fly out of the classroom and book it to the cafeteria, making sure to wave hello to Henri, who I see milling around with a rake on the lawn in front of the administrative building.

SCENE EIGHT

CABARET À LA WHITNEY CURRY

Thierry is nervously drumming his long fingers on the table we've started to frequent when I finally turn into the cafeteria for our tutoring session, nearly barreling into a mousy boy with glasses.

I brace myself for the inevitable sour reprimand for my tardiness, but as soon as I throw myself into the seat across from him, Thierry perks up.

"Okay," he says, and even though it's not exactly enthusiastic, his voice doesn't have the dull-as-pennies tone he usually favors. He slings a backpack that's half open across his shoulders as he stands. "Let's go."

"I'm sorry, what?" I ask, hopping up and scrambling to follow him. Damn Thierry and his long legs! "Didn't you see that I was late? Aren't you going to, like, I don't know, glare at me moodily or something?"

The boy shrugs and keeps walking, straight through the cafeteria doors and through the courtyard, until we reach the street; then we take a left and walk along the hedges in front of the school.

He's dressed differently today, I notice as we quickly cross a street before a man on a vélo tries to flatten us. Thierry has ditched his plain joggers for jeans and has on the red shoes from the day we met instead of the slides I've seen him wear every day since.

I'm trying to infer what the occasion is, but he's striding so fast that I am not going to be able to think and keep up at the same time. All my energy has to be on not getting lost in Paris . . . again.

But after the third time I get caught by a pedestrian light with Thierry on the other side of the intersection, waiting for me with his arms folded across his chest, I admit defeat.

"Do you think you could slow down?" I huff when I finally make it across.

"Oh," he says, and I see in his eyes that Thierry actually didn't realize I couldn't keep up until now. "Yes. I'm sorry."

We set off again, but at a much more manageable pace, one that allows me to do things such as think and admire the scenery as we go. I haven't had time to go far off campus since my first disastrous excursion during my first weekend, so I try to make note of the landmarks I pass so I can make it back to the school without having to send up a flare.

"Where are we going?" I ask finally. It briefly occurs to me that even though I technically know Thierry, I don't know this boy *well*, and following him through a city I don't know—hell, any city at all—sounds like the perfect way to end up on a "Missing" poster. But as I watch him, his profile softer than his expression when I face him straight on, I figure if he meant me harm he wouldn't have seen me safely home from Montmartre.

"Montparnasse, to see your placard," Thierry replies as we approach the entrance for the Cardinal Lemoine métro station.

"I mean, I know that, but I just mean, like *where are we in the city?*" I hesitate as he takes a couple of steps down.

"At the métro, évidemment." He turns back, eyeing me quizzically. "Are you coming?"

Even though Parisians also trying to catch a train are brushing past us, Thierry stays still as he waits for me. He doesn't touch the railing, but he does edge closer to the wall to make way for passersby.

Then his mouth and his eyebrows quirk up. "Miss American Princess is nervous?" He offers me a hand with a bit of a flourish, as he might to actual royalty.

I secure my bag over my shoulder and march decidedly past him straight down into the métro, pushing his arm away as I go, saying "Absolutely not."

When we reach the inside of the station, I turn back quickly.

"And it's *Mademoiselle* American Princess to you."

Thierry chuckles behind my back and follows me to the turnstile.

After he motions for me to hop off the métro, I follow him up the stairs until we reach the street and then walk alongside him. A couple of minutes later, we arrive at a fairly nondescript square in the city.

There's an outdoor section of a restaurant, Bar à Fruits; a few trees and typical Parisian batîments surround the area, with eggshell-colored shutters around windows five stories above the stores at the street level.

I'm about to ask Thierry why he brought me to this random part of Paris, when a fellow pedestrian accidentally jostles me to the left as he passes.

"Désolé," the man mutters, barely acknowledging me. "I—"

My words catch in my throat when I see a blue sign with a green border secured to a black post. My eyes scan the white writing. The sign is similar to the historic markers you'd find in the US.

Except you wouldn't find this specific sign in Virginia:

14E ARRT

PLACE JOSÉPHINE BAKER

1906–1975

ARISTE DE MUSIC-HALL

SOUS-LIEUTENANT DES FORCES FRANÇAISES LIBRES

PHILANTHROPE

Quiet reverence takes over my body as I inspect this tribute to my heroine. My fingers find the pole, and even though I know it's just a placard, it feels like so much more. I turn to find Thierry, who has lost his sharp edge and is looking anywhere but at me. I smirk a bit. Pity, since I'm such a ravishing creature; he's definitely missing out.

I step over to him and hold out my phone, which I unlock as I go.

"Will you take a video of me, please?"

Thierry pauses to check out my phone case, which has

gold Art Deco patterns on it. I think I may have to pull out my best eyelash batting, but he eventually accepts the phone, grateful to be out of the spotlight that I accidentally shone on him by asking him to be my photographer.

"What are you going to do?" Thierry asks.

"I'm going to sing something."

He cocks his head. "Why?"

"So I'll have a video of myself paying tribute to Josephine Baker during my first time in Paris for the director of the documentary they will inevitably make about my life when I'm famous, obviously," I say. "I've also choreographed this song to perform as part of my play."

"Obviously . . . ," Thierry repeats with a good three cups of skepticism in his voice.

While he busies himself with finding a decent spot to stand, I get closer to the post with the placard, drop my bag, and smooth out my shirt.

"T'es prête?" Thierry calls. He's standing on the low edge of a planter box, holding the phone gingerly in front of him. The way he's grasping the thing like it's going to explode reminds me of how my Grandpa John, Nana's second husband, acts whenever we tell him he has to use the internet for something. It makes me giggle.

"Quoi?" he asks gruffly.

"Nothing," I call back. "On y va!" Thierry looks half like he wants to press me for more details, and half like he's impressed that I used a French phrase correctly and without prompting.

I watch him tap the record button, and I start moving without thinking.

I grab the post with one hand and swing myself around

at the tempo of Josephine Baker's song "J'ai Deux Amours" for a four count; then I start singing:

> *"J'ai deux amours*
> *Mon pays et Paris*
> *Par eux toujours*
> *Mon cœur est ravi . . ."*

I twirl and dance as I sing, moving around the post as if it were a partner standing stock-still. The sun is shining down on me, and it feels like I'm pulling energy from it; I let it fill up my cells and send electric currents through my body. I make sure to flash a bright smile at the camera a couple of times as I go. Finally, when I'm done, I grab hold of the post, let myself lean back until my arms are outstretched, then pull myself back up, gazing directly into the camera.

Once I've held the last pose for a couple of seconds, I release it and wave my hand so Thierry knows he can stop recording. When I am famous, documentarians will go nuts over this early-years footage. Around me, I notice that a couple of people have stopped walking to watch me. There's a very small smattering of applause before they continue on their way.

"Oh, uh, merci!" I say with a quick bow, then a modest wave.

Everyone's gone in a flash, though, as if nothing happened at all, and when I turn, Thierry's next to me, holding out my phone. I eagerly take it, ready to check out the video.

"I didn't know that you could sing," Thierry says, blinking enough that it's noticeable—like he's trying to shake himself out of shock. "Or . . . dance. I thought you were only an actress and writer."

"Oh, yeah," I say, pocketing my phone as I shake my head modestly, trying to downplay the whole thing. I didn't felt shy when I was singing and dancing in public in Paris moments ago, but now I suddenly feel very exposed. "I'm no Ella Fitzgerald, but I can carry a tune well. I took a lot of dance lessons for a while, so I'm good at tap. Technically, I'm good enough to land decent roles in musicals and stuff, when they come up, but I'm working to be better. In order to be a triple threat, you have to be prepared for anything."

Thierry's lips part, and I can't read his expression. It makes me shift my weight from leg to leg to occupy myself. I'm about to say something, anything, just to break the silence, but then Thierry says, "I . . . don't know much about . . . performing, but that was better than 'good.'"

His words feel so sincere that I swear I feel my heart swell and press against my rib cage. And even though I could live in this moment, live in the warmth of it all, it also feels too large to fit in my body, and I'm scared of what might happen if I let that big feeling steer the ship. I don't think I'd know what to do with it.

I deflect instead.

"You know you don't have to compliment me to get your good review," I say lightly, pushing a braid behind my ear. "It's in our contract. I don't go back on my word."

"Of course," Thierry says abruptly. "I know."

The moment his face clouds back over, I regret saying anything. Maybe this unidentified tidal wave of warmth that hits me isn't my favorite feeling in the entire world, if only because I don't know exactly what it is, but at least I was in it with Thierry, and being on the outside now, seeing his closed-off expression, feels lonely as hell.

Thierry waits on a bench as I finish roaming around the square, taking pictures with my phone; sending the video and a few pictures to Mom, Nana, and Archi; and committing this place to memory.

"Okay, I'm ready," I say, walking toward him. "Are we headed back to the school?"

"Yes," Thierry says, rubbing his palms on his knees, then pushing himself up to standing. "Do you want to see one more thing? It is on the way."

I check my tiny wristwatch. Even if I stay out another two hours, I can still get home to read for a decent amount of time before heading to bed—Nana recently gifted me a book about Ntozake Shange, poetry, and dance that I'm devouring. So I nod, and within moments, we're headed toward the métro.

SCENE NINE

I MAKE SOCCER CLOTHES EN VOGUE

We end up getting off Line 10 at "my" métro stop, but instead of walking straight ahead, as I've managed to do most of the few times I've returned home from any outing, Thierry takes the steps two at a time and swings himself around the railing, heading in the opposite direction.

I deliberately ascend at a leisurely pace and ignore the red sneaker I see tapping against the sidewalk as I come up. I make a show of letting my ivory kitten heels clack against the grate as I come to Thierry's side, giving him a simpering smile.

He wants to laugh—at least, I think he does by the way his mouth twitches, his dimples trying to make an appearance. But Thierry only shakes his head and leads the way down a new street.

"Your French is very good when you sing," he says as we dodge businesspeople in neutral suits and collared shirts.

The compliment is unexpected, and it seems he has more to say, so I suck in my reply.

"Maybe . . . you could learn more songs," Thierry says, stuffing his hands in his pockets. "Do you think it would help?"

I consider it as I watch a blond toddler pirouette at her father's side up ahead.

"It might," I tell him. "It can't hurt to try, right?"

We both fall quiet, letting the sounds of the wide boulevards wash over us. In this spot, it's quieter than the big squares or roundabouts where the streets open up. In those areas, cars honk nosily and bikers weave through the standstill traffic. Folks talk in their cars, laugh on the streets, and call at each other from the bumper-to-bumper gridlock. Even so, those areas are not as debilitatingly noisy as some US cities. The buildings don't go as high here, so you don't feel pinned down with the noise, and you can see where the birds go when they zip by. More sky makes me feel like there's more space.

"It's easier to sing in French than to speak it," I say to Thierry finally. "I just pick a song that matches what I'm feeling, and the words are already there for me."

He squints at me. "And what if there is no song for what you are feeling?"

I shrug and laugh. "Are you kidding? There's a song for everything."

"No," Thierry presses, "what if you are feeling something different? Something there is not a song for yet?"

I know what my response is, but it doesn't make its way out. The street has opened up, and the buildings that line

92

the street have fallen away, making space for a huge structure that captures my attention. It's neoclassical in design
with six tall columns that hold up a triangular roof, which
has an intricately sculpted front. On the top is a large dome.
From the street, the French flag on the roof, which I know
must be big, looks about the size of a candy wrapper.

"I knew the Panthéon was close by, but I haven't gotten
a chance to visit it yet," I say.

"What's so special about it to you?" Thierry asks.

"Josephine Baker was recently inducted here. She's the
first Black woman to hold this honor," I say, tripping over
the word *honor*. "I struggled with the news for a long time:
on the one hand, it was a national, even internationally
recognized honor, and Josephine probably would have
been touched. But I hate that many Black women don't
get their flowers until after they are dead and gone. My
girl Josephine's been cold in her grave for almost fifty
whole years!"

My chest is getting tight as I stand at the end of the
street across from the bollards that demarcate the beginning of the property for the Panthéon, and I know my eyes
are starting to water, so I turn away from Thierry. Plus, he
might look at me with that soft expression he had at Place
Joséphine Baker, which would cause my brain to short-
circuit and melt down.

I'm not usually a weepy mess anyway, but I certainly
won't become one in front of Thierry Magnon.

His words linger at the periphery of my brain: *What if
you are feeling something different? Something there is not a
song for yet?*

A wave of emotions floods over me as I stand on the streets of Paris. Discontent and pride and rapture and . . . something warm but still undefinable. None of the feelings match, and they're all taking up so much space, trying to exist together in my one body.

I can't be the first person, the first Black girl, who's felt this.

And even though I laughed at Thierry mere moments ago, I have to admit that maybe there's not a song for every emotion.

"But to your initial question . . . I'll find the words," I say quietly, so quietly I'm not sure he hears me. But he shifts ever so slightly next to me, so I know he does, and for once, he doesn't chime in with his two cents.

"Do you want to go inside?" Thierry asks me.

I nod and take a few steps toward the Panthéon. But as I'm stepping down off the curb, about to cross the street onto the plaza, my shoe sinks into something soft before it hits the ground.

Shocked, I raise my foot to shake off whatever I landed in and immediately lose my balance, falling back onto my butt into a decent amount of mud that's been made particularly icky from the recent rain.

"Merde," I say, pinching the bridge of my nose in distress.

"Are you okay?" Thierry asks from somewhere above me.

I force myself to nod even though my face definitely belies my words.

"I think you should get out of that," Thierry tells me, a semisympathetic grimace on his face. He offers me a hand. *Great,* I think, *I am still sitting in a pile of mud. If ever I could just slither down a drain and disappear, now would be a great time to do that.*

I finally, gingerly, accept Thierry's outstretched hand and get to my feet. I touch my braids to make sure I don't have any grime in my hair, and thank goodness, I'm saved from that particular humiliation. As for my outfit, from the front, it looks totally fine. But from the back . . .

My neck will only crane so far around to let me assess the damage. I have to ask Thierry.

"How bad is it?" I ask, distress leaking into my voice. I don't even care that I sound like a woman on a soap opera asking her doctor how long she has to live. I angle myself so that he has a full view of my backside.

Thierry steps away from me a bit, evidently uncomfortable.

"You *cannot* be embarrassed that I'm asking you to check out my ass right now!" I say loudly, grabbing the interest of a few passersby. I lower my voice to a more reasonable level. "Help! *Please!*"

"Ça va, ça va," Thierry says in what I'm sure he thinks is a soothing tone, lifting a large hand in surrender. He takes a sharp inhale that tells me I look like the hot mess I fear I am. "I have football clothes; you can wear them." Then he glances past me, and when I turn to see what got his attention, I notice a small gray structure made of what appears to be a sturdy plastic in his line of vision. "Toilettes" is written across the side.

"Praise the goddess Ntozake Shange," I say in a single breath. Time is of the essence, so I don't repeat myself for

Thierry, though he's staring at me with his brow furrowed. What else is new? "Where are your clothes?"

"Voilà." He fishes a wadded-up bundle of clothes out of his bag and hands them to me, and I'm moving toward the public toilet as fast as my chunky little legs will carry me. I do hear him tentatively call me—"Whitney, are you sure you want to . . . ?"—but I need to get out of these clothes.

It takes me a second to wrench the door open, but I get in and lock the door behind me. It's cramped, and the smell inside isn't exactly fresh-cut roses (hence Thierry's warning, which I soundly ignored), so I make haste to shimmy out of my formerly fabulous outfit. I somehow manage to hold the mud-soaked clothes in one hand so they don't touch the floor of the bathroom as I untangle Thierry's gym clothes: a navy-blue shirt with the letters "PSG" printed across the chest in bold red letters over a stylized illustration of the Eiffel Tower, and a pair of white shorts.

If I was hesitating to throw them on, I forget about it the second I pull Thierry's shirt over my head. Despite having been stuffed in a teenage boy's book bag, it smells refreshingly clean, like laundry detergent but with a lingering scent of sugar, probably picked up from his parents' shop. I breathe it in deeply before I stop, silently reprimanding myself for behaving like a creeper.

When I'm dressed, I admire myself in the tiny mirror. Thierry's tall and lean, so a smaller girl might've drowned in these clothes, but my thick thighs and butt fill out his shorts. His shirt, however, is long, and when I look down, I see falls loosely down to my thighs, leaving only a sliver of white from the shorts visible.

"This actually wouldn't be a bad outfit if I had a belt," I muse, pulling the fabric of the shirt from the back so it cinches at the waist. I find a scrunchie in my bag and tie the shirt in the back. Then I consider my braids, which are too elaborately pinned and tucked for my current clothing situation. So, one by one, I pluck the bobby pins from my head and drop them into the side pocket of my messenger bag.

I look . . . different. I can't put my finger on it, but somehow, this Whitney, this Parisian Whitney, just looks like she can handle anything.

There's a soft knock at the door, and I hear Thierry calling me to check if I'm okay. I grab my bag and my soiled clothes, then emerge back into the late-afternoon sun. I've been inside for a few minutes, so the golden light seems ethereal and throws the buildings into sharp relief, dancing off the windows. The fact that I'm in Paris, experiencing this beauty, once again nearly knocks the breath out of my body.

My gaze finally lands back on Thierry, and he's staring at me, barely bothering to hide it. I'm suddenly overly aware of how visible my legs are, and it takes every bit of control I have not to peer down at my knees to make sure they aren't ashy. I basically take a second bath every morning in shea butter body lotion, but today would be the day my rituals failed me.

We stand there for a few more seconds before I blurt out, "I know I look ridiculous, but this is so much less humiliating than walking back to LIA covered in mud."

Thierry smiles a little, bringing his fist to his nose to cover the expression. Then he gestures for me to follow him.

"We can come back another day to see inside," Thierry assures me as we walk away from the Panthéon. I'm distracted by the sharp sound of my heels landing on the pavement and the swish of Thierry's shorts as the jersey fabric rubs together between my thighs. I lift my chin higher, as if trying to convince everyone around me I *meant* to dress like this.

"Okay," I say, my mouth puckering at the thought of what I want to say next. "Thanks. For this. You're basically my hero. Again."

Thierry's shyness is falling away and is slowly being replaced with smugness as he peeks at me from the corner of his eye.

"I am?" he says, clearly fishing for more praise. I push him lightly on his shoulder.

"Don't get used to the compliments," I warn him, cutting him a dangerous look both my mother and grandmother would be proud of.

Thierry nods, grinning, with his hands raised in surrender again. "I understand." But he still appears a little too pleased with himself for my taste.

"You just happened to have practice clothes with you today? Even though you're suspended from the team?" I ask him.

Seriousness falls over him again, but it's not as complete as it was. Thierry keeps talking, to my surprise.

"I play for fun with my friends sometimes when there are no games or practice," he says. "We are going to play tonight. I was going to go there after I walked you back to school."

"Oh my gosh. I'm so sorry. I totally wrecked your plans," I say.

"No, no, not at all," Thierry says quickly to reassure me. "It is okay. I can borrow shorts from someone. I still have my shoes. It is okay."

I try to gather myself, because I—who have never cared about sports a day in my life—suddenly want to see Thierry playing soccer in just gym shorts. I'm actually about to do something wild and ask if I can come to the game with him, but as I'm opening my mouth, he jogs in front of me, hooting and calling in French.

As we cross the street, a soccer field becomes visible. It's surrounded by a black wrought-iron fence that curls at the top several feet above both of our heads. Thierry has fitted one of his feet into one of lower openings on the fence, and hoists himself up. A few guys about our age milling around on the other side of the field near the benches look up when Thierry calls.

They return his greeting just as warmly—and loudly. Thierry yells something at them that I don't understand, but I hear my name, and he gestures to me. I decide to wave.

Possibly the wrong move, because regardless of nationality, teenage boys act stupid when girls are involved.

"Ah, la princesse américaine!" one boy yells. He has curly sandy brown hair that is shaved down on the sides and matching skin that is peppered with so many gingerbread-colored freckles I can see them from here. He's hooting as he nudges the guys next to him, one of whom I recognize as Amir from the kebob stand and one of whom says something that causes them to break into riotous laughter. He pulls at his shirt as he laughs, and the other boys start pulling off their shirts.

I am now painfully aware of the implication of Thierry walking me home in his clothes, and even though it's mild outside temperature-wise, I think I'm going to melt from the molten heat taking over my body.

"Ta gueule!" Thierry shouts back, which is, without a doubt, something very rude. But he's got a smile in his eyes as the boys trade insults and jokes.

As he climbs down off the fence, he calls, "I am coming back," but the boys barely acknowledge him, already moving on to something on one of their phones.

Thierry starts walking back toward the school, which I know is close now that I've seen the soccer pitch, and I am moving sluggishly, my embarrassment apparently filling my joints with molasses. He turns back and studies my face for a second before he says, "That is just Fabien. We have been friends since we were very young. He is not so bad."

"I'm sure he's delightful," I say, grateful that Thierry is taking his strides at a more manageable pace, "but I feel like I just got made fun of, and I have no idea what anyone said."

Thierry's quiet for a minute as we walk.

"I told them I am coming to play but I need to walk you home first," he says. "Fabien noticed that you were wearing my jersey, and so . . ." He drifts off, but I don't need him to translate the rest.

"And you just . . . let him say that?" I ask. We're two blocks from the soccer pitch, at the start of the fencing that runs around the periphery of LIA.

"No," Thierry says firmly. "I did not think you wanted

strangers to know about your . . . accident. I told them you'd fallen and ripped your shirt and to shut up."

"Ta gueule," I repeat as we get to the gate and turn onto the wide pebbled walkway that leads to the dormitory.

Thierry turns to me, his eyes wide, his expression stuck somewhere between shock and amusement. "I'm sorry?"

"Ta gueule," I say again. "That's what you told him."

He throws his head back and laughs. I smile in spite of myself.

"That's not very polite, Whitney Curry."

And then I'm laughing, clutching my side, trying to catch my breath. When the giggles finally subside and I clear away the tears that are blocking my vision, I see Thierry taking big breaths trying to get himself together, too. The two of us are laughing like maniacs, and with me in this ridiculous outfit, I'm not surprised when a few girls who I think are in one of my classes walk by, eyeing us suspiciously.

"Okay, well," I say finally. "This was . . . fun."

Thierry's eyebrows quirk up. "Really?" His energy shifts, and he has a tiny bit of hopefulness written on his face, which makes me suddenly overthink what I was going to say next.

"Yeah," I say slowly. "Though I admittedly did not learn very much French."

"You learned how to tell me to shut up very rudely," Thierry says solemnly. Then he grins and his dimples pop out. *God, those things should come with a warning.*

"I have a feeling that phrase is gonna come in handy," I tell him with a light laugh, tossing my braids over my shoulder as I start walking again until we're on the steps at the front door of LIA. "Are you sure you don't want these clothes back? I can run upstairs and change and bring them down to you. It'll only take a minute."

"No, really," Thierry says, shaking his head. "I can get them later."

"Okay . . ."

I feel myself lingering. I'm home. I should want to get upstairs to take a shower and wash my clothes, then hang them out to dry. (Drying loads of laundry is weirdly expensive at LIA. Our welcome packet recommended we air-dry as much as we can.)

I should want to call Archi or my cousin and other best friend, Becca, and recount this entire ordeal. I should want to get as far away from moody, surly Thierry Magnon as possible, but I am inexplicably still on these steps.

Then Thierry surprises me.

"May I see your list?" he asks as we idle in front of the school.

"What list?" I say stupidly, as if I don't have at least twelve in my journal right now.

"Your list of things that you want to see in Paris," Thierry says. "If you show me, I can show you which things are close together, things that you can see all at once. It will help me plan for tutoring . . . field trips?"

I'm hung up on the way "field trip" came out plural. I know leading me around was part of the agreement, but after falling in mud and having to steal his clothes, I wouldn't be surprised if he went back on his end of the bargain. Or at least was thinking about it.

Thierry's still waiting for my answer, so I dig into my bag for my leather journal, open it to the first page, and hold it out for him. The list goes on for another two pages, so I flip it to show him.

"You'll also want to see my annotated map," I say briskly.

"Your what?" Thierry asks blankly.

"It's kind of like a supplement to the list," I tell him, taking that out, too. "But more visual, with notes and highlights, potential routes to and from locations. Very casual."

"But why would you do this?" Thierry asks genuinely, like he can't understand why anyone would make a color-coded list and annotated map.

"It's how my brain works." I shrug. "It's how I keep important things organized and prioritized. Don't knock the system."

"Okay . . ." He digs his phone from his pocket and gestures as if he wants to take a picture. "May I?" When I nod, he snaps a couple of shots of both the list and the map.

Whitney Curry's Parisian Bucket List
(Thrice approved by three generations of Currys!)

TOP PRIORITIES
See the Eiffel Tower
    - Related: See the Eiffel Tower lit
      up in the evening
    - Have a picnic under the Eiffel Tower with
      cheese and wine
Visit a chocolatier and take a class
Tour the Panthéon
Go thrifting!

- Chinemachine
- Nuovo

MUSEUMS

The Louvre
   - Get a picture in front of the Mona Lisa!
The Musée d'Orsay (to see the Monets!)
The Centre Pompidou (to see the modern art!)
The Musée Rodin
The Musée de l'Orangerie

CHURCHES

Notre Dame
Sacré-Cœur
Sainte-Chapelle

HISTORICAL/EDUCATIONAL

Visit Versailles
Take a Black Americans in Paris tour
Visit BNF (the Bibliothèque Nationale de France)
Tour the Sorbonne
Find a way to visit the Château des Milandes (where
Josephine Baker lived)
See the Josephine Baker historic plaque

ART/THEATER

Go to the Moulin Rouge
Watch a performance at the Palais Garnier
   - Try not to break into a rendition of
     "Phantom of the Opera"

Visit theaters on the Grands Boulevards
Dance at the Caveau de la Huchette

FOOD
Have a hot chocolate at Angelina's
Take a cooking class

MISCELLANEOUS
Visit the Champs-Élysées and the Arc de Triomphe
Read in the Jardin de Luxembourg
Take a boat ride down the Seine
Go to Shakespeare and Company
Shop at the Galeries Lafayette and Les Halles
   - Les Halles in particular because it is the
      original fresh food market of Paris
Visit a parfumerie
Check out flea markets!

I feel kind of exposed, with my private journal opened up to a guy I met two weeks ago, but it's not uncomfortable. Though I regret thinking this as soon as Thierry reads my list, taking pictures and chuckling. I roll my eyes, but if he's keeping his commentary to himself, so can I.

Eventually, of course, he can't help himself.

"Your list . . . it is very 'tourist.' The Eiffel Tower, the Champs-Élysées, Shakespeare and Company . . ."

"I *am* a tourist," I reply, pulling my journal back to my chest.

"No, you live here," Thierry says. "Maybe not for a long time, but for now, you live here. You should act like it."

He's quiet but is challenging me in a way that makes me feel like there's electricity running up and down my arms. I bristle at the words and the conversation we're having. Yet I'm trying to think up an excuse to stay out here and prolong it even more.

That's the thought that brings me back to myself as I realize we're stuck, neither of us making any effort to move.

"Well, thanks for the advice," I say, dropping my journal into my messenger bag and putting my other hand on the doorknob to my dorm. "I'm . . . I'm gonna go . . . get cleaned up."

"Of course," Thierry says, taking the smallest step back from me, breaking our connection. "Good night, Whitney."

"Bonne soirée, Thierry," I say, slipping inside before I change my mind.

From the lobby, I can see Thierry biting his bottom lip thoughtfully as he tilts his chin up at the school for a few moments. Then he pivots on one foot and does a light jog away.

I head toward the beautiful staircase on the left side of the building, breathing in the lingering smell of sugar on Thierry's clothes and letting the loud clack of my heels drown out the thudding of my heart.

SCENE TEN

I BEFRIEND SOME SKULLS

> **Thierry:** Would you like to see something that is not on your list of Parisian sights?

It's the next Thursday evening, and I'm in my room with books for my thesis, a few plays, and my journals spread out over my desk. A few books that won't fit on the desk are open on the floor next to me, covered in the wrinkled foil remains of my brain food—half of a box of truffles— when my phone lights up with the message from Thierry. I raise my head, which I've been resting on my palm, to read it and chew on an orange-filled chocolate, my eyebrows threatening to disappear into my hairline. I accidentally knock the two small journals I've filled with notes from my adventures around Paris since my arrival to the floor in my haste to grab the phone.

He hasn't messaged me first since the day I got lost and he saved me. There's no real need. We met three times this week in the cafeteria, plus last Wednesday, when Thierry took me on the field trip that ended with me looking like I was doing a walk of shame back to the dorm. And I've had to put that out of my mind by zeroing in on my play, but the organization of it all is muddy. Or at least, I think it's muddy *now*. I sigh, scanning my work schedule.

<u>Whitney's Research and Rehearsal Schedule for *The Loves of Josephine Baker*</u>

<u>Mondays, 7–9 p.m.:</u> Reading/research, writing, and editing time

<u>Tuesdays, 7–9 p.m.:</u> Vocal and dance rehearsal (eventually blocking) time

<u>Wednesdays:</u> Off, for tutoring adventures with Thierry

<u>Thursdays, 7–9 p.m.:</u> Reading/research, writing, and editing time

<u>Fridays:</u> Rest day

<u>Saturdays, 9–10:30 a.m.:</u> Vocal and dance rehearsal (reserve practice room in the annex)

<u>Sundays, 8–11 a.m.:</u> Vocal and dance rehearsal

Madame Hassan told me my current plan of a one-woman show was "mundane" and my rehearsal schedule was "likely insufficient" when I mentioned it in class this morning, so I've been rearranging the section of my show outline composed of half-written monologues about Josephine Baker's love life, with breaks to practice some songs. I complained to Monsieur Laurent later when I saw him for class, but he didn't have the technical expertise to back his assurance that he thought it was "fine."

I have been locked in my room ever since.

Which is all to say, I'm surprised and grateful that I have this text message.

Also unexpected: the way I'm suddenly jittery, like I've had three of Mathilde's best espressos.

I tap the fingers of my other hand on the wooden desk and bounce my leg as I try to decide what to do. Nora's out, but my eyes dart over to the other side of the room, where Sophie is lounging on her navy comforter dotted with gold stars, eyes closed, headphones covering her ears. She probably can't deal with a dose of Whitney today. I can't help but think she'd have the time and patience if I were Fatima, the best friend she brings up at least once a conversation. . . . Sometimes I feel like we've moved on from the initial rough patch, but there are moments, especially if I see her when I'm out with Thierry, that make me think something else is going on.

Plan A, it is, then, I think as I unlock the phone and scroll past the new message from Thierry to find my thread with Archi and send a new text.

> **Whitney:** Arch, we have a problem.

> **Archi:** Hi, Whitney!!! How's Paris?!

> **Whitney:** Beautiful, wonderful, my first true love.
> **Whitney:** BUT ALAS, it's not perfect.

Archi: . . . Do I want to know why?

Whitney: YES, you do!

Whitney: Have I told you about the boy that's tutoring me? Thierry?

Archi: Your French tutor is a Parisian boy?! OMG! Is he cute?!!!

Whitney: . . . yes.

Whitney: But you're missing the point!

Archi: Babes, you're getting tutored by a hot Parisian boy. I think *you're* missing the point.

Whitney: Archi, nobody has time for that!

Archi: Right, right, because you're on a mission to write the best one-woman play in the history of Western civilization.

Whitney: Right.

Archi: But aren't you the self-appointed queen of multitasking?

Whitney: *deep sigh* Make friends, they say. They'll support you in all things, they say!

Archi: Okay, Whit, what's the issue?

> **Whitney:** Thierry wants me to go somewhere with him . . .

I fill her in on our first outing to Place Joséphine Baker and the Panthéon, making sure to detail having to wear his soccer clothes home and also how he doesn't usually text me. His clothes have been washed, air-dried on my windowsill, and folded, and I can't help but glance at them on top of my steamer trunk as I wait for Arch to heart all my messages and reply to each individual text with a string of exclamation points and tons of emojis, a process that takes her several minutes.

> **Whitney:** Are you done?

Archi:—Nope. 😮😮😮😮😮😮 ●●●●●●●●●●●●●●
😩😩😩😩😩

Archi: He likes hanging out with you!

> **Whitney:** Archi!

Archi: I didn't say he *likes* you. I just said he probably likes hanging out with you. He seems kind of shy and mysterious so maybe he doesn't have a ton to say.

Archi: But he clearly wants to spend time with you.

> **Whitney:** So you think I should go?

> **Archi:** I think you should at least respond to his message, babe.

The clock tells me that I have now spent a half hour frantically texting my best friend about a boy I am decidedly uninterested in. Sure, hanging out with Thierry is fun, but there *can't* be anything more to it. It would be too much of a distraction from the plan: platonic sightseeing with him for research purposes and getting this one-woman show in tip-top condition. But after talking to Archi, I realize *something* is happening, whether I want it to or not. If it wasn't a thing before, I'm absolutely making it one by spending all this time on it.

It's just a text, I tell myself. *Stop sweating the little things, Curry.*

> **Whitney:** Thanks, Archi. 💀💀💀💀💀💀💀💀
> **Whitney:** We'll video chat soon

I thumb back over to the message from Thierry, smiling at how the only other messages are from the day I got lost at Montmartre: my desperate plea for help and his short reply.

> **Whitney:** Is this some sort of surprise, or are you going to tell me where we're going?

Three little dots dance on the screen moments after I send my text, which is a relief because I can skip the inevitable panic that comes with sending a risky text. Not that anything about this is risky . . .

Thierry: You do not like surprises?

Whitney: I like to be prepared.

Thierry: This place is not on your tourist list. So wear shoes for walking.

I snort. Leave it to Thierry to still not tell me what's happening.

Whitney: I never said I was going with you.

Thierry: You say the best way to learn is by experience. We will have a real Parisian experience tomorrow.

Ugh, I hate when people use my own genius words against me. And now I am very invested.

Whitney: Okay.

"No."

"Whitney."

"No!"

Thierry would probably be exasperated if he weren't so busy laughing. I fold my arms over my chest because I hate being laughed at.

He convinced me to go for a vélo ride to Montparnasse, and I obliged, thinking that was the whole adventure, only to find myself standing at the entrance to the Catacombs.

"It is going to rain. If we stay out here, we will get wet," Thierry says, gesturing to the stormy gray sky, as if there were any weather report on God's green earth that would get me to go underground into a huge mass grave. There's a reason I intentionally left this particular landmark off my bucket list. Whitney Curry does *not* do dead people in any way, shape, or form—especially not in skeleton form! Honestly, it could rain fire right now, and I still wouldn't go down there for cover. Imaginary roots have grown out of my feet, hooking me to the ground; that's how unmovable I am.

"Whitney," Thierry says evenly, moving closer to me. I can smell his cologne, which doesn't quite mask the ever-present scent of sugar and butter on him. Between the sound of my name and the smell, my brain suspiciously goes blank, and I have to blink a couple of times to get everything back online. "Not everything in Paris is warm and beautiful. This is Paris, too." He moves closer to the entrance. "Plus, this is cool."

Thierry's daring me to do this. But there's also something a little hopeful in his eye that eventually makes me give in.

"Fine," I say, "but you owe me a trip to Notre Dame and a box of chocolates. I still haven't been to your family's shop, and I have to try the goods."

Thierry snorts and replies with a joking, "Bien sûr, princesse."

This isn't so bad, I think a while later. Sure, we had to go down about a million steps to enter the Catacombs, and there was a sign over the entrance that read "Stop! This is the Empire of the Dead" (but in French), and now we're underground, and it's chillier than I expected . . . but so far, it's not terrible. Where we—the other visitors to the Catacombs, Thierry, and I—are, the walls are just light brown dirt and sand with lanterns wedged into them every few meters. I start to ask where the skeletons are, but I close my mouth and figure that's a problem for Future Whitney.

The cavern here is tight, so Thierry and I can't walk side by side. I have to trail just behind him, and I tell myself that the narrow space is why I keep drifting closer to him, not my fear or any other impossible feelings.

"Ça va?" Thierry asks me after we've walked a bit farther. We're about to turn a corner that I'm pretty sure is going to put me face to face with an experience that'll give me nightmares for a few months, but I nod.

"Oui," I breathe.

The cavern opens up, and I feel my stomach turn and then threaten to rise up my throat. The walls, which were previously made of dirt, are now made of bones, with mostly the jointed ends protruding. I attempt to calm myself by taking a few breaths; after all, they're bones, which means that whoever they belonged to is dead and can't hurt me. Still, I make certain that no part of me even accidentally brushes up against the wall of human remains.

I'm so focused on not touching them that I accidentally bump lightly into Thierry.

"I told you, it is not so bad," Thierry says, trying to keep his expression serious but failing as I see the humor dancing in his eyes.

"I guess . . . but—" I stop, horror twisting my face. *"Is that a skull?!"*

"Yeah," Thierry says, sounding as though he's just discovered a twenty-euro bill on the ground and not something that used to belong inside a human's head.

I try to listen to the audio guide Thierry got us, but I can't concentrate.

"It's just . . . ," I say, tapping Thierry's shoulder, causing him to cock his head and widen his big dark eyes. "The only time I've ever been this close to a skull was when I was Ophelia in *Hamlet* in tenth grade and the 'Alas, poor Yorick' skull was *plastic,* and I wasn't even *in* that scene, so you can see I'm not—"

I stop babbling long enough to whimper. Now, not only are there skulls in the wall, but there's also an entire column of them in the middle of the passage.

"Whitney," Thierry says seriously but with a smile that's strangely comforting, "Tout va bien."

And then he gently squeezes my hand, which somehow got itself wound around one of his.

Well, at least if I die of embarrassment right now, I'm already in a mass cemetery, I think as I spring away from Thierry, but not so far as to rub up against the wall of bones. I make sure to drop his hand carefully, so as not to draw attention to the fact that I grabbed it in the first place. But Thierry cuts me an entertained look out of the corner of his eye and purses his lips so he doesn't smile. *They could just leave me down here.*

We walk for another half hour, and in that time, I calm down considerably. I even listen to the audio guide tell us how bodies were evacuated from Saints-Innocents cemetery and dumped here and how more evacuations occurred during Haussmannization, the period during the nineteenth century that created the wide boulevards that form the basis of Paris's layout. Thierry listens and walks solemnly next to me but stops from time to time for some selfies in front of the bone walls.

Fortunately, I listened to Thierry when he suggested I wear walking shoes, so I ditched my kitten heels for a pair of brown loafers that go nicely with my matching brown-plaid-pants-and-vest combination. I was not, however, warned that the Catacombs would be this cold. The chill is striking my skin through the thin chiffon blouse with loose sleeves I'm wearing underneath the vest.

There are only a few minutes left of the audio tour; then we'll be back on street level, where it'll likely still be cool from the rain, but at least warmer than down here. My body clearly can't wait, though, because my teeth start chattering within moments.

And it's like Thierry can hear my mind—or at least hear my teeth chattering so loudly they start to echo in the cavern—because he turns around and asks me if I'm cold.

"N-no," I say stubbornly, but once again, my body betrays me as I stutter my answer.

"Take my hoodie," Thierry insists, already pulling it over his head in spite of my weak protests.

Heat rises to my face as I realize I am entirely too focused on the bit of his stomach I can see when his shirt rises.

He hands the navy hoodie to me with a quick nod, and I stop my hemming and hawing when I feel that it's still warm from his body heat. I slide it on, pulling my braids out from the neck and sticking my hands down into the front pocket, sighing contently. In addition to being bless-edly warm, it smells of him—of sugar and vanilla almost masked by his light cologne.

"I'm glad you are no longer cold," he says, glancing over at me as we continue moving forward. "But I think you are trying to steal all of my clothes." The safe feeling of being wrapped in Thierry's hoodie is warring with impulse to keep him at arm's length. We have an agreement, and I, for one, am planning to stick to it, no matter how much he tries to rile me up. No distractions.

I snort. The few people down here in the Catacombs with us glance over. It's not a library, but it seems as though the general consensus is to walk through quietly, as if loud talk and laughter will disturb the spirits.

Personally, I'd guess that being removed from their graves already did that, but what do I know?

"Or one might say you were putting me in situations where I'd *have* to steal your clothes," I retort. Thierry doesn't immediately respond, so I face him and find that he's got a marginally guilty look on his face. I grin. "Oh, my gosh, you *are.*"

"That is silly," he says, fixing his expression in a dead-pan stare. "How was I to know you would fall last week?"

"Okay, yeah, but today?"

Thierry huffs out a laugh and throws up his hands. "How was I to know you would be cold?"

I snuggle farther down into Thierry's hoodie.

"I have your soccer clothes, by the way," I tell him. "They're in my room. I washed them and everything. I can get them for you when we get back to school." I don't mention that the wash was recent; I inadvertently turned his shorts into loungewear last week. In my defense, they are extremely comfortable shorts.

Thierry shakes his head and stretches himself, arms going high over his head, raising his shirt again. I really need him to stop that.

"It is okay. I have many clothes for football."

"Honestly?" I say. "Great, because your clothes are so much more comfortable than mine." I pinch my lips. My incomparable ability to let my mouth run off without my brain wins again.

But it's Thierry's turn to attract attention. He laughs loudly. He doesn't seem to mind. I consider backtracking over my words, but decide I'll just let him have this.

We walk in a comfortable silence for a few more minutes before I bite my lip, trying but failing to keep in what I want to say.

"Uh . . . about . . . back there. I grabbed your hand because I freaked out. . . . Sorry," I say, developing a sudden and intense interest in the dusty bones.

I chance a peek at Thierry to find that he appears . . . satisfied. His eyebrows are raised as he peers down at me, and I sort of want to disappear into his hoodie.

"It's okay." His voice is low and soft, with a tone one might take to mean that a repeat of the offense would be . . . welcome.

His hand, dark brown with a few prominent veins, swings gently by his side as we walk, and I consider reaching for it again, even though I'm not scared anymore and I'm warm now, and it's dark down here so no one would know I held Thierry Magnon's hand in the Catacombs—

But he slows, and I see that we've made it to the other

end of the Catacombs. We stand at the base of a staircase that we'll climb to get back to street level, and as we go and we get closer to the sun again, I can't help but feel I've missed an opportunity I didn't think I wanted in the first place.

7 Things I've Noticed About Thierry Magnon

1. Thierry really likes sneakers. They might be his favorite things. I can see him in slight variations of the same outfit several times over the course of a week, but he will always have on a different pair of shoes.
   a. The red Air Force 1s I saw him in the first day are probably his *all-time* favorite.
2. In addition to the soccer thing, he runs a few miles most mornings. I discovered this when I accidentally texted him at six a.m. one morning to ask what one wears to the Palais Garnier for our school trip to see a ballet. (Okay, so it wasn't an accident; I was awake tearing up my closet and figured he'd see the text when he woke up.)
3. He likes coffee but tries not to drink a lot of it. He almost never takes a second espresso, if he has one at all, usually opting for room-temperature water. (I still haven't quite gotten over the French distaste for ice cubes in drinks.)
4. While he may not like talking about his parents, Thierry decidedly lights up when I ask questions about his sisters—well, as much as Mr. Grouchy Pants can light up. This is how I found out Célestine was briefly in an all-girl rock band that

she almost dropped out of college for, and Lucie
has an unholy appetite for chocolate. A girl after
my own heart, honestly.

5. Thierry likes numbers. Specifically, finance. The
day he accompanied me to Versailles, I passed the
time by asking him every question I could think
of, including what his best subject was at school.
Color me shocked when it wasn't French, since he
loves to be a know-it-all in that area.

6. When traveling, Thierry needs to stand, or he
will rest his head against the window and fall
asleep almost immediately. Considering we almost
missed our stop at Versailles because he was nearly
impossible to wake, I will never forget this fact.

7. He doesn't mind when I hum show tunes
absentmindedly on the métro. In fact, judging by
the way I caught him smiling the last time I did
it . . . he might even kind of like it.

SCENE ELEVEN

I DEVELOP MY TEMPO

"Ooh, a thrift shop!" I gush, quickening my pace to pass Nora and Sophie.

The three of us decided we needed to spend a little more quality time together as roommates, so I told Thierry we wouldn't need to meet over the weekend and booked a riverboat ride along the Seine with the two of them instead. We giggled loudly and took a lot of selfies on the water, bundled up in our fall jackets, letting the river air whip our hair around our faces.

Now we wander aimlessly, not quite ready to head back to school. As we walk, I send my nana a quick photo of me with my friends from the boat.

Whitney: Just me, my friends, and my favorite river in the world. Miss you!

Nana: How charming!

The girls follow me into the thrift shop, a comforting scent of aged leather drifting to me as soon as I open the door while a bell tinkles brightly overhead.

"Bonjour, mesdemoiselles," the woman behind the counter says, boredom written all over her face.

"Bonjour," we chorus back. I notice that the shopkeeper doesn't do a double-take at me when I speak, as most French people I encountered did in the first couple of weeks after I arrived. It was like they could hear in two syllables that I didn't belong.

I don't know if my accent is hidden beneath Nora's and Sophie's or if the shopkeeper simply doesn't want to acknowledge us further, but either way, it's nice to feel like Paris and I are settling into each other.

Now that it's October, I found that I've started to fall into a rhythm. My classes take up most of the day during the week, and during free hours I find corners and hideaways to study in all over the school and around the Latin Quarter. I meet with Monsieur Laurent on Tuesday afternoons at four for cookies and a quick espresso from the vending machine outside his office while I give him updates on my writing; he always sends me off with about four new books to read and an encouraging smile. On afternoons that I don't have tutoring with Thierry and I decide to leave campus to study or edit my play, I stop by the cafeteria to say hello to Mathilde and then bring Henri his afternoon espresso in the administrative building.

Somehow, in all my routine building—which has included more time with Thierry than I'd like to admit—I haven't had much time to devote to making new friends, and I found myself missing both having people in this place and all the folks I had back home.

I'm glad to have this afternoon outing with my room-mates, but Nora's breezy laugh and Sophie's reserved smile as they discuss a plaid vest likely from the '90s make my heart ache for my people back in DC—Mom and Nana, Archi and Becca.

I manage to ask the shopkeeper about the price of a ruby-colored circle skirt in French without pausing and am delighted when she tells me—"Cinq euros"—with barely a glance.

"Merci," I reply, then turn to Nora and Sophie with the skirt clutched in my hand. "I have a favor to ask."

Sophie's eyebrows quirk up. "Would you two be willing to help me with my show? I could use some help with my choreography, Nora. And, Sophie, I'd love for someone to run my sound and lights."

Nora appears interested but doesn't speak immediately, deep in thought over a lacy, flowing white sundress with an empire waist. I press on. "You won't have to do very much. I know you're both busy with your own work. I could just use a hand."

"Sure, if I can make suggestions for the sound design?" Sophie asks, placing an ornate jade straw hat with a collection of flowers and a small cardinal on the side on top of her messy black curls. "I might be able to get extra credit with Monsieur Tsien, my sound production teacher."

Nora puts the dress back on the rack between a sunny peacoat and a violet corset top, focusing back in on our conversation. "Of course, Whitney, I'll help. Maybe once a week?"

"Once a week is perfect!" I say as I approach the sales counter. "Are you two ready to check out? I just want to get this."

"Ah!" the shopkeeper interjects. "Mais vous êtes américaine! Your accent . . . it's very good."

I'm so shocked that I almost drop my skirt.

"Moi? Me?" I ask. She can't be talking to Nora or Sophie.

The shopkeeper nods. "I did not realize you were American until you spoke in English."

"All your tutoring with Thierry must be paying off," Sophie says with a knowing smirk that I want to return, but I decide against it when I see that Nora doesn't smile with us. Instead, she has a new pensive expression on her face as I pay.

"Merci, madame," I say as the three of us leave the shop. She gives me a quick nod of acknowledgment.

As we walk back to LIA, I notice a few of my new favorite haunts. When I'm not interested in cafeteria food, I go down a few streets to a kebob stand Thierry showed me a couple of weeks ago. If not there, I grab a jambon-beurre or a pizza from one of the other shops just a few steps past the stand, both spots we pass as we continue our promenade.

Before long, we're back in our room at school, and it doesn't take long for Sophie to sink into her music-induced silence with her headphones over her ears. Nora, I notice, pulls up a video chat with Fatima.

"I'll give you some privacy," I say, grabbing my phone and my journal and heading for the door. It feels like Fatima is giving me the stank eye through the phone, but I can't figure out what I could have possibly done to offend her, especially when Nora, Sophie, and I have already moved on.

I settle down in the library on the ground floor, which is miraculously always empty, and open my journal to check "boat ride down the Seine" off my bucket list. With a lot of help from Thierry, more than half of the list is checked off, even with all the side adventures he insists we go on. On a new page, I start a list of the places I've gone with Thierry that weren't on my original list, including the most recent.

Thierry's Additions to Whitney's
Parisian Bucket List

A trip to le Ballon de Paris Générali
A trip to La Tour de l'Horloge
A trip to The Belleville neighborhood

In Belleville, we walked through the streets slowly, Thierry pointing out his favorite street art pieces on the sides of the buildings: profiles of a Black man and an abstract piece so vibrant that the oranges and greens threatened to jump off the wall. I took lots of pictures of them, with my Polaroid camera and my phone, and Thierry always offered to get shots of me in front of them as well. I convinced him that he needed to be in a few pictures with me. He grudgingly let me pull him toward me by the arm and didn't quite smile, only raised his eyebrows, which was not ideal, but it'll do.

I pull that particular Polaroid out of my journal and scan it, remembering that day's adventure. How he told me Belleville is not a part of the city tourists go to often.

How I then noticed that once you push beyond the art, the storefronts aren't as clean and sharp as the ones in the parts of the city I've spent the most time in. People are dressed well but in clothes that don't scream "luxury," as I typically see in the more touristy parts. And there are many more Black people, Middle Eastern folks, and younger folks in general who I see in clusters, vaping. With Thierry's perspective on Paris, I have a new appreciation for the city I made into a fantasy. Thanks to him, I now wonder what it must be like to live in one of the most visited cities in the world, but in the part no one would have you see.

I put the photo of Thierry back in my journal and close it. No matter how Fatima was looking at me, seeing Nora call her best friend almost weekly turns my stomach into a little knot. I miss my family. I miss my friends.

It's a reasonable hour on the East Coast on a Saturday, so I let my finger hover over the contacts in my favorites list. I already spoke to my mom via text a few hours ago, and Archi mentioned she's going to an artisanal fair, so I decide to call Becca, tapping her name and smiling when a photo of us wrists-deep in cake at her third birthday party pops up.

My cousin answers quickly, and her face fills my screen with a blinding smile. She has more freckles since I've last seen her, and I fight the urge to use her childhood nickname, Cookie.

"Whit!" She greets me happily with a wave. "How's my world traveler? I am stanning how brave you are, traveling alone!"

My smile breaks, just for a second; I don't want to admit to my cousin that I'm worried about traveling on my own now, after getting lost in Montmartre my first weekend. My classmates organize quick weekend trips to various locales around France, and even though I went with them to Annecy, a quaint lake town in the southeastern part of the country, I often stay behind to wander around Paris and work.

"She is fabulous, as you might have guessed," I reply after a moment, injecting my voice with more bravado than I feel at the moment. "How are you? How's rugby?"

"Rugby's good," Becca tells me. "We actually won our game this morning." I don't have time to cheer much before she cuts me off. "We can talk about that any old time. You have to tell me more about France!"

I do my best to tell my cousin as much as I can without giving up information about Thierry, not because I don't want her to know who he is, but because I'm starting to realize there's very little I can say about my time here that doesn't involve him.

In general, I do my best to get as much work done as I can before texts from Thierry chime on my phone. They usually come with an invitation to go somewhere during or after tutoring, or in the afternoon on Saturdays when he gets off work at the chocolate shop. We venture out at least a couple of times a week, and at the end of every excursion, Thierry makes sure to walk me all the way back to the front steps of the school before heading back toward Cardinal Lemoine. And about a half hour later, I text him, just to be sure he's gotten home all right.

Because of all this, I talk for approximately two minutes before his name slips out of my mouth, and Becca's eyebrows rise suspiciously.

"And who is *Thierry*?" my cousin asks.

There are a million things I could say about Thierry—about who he is, who he is *to me* . . . but all I can manage is "He wasn't on the list."

Becca's face softens as she begins to understand all the things I can't make myself say, all the confusing things I don't have words for yet.

"Well, Whit," she tells me, "the best things in life usually aren't."

Everything I Need to Put on an Unforgettable
One-Woman Show

1. A small, elite technical crew (Check! Nora and
   Sophie are on board!)
   a. A one-woman show is a bit of a misnomer
      because I still need folks to run lights and
      sound . . . and maybe a stage manager and
      costume change helper.
2. Costumes! Obviously I need:
   a. A trench coat
   b. Some prop bananas so I can DIY Josephine's
      iconic skirt
   c. A gown for the opening number—I'm thinking
      something red, sparkly, and floor-length.
      Probably can thrift something close and bead
      it myself if necessary.
   d. Related: A bigger sewing kit or access to a
      sewing machine. Maybe one of the design
      students will have one I can borrow?
   e. Hats. Fascinators specifically. Another thrifting
      project!

3. Some props:
   a. A cheetah plushie
   b. Sheet music, and lots of it
4. Instrumental recordings of some of Josephine's songs for rehearsal and performance
5. An updated rehearsal schedule

SCENE TWELVE

JAZZ HANDS

It's a Friday evening, so the Latin Quarter is illuminated by streetlights, and people stumble by, girls clinging to each other and young couples walking with linked hands. Many of them pass me to join the relatively short line below the glowing red Caveau de la Huchette sign jutting out from the building. I stand far enough away from the wall that no one will think I'm waiting to go in, but not so far that Thierry won't see me when he shows up.

If he shows up.

No, don't do that, I tell myself sternly. Sure, Thierry was not particularly enthused about visiting an old jazz club on a Thursday evening, but when I reframed the outing as a belated birthday adventure for myself, he caved.

Granted, my birthday is in August, and it is now well into October, but he doesn't need to know that.

And at any rate, Thierry has yet to leave me hanging thus far. Why would he start now?

While I wait, I decide to take a few selfies that showcase the Caveau de la Huchette sign in the background, the left side of my face washed in red light. Even though I like the glow, I try a few different angles to see which one works the best.

I'm on my fifth pose adjustment when I hear Thierry's voice coming from somewhere to my right. I'm a little annoyed at how fast my heart is fluttering around in my chest but also grateful no one can tell but me.

"Here, let me," he says without saying hello. He looks comfortable as he takes my picture, a black bomber jacket stretched over his shoulders with a white shirt underneath and blue jeans. He's opted for black leather boots that stop at the ankle, and it's definitely a vibe. When he's done, Thierry hands my phone back.

"You look great, by the way," Thierry says, stuffing his big hands into his jeans pockets.

I shift, then look down at the carefully curated outfit I put together—a red 1950s-era long-sleeved wiggle dress with cold shoulders and a pair of black heeled Mary Janes. Even though my first instinct is to reply *Damn right I do*, I'm suddenly a little self-conscious. I go to tuck my braids behind my ears before I remember that I carefully wound and twisted them into a bun at the crown of my head.

"Thanks. You never told me how you happen to be such a great photographer," I say to change the subject, glancing up quickly at him as I thumb through the photos he just took. We take our place in the line, which is maybe ten people deep. "These are so good."

I pause on one in which I happen to be gazing off to the side, with a hand on the chain of my beaded clutch and one thick leg forward where the sign for the club is pulsating in the background. *Wow,* I think, *I look amazing.*

Thierry hasn't spoken yet, so I nudge him to let him know I haven't forgotten him.

"My . . . ex-girlfriend is something of an influencer," he says, a little like the admission is going to strangle him. He taps his fingers against the side of his jeans. *Ex-girlfriend,* huh? I vacillate between wanting to laugh at how uncomfortable he seems and trying to dig deeper into why he seems to be so embarrassed. And it occurs to me that my nosiness could be attributed to something else . . . but I push the thought away and shove the feeling down. "Focusing on makeup. I took a lot of her pictures whenever we went out." He purses his lips like he regrets having said even that much.

"Oh . . . ," I say. The discomfort between us is palpable at this point, and I hate it. "Listen, this conversation doesn't have to be weird unless we make it weird. And, you know, I get it. You don't really want me to know about your personal life because this is, like, a professional relationship." I make an awkward gesture, pointing back and forth between us to indicate our working relationship.

The line moves forward, and I move with it, but Thierry stays rooted to his spot for a few more seconds, blinking slowly.

"Um, hello?" I say, waving for Thierry to join me. He regards me cautiously, and I think maybe I broke him, but he eventually steps up next to me.

Thierry's quiet for another moment before saying, "I don't think that going to a nightclub together is only professional."

He gazes down at me, and suddenly I'm wishing I had let him stay a couple of steps behind me, because now I can see his thick eyelashes falling on the top of his cheeks and smell the faint aroma of butter and sugar that always clings to him, and all of it is very distracting. I'm finding it very hard to get my brain to work properly, and you *have* to keep your wits about you in a foreign country.

"Of course it is," I manage to scoff finally as we move forward again. When I glance back, I see Thierry has his hands shoved in his pockets and he's biting his lower lip thoughtfully. *Still distracting.* "You're helping me with my project by coming with me to a club where Black American jazz performers played in the 1950s and 1960s. Purely transactional."

The minute I say that this outing is "purely transactional," I know it is a bald-faced lie, but I can't take the statement back now.

"Maybe . . . but I think you could have come here by yourself," he says, pulling his hands out of his pockets and clasping them behind him. "It's close to school. Or you could have asked friends." Thierry has recovered from the shock of the original comment, and I think he's fishing, trying to draw a particular response out of me, but I won't give him the satisfaction. I can't. Getting to Paris, into this program, was a moonshot for me. I can't throw it away, lose my focus, and get distracted by a handsome boy who smells of chocolate and light cologne.

"Nora and Sophie were busy," I say. Another lie. I didn't ask them. I asked Thierry and only Thierry. My face warms, but I attribute it to the heat coming off the neon sign we're now under. "Besides, I spend most of my time working on my show . . . or with you." *That* admission bothers me, too, because that time is not the drag I've been making it out to be at all.

Thankfully, I don't have to see Thierry's smug face, because we've now reached the front of the line and are able to make our way into le Caveau de la Huchette.

The inside of the club takes my breath away. It's a decent-sized space but feels small with all the people packed inside, bodies swinging to the music. True to its name, the first floor has a cavernous appearance, the gray stone walls sloping together toward the middle, and I can see a set of stairs that must lead to a second floor. Toward the back of the space, I can see where the music is coming from. A jazz band is set up on a stage with a young woman with huge curly hair singing into the mic. To the right, there's a bar and a line of stools, but most people are up, dancing.

I don't know the song, but my feet are already tapping, and I'm dying to get out onto the floor and dance. I turn to Thierry, who seems shy so stays close to me. I reach for his hand and nod toward the floor.

To my surprise, he pulls away, gently but firmly.

"No, you go ahead," Thierry says, checking out the bar as if to see if there's an empty stool he can occupy.

"Absolutely not," I tell him, letting my voice rise above the music. "You did not come out here to let me dance by myself, Thierry!"

"Dancing is not in the contract," he reminds me with an eyebrow raised. His arms fold over his chest, and he waits for my response.

I swallow because now I think I know what's bugging

him, and we're going to have to talk about it. Or at least . . . we're going to have to talk about *something*.

"So? We've been doing stuff not in the contract for weeks!" I retort.

"Yes, which is why I'm not sure why you think this is just 'professional,'" Thierry tells me. If I'm not mistaken, there's a little hurt in his tone.

"I'm sorry I said our relationship was purely professional. That was really dismissive of everything you've done for me over the last few weeks," I tell him, trying to make sure the apology is evident in my tone. "But, Thierry, I didn't think you liked me very much! I figured I've been getting on your nerves. Plus I'm the one thing standing between you and returning to soccer."

"I didn't think *you* liked *me* very much," Thierry replies, shrugging. He's trying to play nonchalant, but I can see something in his eyes just past the wall he puts up. Nervousness, and hope for acceptance. I didn't think that he *wanted* me to like him. But for whatever reason, this admission helps me to see that I matter a little more to him than I thought . . . I'm not an inconvenience to him after all.

"I didn't know you *wanted* me to like you," I say. "I'm sorry if I made you think I haven't liked having you around. I . . ." I stumble over my words for a moment. "I actually really like having you around. You're the person I'm closest to in Paris."

He regards me quietly, intensely, as Thierry does, but he doesn't make any sort of gesture of affirmation or acknowledgment. His stillness lets me know he's listening carefully, like he doesn't want to miss a word.

"But you know . . . you didn't really act like you wanted

to be around me either," I press on. "And you've been call-ing me 'la princesse' behind my back and to my face. What was I supposed to think?"

My arms are folded tightly across my chest, too, now, and it's becoming clear to me that this uneasy truce I've had with Thierry has been causing me a lot of unconscious stress, but things are starting to make more sense. Sure, we agreed to be civil, at first. But somehow, we developed something like a friendship that the terms of our contract couldn't have prepared either of us for. I don't quite know how to handle it. And that's without considering the shock of electricity I sometimes feel when I unexpectedly lock eyes with him. . . . One thing at a time, though.

Finally, he uncrosses his arms, then brings a hand to cup my elbow. I feel the aforementioned electricity shoot up my arm. "I'm sorry, Whitney."

I hold his gaze for a moment, then stretch out a hand. "Well, since we've apparently moved beyond professional partners, do you think that we could try being friends? Officially?"

"Friends." He shakes my hand but keeps it in his longer than I expect him to. And I let him because I like the way it feels. We lock eyes again, and it doesn't feel friendly at all. I want to both run from the intensity of the moment and stay here forever.

Even though the intimacy scares me, I decide to use it to my advantage.

"So does this mean you'll dance with me? *Friend?*" I ask, stepping closer without letting go of his hand. I sud-denly feel much braver right here next to him, like all of my sense has jumped out of my brain and into the Seine.

Thierry stares at me, a little mesmerized, and has to shake his head to come back to earth. He releases me, leaning on the bar and away from me. The moment we've created in this crowd of people is not gone but has shifted.

"It does not," Thierry says stubbornly. But a light is ignited in his eye, and I think if I push just a bit more, I'll win this round.

"But it's my birthday! Well, *was* my birthday," I protest, and I know I'm one single notch away from whining. "I mean, I have a tiara and everything I could have brought with me, but out of concern for you and how you would feel about walking around with a girl in a tiara, I left it in the dorm."

"When was your birthday?" he asks, suddenly concerned. "I should have gotten you a present."

"August twelfth," I say hurriedly, hoping he doesn't catch the date. "And your present can be dancing with me. Come on!"

Thierry laughs and allows himself to be led to the middle of the mass of dancing bodies.

My new-friend-turned-dance-partner is stiffer than a pair of starched Sunday trousers on the dance floor and looks lost. I smile exasperatedly at him and gesture for him to at least sway or something, shimmying my shoulders closer to him. When he still doesn't move, I grab for his hands so that he has to move in time with me. I'm surprised he lets me raise his arms and twirl underneath them, and even more surprised when he smiles shyly at me.

In spite of his reluctance to move, I find I'm having a blast, and Thierry makes it three songs in a row before we decide to take a quick break.

"Oh, my gosh," I say breathlessly, dropping myself into a booth upholstered in red vinyl. "That was so fun. Jazz at a club in Paris, just like Josephine Baker." I nurse a colorful (and expensive) virgin cocktail while Thierry sips on a soda.

Thierry is more relaxed than I've seen him yet. He seems to enjoy the music better from a seat than he did from the dance floor.

"Why Josephine Baker?" he asks finally, slumped back against the booth as he turns his glass between his forefinger and thumb. "She is just a singer, right?"

Just a singer? I repeat in shock. He might as well have slapped my mother, the way my jaw unhinges and drops. "No, no, no, Josephine Baker is not *just a singer.* She is an *icon.* An entire *moment.* Everyone wanted to be Josephine Baker."

I start to tick off all the things she did on my fingers. "Yes, she was a singer, but she was also a hugely popular performer. Totally eccentric, too. Made fashion history with her banana skirt. And her pet cheetah? Legendary. And even though she was a spy for the French Resistance in World War II, she could have also been even bigger in the American civil rights movement if she'd wanted to. Leaders offered her formal roles, and she declined.

"Plus, she basically invented sex appeal. She had so many lovers, men and women, and a whole mess of kids she adopted from all over the world." I lean forward conspiratorially. "She was even in a relationship with Frida Kahlo. The *taste,* honestly."

Thierry listens intently, like he does basically everything else. He's so serious all the time, even now, when we're at a nightclub. But he's nodding slowly, like he's processing each sentence. I can see him filing each tidbit away. He also makes sure to take a few beats when I'm done to make sure I'm finished speaking before he adds anything.

"You love her because she was a Black bisexual activist and performer in Paris?" Thierry asks, as if trying to make sure he's gotten it right.

"Yeah," I say slowly, twirling my straw around. "But it's more than that. Maybe I'm not explaining it well. But Josephine Baker . . . she did whatever she wanted. She was so good at everything—immensely talented, yeah, but also just a really cool person. She was too much for this world. She's the standard when I say someone's a genius."

Thierry waits, knowing that there's more.

"It's like . . . if there was space for someone who was as . . . much . . . as Josephine Baker, maybe I'll find a space for me," I finish, letting an exhale relax my shoulders.

"I would never have thought you feel like you don't belong," Thierry says, leaning forward, putting his elbows on the table so our faces are inches apart. I briefly worry about his jacket—the table is a little sticky. "You come across very confident."

The flush on my face that I had from dancing moments ago returns.

"I am," I say, summoning some bravado. "Doesn't mean I don't also want to belong to something." I cock my head and gaze at the low lights around me. "But I'm starting to think at least I belong to Paris." The thought carries me away, so it's a second before I am able to return to the table, to the conversation, to Thierry. When I do, I take in his eyebrows furrowed and his mouth pursed like he wants to say something but changes his mind. He raises his glass toward me, and I return the gesture.

"À Paris," he says before taking a sip.

"À Paris," I echo, comfortably holding his gaze.

~~Things I Don't Hate About Thierry Magnon~~
Things I Kind of Like About Thierry Magnon

1. He's a surprisingly good French tutor. That is, when he's not judging my desire to see all the tourist sites Paris has to offer or laughing at my pronunciations.
2. He has a very . . . morbid . . . but cool . . . idea of fun.
3. He is actually a very good videographer. He could make a side career out of filming stuff for influencers if he really wanted to.
4. He's a pretty decent tour guide.
5. He doesn't mind sharing his clothes.
   a. Clothes that actually smell so good, I want heaven to smell like them when I die.
      i. But also, what teenage boy has clothes that smell that good? *Suspicious,* if you ask me.

SCENE THIRTEEN

PARTY PEOPLE

"Whitney?"

I hear Thierry's voice coming to me distantly. Whoops, I've zoned out again. The two of us are having a tutoring session after both our classes that's not tied to a field trip, but fortunately we've upgraded from posting up in the cafeteria to sipping some of Mathilde's famous coffee from to-go cups in the garden as I try to remember where the adverb *y* goes in sentences. Let me tell you, it is not intuitive.

Nora and Sophie walk by, dressed in athletic wear and toting yoga mats held together with strings and slung over their shoulders, calling hello to me and Thierry. The two of them were in our room when I got home from my trip to le Caveau de la Huchette with Thierry last week. I hesitated to tell them about it, but Nora enthusiastically encouraged me to open up, and I spilled major details, chatting with them well into the night. It felt good to have some girlfriends again, but I do feel a little bothered by my lack of invite to the yoga class.

They walk to a far corner of the garden, almost obscured by a few topiaries, toward some other students I recognize from Madame Hassan's drama fundamentals class, and judging by the mats the rest of them are clutching, they've organized a pickup yoga session.

"Whitney?" Thierry tries again, and this time, I'm back with him in seconds.

I try to paste on a smile, hoping that even if he doesn't believe it, he'll have the decency to pretend not to notice the dip in my mood.

Infuriatingly, and to no one's surprise, Thierry does not do what I want him to.

"Ça va?" he asks, gently closing the book on the garden bench between us.

"Mhm," I say tightly, and even though I know my smile now is painfully strained, I open the book back up. "Oui, ça va."

Thierry doesn't say anything, only gives me a "Really?" expression with his eyes while his mouth is set in disbelief. He closes the book again, then folds his arms across his chest and waits expectantly.

"Ugh, fine," I cave, rubbing my temples. "Nora and Sophie," I tell him. "Do you know them?"

"Sophie? Not well," Thierry replies. "But Nora Belaïdi, I do. She is a friend of my—" Thierry pauses, quickly tugs at his shirt collar, then clears his throat. He almost seems nervous, but then he carries on like the hesitation never happened. "She is a friend of a friend. They went on a summer program in Morocco last year. Why? What's the problem?"

"No problem really," I say. "I've just been so busy with"—I catch myself before I say *you*—"with my play, I think I haven't been the best roommate and friend. They're helping me with my show, but I want to spend more time with them for fun. We've had good times together recently, and I want as many of those moments as possible. I'm only here for a semester, you know?"

Thierry nods in agreement. "Fun is good," he says. "And you do spend a lot of time on your show. You've been sending me quite a lot of costume ideas."

I'm momentarily embarrassed because I have in fact texted Thierry at least twenty costume ideas—obviously the famous banana skirt outfit, but also trench coat inspiration for when she is a spy and a number of midcentury hats Josephine Baker might've worn—in the last week, but then an idea strikes.

"Monsieur Magnon, how do you feel about costume parties?"

A couple of hours later, I open the door to my room with a flourish, dancing my way inside. Sophie and Nora are both there when I do a quick sweep of the space. On one side, Sophie is listening to music in her typical lounging position—sprawled across the bed with headphones on and one foot tapping—and Nora is on the floor in front of her desk, polishing her toes with a seafoam blue that matches her eyes.

"Bonjour!" I call, striding across the floor and setting my bag down on my desk chair. "Ladies, I have a question."

My roommates look up at me. Sophie even flips herself over onto her stomach and props herself up on her elbows, pulling down her headphones as she goes.

Well, I think, *this is already going better than I thought it would.*

"I had an idea," I say, clasping my hands together, mustering up a bit of courage. "How would you feel about throwing a Halloween party?"

They glance at each other, and I feel my stomach start to sink, so I rush into the silence to try to convince them.

"It could be fun!" I continue. "We could do it up American-style! I can get my mom to send us a bunch of candy. We could decorate, make brownies, dress up, and have a costume contest. Just for us LIA kids. What do you think?"

When they hesitate, I press on. "Listen, I know I haven't been the most present, but back home, I was known for throwing a good themed party. This is a chance for me to be more *here and now* and make some space to hang out with my friends in the best way I know how."

"Ouais," Sophie says slowly, bobbing her head. My stomach rises back to its original position in my body, buoyed by the one word. "It sounds fun."

I smile gratefully at her. Then I turn to Nora, who is nodding in agreement as well, the messy blond bun on top of her head wobbling.

"Do you want us to help plan it?" she asks.

"Of course! Bien sûr!" I say eagerly. "I was thinking this could be *our* party. Like, 'courtesy of les filles de cinq A'!" I mix up my English and French, but I like how cool I sound ending the sentence with a strong French accent.

"Really? Are you sure you are not too busy with your play?" Nora asks, screwing the top back on her polish, extending her long tan legs, and wiggling her freshly painted toes.

"Yeah," I assure her. "I thought we could all do something fun together. I'd like to spend more time with you both."

"That would be nice," Sophie agrees. "I want to pick the music!"

"Évidemment," I say, gesturing to her headphones. My conversational French is still developing, but after a few weeks of tutoring with Thierry, I am now much better at sprinkling in a few words and phrases. I puff up like a peacock.

The prospect of a party generates a lively conversation. As Nora and Sophie chatter, I sink onto my bed and pull a notepad close to me to jot down our ideas, lost in the daydream of what surely will be a night to remember.

It's pretty easy to get the space for the party and food. I ask Cécile to let us use the cafeteria for our party, and with Cécile's blessing, Mathilde offers to leave us some snacks but promises to murder me if there is so much as a spot on her floor the next morning.

"Whitney, you are so resourceful!" Sophie says a few days later as we lounge in le Jardin des Plantes.

I toss my braids over my shoulder with a smug smile, then recline on my elbows.

"Music is going okay?" I ask Sophie.

She taps on her phone a few times, then turns it out to face Nora and me. She scrolls through the music, and we both murmur our appreciation as we read, though admittedly, I don't know half the songs. But I trust Sophie's judgment; no one who listens to as much music as she does could possibly have bad taste. It's just the rules.

"Okay," Nora jumps in. "What about the guest list?"

"All of the international students who live at the dorm, of course," Sophie says, flicking her pointer finger as if she's going to start counting. "Who else?"

"Maybe some of the students from the public school. Like . . . Thierry?" Nora cuts me a sly eye. "You've been spending a lot of time with him, no?"

Sophie's eyebrows rise into her bangs until they disappear, and she lightly nudges me with a laugh.

"Oh, no," I protest, twirling the end of a braid around my finger, even though it feels like something is doing cartwheels in my stomach at the mere mention of Thierry's name. "I mean, yes, invite him. But no, it's not like that. Thierry is tutoring me . . . and helping me with my senior project."

"That's interesting," Nora says. "I didn't think he was *that* invested in school."

I shoot Nora a look. "What are you saying?" I don't *think* the implication is that Thierry is bad at school, therefore there's no reason to believe Nora is accusing him of being stupid, but I have to ask. I prepare myself to snap back with a cutting remark on Thierry's behalf, if need be.

She meets my gaze, but her tone doesn't match the bite in mine. "You misunderstand," Nora tells me calmly, sweeping her long blond hair off the nape of her neck and fanning it. "Thierry is *very* smart. He barely has to study. So now you tell me he is very interested in tutoring and a senior project? Bon, I do not think it is the books, but the girl reading them."

Nora points a finger at the book in my lap and smiles serenely at me.

It's a perfect juncture to turn the conversation around, head back in the direction of party decorations and music and guest lists, but Nora's comment ignites my curiosity. I ignore my better judgment and press ahead.

"How do you know?" I ask. "I mean, how do you know that about Thierry? I thought you were new here this year?"

"His old girlfriend, Fatima, studied at my boarding school in Belgium for a while, and you might remember we were supposed to be roommates," Nora says. "We were good friends there." She's quiet for a moment before she adds, "You might want to be careful. I'm not sure Fatima has accepted that she's an ex. . . ."

A tiny alarm goes off in my head, complete with a flashing red warning sign. Details start to click together, especially why Fatima looks at me like I'm dirt every time I happen to be in the room when Nora is video-chatting with her. Nora and Sophie seem nice enough now, but if Nora is friends with Thierry's ex-girlfriend, it might be wise to approach our friendship with at least a spoonful, if not an abundance, of caution.

The alarm goes off again: I told Nora and Sophie everything about my night out with Thierry. I'd been missing Archi and Becca so much, I needed girlfriends in the city to chat with, and I may have been a little too forthcoming. Maybe I should've just told them our evening was fine and waited until I had a chance to talk with my girls at home.

For a third and final time, the alarm goes off. Thierry told me that Nora was just a friend of a friend. Why wouldn't he tell me that Fatima was his ex, and that Nora was her close friend? What else isn't he telling me?

I've stumbled onto a ton of information at once, and all of it is messy. The last thing I need is to stir up drama between two old lovers, especially when I'm supposed to be here with the singular mission of getting through my Parisian bucket list and killing my show.

Not to mention, I am *not* interested in Thierry.

Much.

Not *at all.*

Nora must mistake my conflicted silence for apprehension, because she leans over and places her hand on my knee.

"Listen," she starts, "I am Switzerland. I don't get involved in these things. Besides." Nora draws back. "Thierry seems happier when he's with you."

"Happy?" I snort, wondering how "Switzerland" Nora actually is. "You must be referring to his twin from a parallel universe, because 'happy' is not a word I would use to describe how Thierry Magnon is around me."

Sophie, who has been quiet while Nora and I have this back-and-forth, makes a gentle *tut* sound as she shakes her head. "Have you considered you are not very observant?"

With her deadpan expression, it takes me a second to realize that Sophie is joking. Then, all at once, she and I break into peals of laughter that likely carry over the trees, joining the faint sound of acoustic guitar and singing.

SCENE FOURTEEN

JOYEUX HALLOWEEN!

"Tug it up a bit more on your side."

"Okay."

"Wait, no, too much! Now it's crooked again."

"I think it looks okay."

"Of course you do, Thierry, but I assure you, a crooked sign will ruin the ambiance."

An exasperated huff escapes Thierry. "Okay, then . . . I should lower it?"

I use a piece of shipping tape to secure to the window my end of a huge orange "Happy Halloween" banner my mom sent, then hop down off my chair and hustle to Thierry's side, dragging the chair with me.

"No, just hold it there for a second." I'm standing on the chair again, though this time, I'm close beside him, my heart thudding loudly in my chest. I'm worried he'll hear it, so I take a few slow, steadying breaths without drawing attention to myself, before busying myself with adjusting his end of the sign. He stands without moving, though I can feel his eyes on me.

It's nine o'clock, and we're the only two in the cafeteria. Nora and Sophie left a few minutes ago to get dressed for the party after testing the music on a makeshift stereo system they borrowed from Stefan from Germany, who lives on the third floor. They were also able to lay out snacks on a few tables pushed close to the windows to make room for a dance floor. They'll be back before nine-thirty to welcome our guests, and then Thierry and I will go get changed. Considering how I love a dramatic entrance, it's a plan that works for me.

What I didn't account for is being alone with Thierry in the meantime.

It isn't like I haven't been spending time alone with him for weeks now, but this feels different, especially after our night at le Caveau de la Huchette. Before, I was meeting him strictly for tutoring, not for parties and after spending a few nights innocently texting.

Once I finish adjusting the banner, Thierry offers his hand and helps me down off the chair. Suddenly, I find myself very worried that my hand is clammy, but a glance at him shows me that if it is, Thierry isn't worried about it. It makes me remember what Nora said at le Jardin des Plantes: *Bon, I do not think it is the books, but the girl reading them.*

But even if it is true and I'm reading Thierry correctly, there are so many reasons not to act on it: he hasn't made a move, I won't be in Paris much longer, and I need to focus on my work. . . .

"I see Sophie and Nora coming. Shall we go change?" he asks, breaking me out of my reverie.

"Oh, yeah," I say. "Let's head back to the dorm."

We leave the cafeteria as Sophie and Nora walk in to take over for us, dressed as a vampire and an angel, respectively. When we let ourselves back into the building, Thierry excuses himself to one of the public bathrooms on the first floor, carrying his costume bag, and I trek up to 5A.

It doesn't take me long to transform myself. I pull on a black cat suit and adorn myself with a gold necklace made of big round discs and a chunky gold belt. I collect my braids into a high ponytail and do heavy liner around my eyes before putting on a black mask. Finally, I step into high-heeled boots and put on gloves with crafted claws on them. When I look in the mirror, I'm satisfied to see that I could be a dead ringer for Eartha Kitt as Catwoman. I don't really like comics, but Eartha Kitt is a goddess, and her contributions to midcentury television need to be appropriately celebrated.

Honestly, this ensemble is impressive, even for me. I take a second to admire myself just a while longer; then I swipe my keys and phone from the table and head out.

I can see Thierry before he notices me when I reach the bottom flight of stairs. From this angle, all I can take in of Thierry's costume is that it involves a long black cape. He's scanning the lobby, humming gently to himself, so I don't think he hears the clunk of my heels against the steps. I put more heft in my steps to announce myself, and when Thierry turns, we react at the same time.

Thierry's eyebrows go up and his eyes widen. I take in the front of his outfit, yellow oval with a black bat in it and all, and laugh.

"There's no way this happened by accident," I say as I

finally make it to the bottom step, clinging to the banister to hold me up because I'm doubled over.

"You didn't tell me you were going as Catwoman," Thierry protests, but there's a smile on his face as he does so.

"Thierry, I could have sworn you said you were going as a soccer player!" I shoot back, wiping a tear from the corner of my eye in an attempt to preserve my eyeliner.

"I thought this might be more fun," he says with a shrug. Then he slips a cowl with pointed ears over his head. I think he winks at me, but with the cowl, I can't be sure. "We look nice, though, yes?"

It feels like a trap if I agree, but Thierry's grin lets me play it off.

"Well, I do," I tell him haughtily before I set off toward the exit. As I push the front doors open with both hands, I turn back. "Try to keep up, will ya, Bruce?"

Less than an hour in, the party is in full swing, and it's going great. I've already had a ton of candy and treats from Mathilde, done a little dancing, and said hello to most everyone.

By now, I've pretty much forgotten how many stares Thierry and I got when we walked in dressed as if we were doing a couple's costume. Sophie and Nora elbowed each other knowingly, but I didn't say anything.

Deep in the middle of the dance floor, Nora is a vision in white, her wings sparkling in the light as she dances to some house music from Sophie's playlist. A few guys from my literature class are flocking to her like bees to honey.

Meanwhile, Sophie appears to be arguing with Stefan about the sound system we borrowed from him. I giggle because in her cape and fake fangs, Sophie is even more intimidating than usual—a thought that Stefan agrees with, by the way he shrinks away from her. Sophie's too busy to notice, but I see the girl with a short black bob from my literature class, Xiomara, eyeing her from a nearby drinks table as I watch from a chair near the window.

There's a flash of black fabric in the corner of my eye, and then Thierry flops down next to me and throws his free arm around the back of my chair, stretching out his long legs, one hand clutching a tiny plate of treats that rests on his thigh.

It's not an intimate gesture—he's literally just taking up as much space as he can as he rests—but it still feels dangerously close.

"Do you see that?" I say, leaning toward him and pointing to the girl checking out Sophie.

"Ah, ouais?" Thierry replies. "Do you think she will say anything to Sophie?"

"Definitely. There's still time left in the evening," I say hopefully. Then I notice his plate, where there is a brownie with only one bite taken out of it. "Omg, why haven't you eaten that brownie?"

"What?"

"The brownie!" I point to the dark rectangle.

"Pffft, because it is not *real* chocolate," Thierry tells me. When I glare at him, he says, "Sorry, sorry! This is . . . It's just . . . this is the best Americans can do with chocolate? French chocolate is the only way."

I fall quiet as the party continues swirling before us,

music pulsing with low lights as everyone walks around in costumes and masks. Sophie somehow found tons of votive-like electric candles to put everywhere, which cast light on the plastic skeletons and witches' hats I strategically placed around the room. Near the music, Sophie has finally left Stefan, and Xiomara, the pixie girl (as in she's actually wearing a fairy costume) has managed to grab her attention. I smile.

"You know, visiting a chocolatier for a class on chocolate making is high on my list of things I have to do in Paris," I remind him, even though he definitely knows. I practically recite my list to him every time we hang out at this point. Of the many chocolate shops in Paris, there's one in particular I want to go to . . . but Thierry hasn't asked me to come. So, with my hint dropped, I wait.

Thierry nods to the music, which has shifted to French rap with words I can't follow. The beat pumps through my chest, though, and it makes me want to dance.

"You could always come to Chocolat Doré," Thierry says, inclining his head toward me so he doesn't have to shout over the music. "If you want. It is in Montmartre. But then . . . you might get lost on the way."

When I shove Thierry away, he's got a full grin on his face that matches my victorious one, exposing teeth and everything. He really *can* smile if he wants to. I mirror his expression before I can stop myself.

"You're finally inviting me? I'm not just inviting myself this time?" I ask.

He nods. "You could come once the shop is closed for the day, and I could teach you to make chocolates. I need to make some for Lucie's birthday—I could use the help."

"Yeah?" I try to stop myself from brightening so much, but even if this didn't involve Thierry, I would be excited to get a private tour of an authentic Parisian chocolate shop. I decide to let my enthusiasm fly.

"Ouais," Thierry agrees. "I just need to make sure it is okay with my stepfather first. So maybe not this week, but I can tell you when I know."

"That sounds great. I can't wait," I say.

Thierry is about to say something else when Nora and Sophie push their way through dancing high schoolers to join us, pulling over chairs so that they are directly in front of us. Sophie, I notice, is clutching a napkin like it's a life preserver.

"This is great, no?" Nora says, wiggling in her seat as if she's still in the middle of the dance floor.

"Some of my finest work for sure. But of course, teamwork makes the dream work," I say, and I raise my cup to cheers with the girls. And because I have to be right, I turn to Sophie. "Is that Xiomara's phone number?"

A delicate blush forms over Sophie's cheeks and nose, but she murmurs "Yes," and I turn to Thierry with my arms raised in victory.

"I told you!"

The rest of the night passes in a haze of laughter, dancing, picture taking, and trying each of the several appetizer/snacks Mathilde left out for us. Thierry is by my side pointing out and naming various cheeses for me and insists that I try olive tapenade. And when he tries to excuse himself as one of Adele's upbeat songs comes on, I grab his arm and smile as I drag him to the dance floor.

He protests the entire way but starts to smile when he

realizes I'm mostly here to sing it. I feel myself slipping into performer mode as he watches, singing with my face, my whole body. The more he watches, the less it feels like a silly bit and becomes more of a private moment, even though we're surrounded by people and he probably can't even hear me.

When the song ends, I figure he's had enough of me and is just waiting to leave the floor, but the next song is Tiwa Savage, and this time, Thierry grabs hold of me. I don't know this music as well, but the beat is so dance-able, and suddenly lyrics about finding love are flooding into my ears, clearer than they've ever been to me before. Thierry spins me and then I'm dancing in front of him, my back to his chest, and his hands slide to my waist. I'm so close to him I can feel the vibration in his chest as he hums along to the song. He's so different from when we danced together the other week, like the walls he puts up are slid-ing down and he's letting loose.

I turn slightly toward him to tease him for knowing such a sappy song, but when I do, I can see him peering at me through his long eyelashes. My body rotates in his grasp until I'm facing him, and I wrap my arms around his neck, fighting the urge to touch the soft skin of his cheek. I settle for moving in closer, letting his arms close around me as I lay my head on his shoulder for a minute.

My body melts into Thierry's, and my eyes travel from his jaw to his lips. I admit to myself right then that, yes, I have thought about kissing this boy, but in the daydream-y, never-gonna-happen way, not in the very-real-could-occur-right-now way. The thought isn't in the background of my mind anymore—it has immediacy.

Right then, Thierry looks down at me, like he heard my thoughts. Maybe he didn't hear them, but judging from the grin on his face, we're certainly thinking the same thing.

The song changes into something bouncier, and I take a tiny step back from him. I worry that the moment was tied to the music and it's gone now, but Thierry grabs my hand and pulls me in for another dance.

We move like that even as the party begins to thin out around midnight, people wandering back to the dorms or off campus for more excursions. When most people have left, we finally break apart, the spell of the night fading but lingering. It keeps us quiet as we turn the lights on to pack up the last of the food and candy and rearrange the tables and chairs. We lock the cafeteria doors.

He walks me back to my building in silence, then lingers at the base of the steps. He's still quiet. Maybe he wants to stay in this moment we created together, too.

I think, more than anything, we're both trying to find words that explain the last few days, but knowing the feeling will get lost in translation, we choose to rest in the space between words as long as we can.

SCENE FIFTEEN

I PRETEND TO LOVE SOCCER

I think my nana would be very disappointed to learn I spent an entire day in France, of all places, doing nothing but watching teenage boys play a pickup game of soccer—the only way Thierry can play until I give him his review. I'm trying very hard to understand the game, but I think I just have to admit that sports is an area in which I will never excel. When Nora—deeply influenced by a cute brown-haired, brown-eyed dancer in her modern dance class—suggested we go watch some boys from school play soccer, I acquiesced only at the promise of pastries after. But I admittedly forgot about éclairs and mille-feuilles when I saw Thierry warming up on the sidelines when we arrived. His eyebrows shot up when he saw me walking up, bundled in as many layers as I could still walk in, but then he gave me a smile.

So now, against my better judgment, I'm still here, an hour later, freezing and confused.

It's too cold to be sitting outside on metal bleachers watching a bunch of teenage boys run up and down a grassy field chasing a ball, even if I am flanked by Nora and Sophie. Occasionally, their commentary makes me laugh, but the cloud of cold air I emit when that happens depresses me all over again. The overcast sky does nothing to help my cold situation, so I wrap my red wool scarf tighter around my neck and try to distract myself.

"And what position does Thierry play, again?" I ask, focusing on him as one of his teammates streaks up the middle of the field and kicks the ball over to him. Thierry dribbles quickly and, without so much as hesitating, kicks it straight into the top right corner of the net. The goalie didn't stand a chance.

"C'est un attaquant," Nora says patiently. "A forward." The girl is a saint and explains the same set of rules to me every ten minutes, not because I've forgotten, but because it seems impossible they can be true given whatever just happened on the field.

"And forwards . . . ?" You would think that by having a soccer player cousin/best friend, I would have absorbed *something* about the game after all these years. Alas . . .

"Mm, mostly they score goals," Nora continues, not taking her eyes off the game. Sure, she came for the cute dancer, but as it turns out, Nora actually likes soccer. The players have headed down to the other end of the field, but apparently Thierry's sandy-haired best friend, Fabien, is on the other team, because he snatches the ball away from someone and the whole mass of them double-time in the opposite direction. It's actually impossible to tell who's on what team when no one is wearing identifying jerseys.

"Okay, that kind of explains why Thierry is so self-important," I say, trying to throw a jab at Thierry, but Nora and Sophie both roll their eyes at me. None of my teasing lands anymore, not after the Halloween party. Even if I hadn't told them that Thierry invited me on what I *think* is a date to his family's chocolate shop, they saw the two of us together with their own eyes, basically attached at the hip all night.

"Allez! *ALLEZ!*" Nora screams next to me, almost blowing out my eardrum. For a girl who barely speaks above a throaty whisper, Nora has *lungs*. On the field, Thierry has the ball again and is focused, dodging everyone, moving so fast it seems easy—effortless. Then there's one person in front of him, but Thierry fakes him out and launches another powerful kick at the goal post. The goalie throws himself to the left, but the ball scoots under him just in time.

Thierry lets out a satisfied roar, running toward his teammates, who greet him with equal fervor by way of quick thumps on the back and chest bumps. He's sweating so hard his shirt is drenched through, but his eyes are lit up like the Eiffel Tower in the evening.

I've never seen him like this. After what he shared about being suspended from the team for fighting, I suspected that Thierry would be difficult to manage on the field, an angry player, his surly nature coming out in full force. But the opposite is true. When Thierry is playing, he is all precision and power. Quick thinking and smart strategy get him through the defense, and raw power gets him the goals. He moves differently from most of the boys on his team, some of whom move swiftly but uncertainly, and from Fabien, who plays like a loose cannon. Thierry plays like this is his calling.

And when he comes off the field, running toward me, Nora, and Sophie, Thierry has a huge grin on his face. The rest of the boys grab water and towels—Amir from the kebob stand falls flat on his back, with his curly jet-black hair plastered to his forehead and limbs splayed out like he's making a snow angel—but Thierry is still playing with the soccer ball, bouncing it off his knees and chest, rolling it across the back of his arms.

"Quel frimeur," Fabien calls, snapping a towel toward Thierry's butt. Thierry only dances away, catches the ball with both his hands, and meets my eye with a wink. I think nobody has seen it, but when I turn around, Nora's blue eyes are twinkling.

"Bon, la princesse, what do you think? Are you having fun?" Fabien asks me, wedging his sweaty body between me and Sophie and spreading his arms out behind the two of us.

"Ugh," Sophie says, wrinkling her nose at Fabien's sweaty body and trying to scoot away from him.

"Why are you calling her a princess?" Nora asks.

"Thierry said she is like Meghan Markle," Fabien laughs. "African American princess."

"I did not!" Thierry replies, laughing, but ducking his head, which I know means even if he didn't say exactly that, he said something like it.

"*Interesting,*" I say, raising my eyebrows in his direction. I knew about the nickname, but it never dawned on me that it was because some part of him linked me to Meghan Markle. I want him to say more, but the conversation has a life of its own and he's saved from having to cut in.

"It's kind of true," Sophie cuts in, saving Thierry from having to explain himself. "Whitney dresses so fancy and chic, and she's an actress, like Meghan. And she's beautiful, of course."

Fabien enthusiastically agrees with this assessment, but I push him away, laughing. Thierry is quiet and is suddenly very concerned with the grass.

Finally, Amir grunts loudly from his spot on the ground and stands.

"Come on, let's finish this game," he says, and heads back toward the field, the rest of the boys following.

Thierry salutes me, the way he did the first day I met him, and I almost laugh as he follows the pack.

When play resumes and Sophie, Nora, and I are left alone again, Nora leans over to me with her phone in her hand.

"So, I didn't want to say anything," Nora says, squinting. "But Fatima has been asking about you. . . ."

"Huh?"

"Fatima. Thierry's ex. Should've been our roommate," Nora says to jog my memory. Then I remember our conversation from the other day, and the alarm bells are back.

"I know. But why would Fatima be asking about me?" I ask innocently, though I already know the answer.

As if she was anticipating that question, Nora unlocks her phone and pulls up a photo-sharing app. She starts with a photo of all of us—her, Sophie, Thierry, and me—clustered together in front of the party from Halloween. I didn't think anything of it when we took the picture, likely because of how Thierry was hovering around me all night and how we'd touched as we danced, but when I see how I'm leaning into him and the way his arm curls around my waist while his other arm goes around Nora's shoulder, I start to grimace. Nora clicks to another picture. It's a shot from above, as if someone stood on a chair to capture it, and smack in the middle of it are Thierry and me, dancing, my arms wrapped around his neck, his snaked around my waist. We seem to be in the middle of a conversation, so our faces are closer to each other than they might be normally. I know, without the evidence to prove it, this is from when we were dancing to Tiwa Savage. I'm embarrassed to report I happen to be grinning like an idiot in the photo. I squint closer, and I see Thierry is tagged, so it will show up on his page.

I bury my face in my hands.

I've managed to piss off a French girl I've never even met.

Then I straighten up and look at Nora. "Okay, show me her profile," I say, holding out my hand for her phone.

"What?"

"I've gotta know who this girl is," I say. "Maybe I'll even reach out, tell her there's nothing going on."

"Why?" Sophie chimes in. She went back to listening to music once the boys resumed play, but she's only got one earbud in, so she's half listening to her playlist, half listening to us.

"What do you mean, why? I . . ." But I realize I don't have a good reason other than I need to know more about Thierry's ex. I want to keep talking, but the rest of my words die in my throat. Nora hands me her phone.

A lot of things strike me about Fatima's profile. The first is that she's got a few thousand followers, which tracks with what Thierry said. The second is that this is my first time seeing her not at a strange angle on Nora's phone or computer, and she's one of the most beautiful girls I've ever seen. Her skin is a deep brown that has a glow, and her hair falls into a straight bob that brushes her prominent collarbone. You could cut diamonds with her cheekbones, and her lips are perfectly pouty. Finish it off with big inky eyes, neatly lined and framed with thick lashes.

When I scroll down a little farther to her highlights, I see labels that say "Get Ready With Me" and "Tutorials" and learn that she is a very good makeup artist, worthy of influencer status.

I scroll down even farther and see the most perfectly curated feed, with posts of her traveling around the world in casual but stylish outfits. She's not decked out in extremely expensive designer clothes, but it's clear she knows how to make an outfit look like it cost several thousand dollars. The other thing I notice is that she also posts pictures of books. Every so often, her feed is broken up with scenic posts of whatever she's reading in front of white sands and blue skies. I see some of my favorite books, so I know she not only has taste—she's got range.

In most of her pictures, she isn't smiling. She and Thierry probably have similar personalities. And though Thierry is nowhere on the feed, I suspect he took many of the early pictures, judging by the angles that are similar to some of the photos he's taken for me.

Whatever desire I had to reach out to Fatima shrivels

up in my stomach and dies. She's practically perfect, and I can't imagine why they ever broke up. They seem like the ideal "it" couple.

I glance up. Thierry is hustling down the field, following everyone as a teammate dribbles the ball through the melee. He positively exudes euphoria, which seems unfair when I feel like my stomach has fallen to my feet.

He catches my eye, and the warmth of his expression scares me. Even if there's nothing going on with Fatima, even if he *is* interested in me, I have to stay focused. I came here with a plan, and nothing is going to distract me from my work. I didn't come to Paris to fight over a boy or to fall in love with anything besides croissants.

Finally, I give the phone back to Nora, my jaw set.

"You can tell her she has nothing to worry about," I say. "Thierry and I are just friends. And I'll be gone in a few weeks anyway. I'm only passing through."

Nora takes her phone, looking like she wants to disagree with me, but I'm not in the mood to debate. So I hook my arms through hers and Sophie's and smile.

"Plus, who has the time for boys when I'm hanging out with my girlfriends?" As I speak, Thierry and Fabien start play-scrapping on the field before they head toward the other goal, throwing a few light jabs at each other's chest and sides, laughing. Thierry glances toward me, and Fabien is quick on the uptake, immediately jabbing him a few more times, saying something I can't make out.

"No time for boys at all," I say, and I wonder if I sound as unconvincing as I feel.

SCENE SIXTEEN

I BECOME LIABLE TO PISS OFF
A FRENCH GIRL I DON'T KNOW

I only have a week, maybe two, to finish writing my play—and I need to buckle down. Every tutoring session now, in spite of myself, I wind up sitting closer and closer to Thierry, finding little reasons to touch his hand or arm. Only sometimes is there a little alarm going off in the back of my head warning that this boy might be someone else's love story. I try to push thoughts of Fatima—and Thierry—away and get to studying.

It doesn't totally work. I find myself replaying conversations with Thierry in my mind so much that eventually I have to externalize them. I message both Becca and Archi to tell them about the Halloween party and going to watch Thierry play soccer, and I'm secretly pleased when they try to convince me I should give him a real shot. As a result, my focus has been wrecked for at least a week, to the point where I have all but abandoned my blocking work for the show.

"Whitney, I just heard about an impromptu dance performance near the Champs-Élysées," Nora says, bringing me back to the present. We're in 5A and she's wearing a leotard-and-tights dance outfit with leg warmers, wrapping herself in a puffy coat. Sophie's already dressed in a black bomber jacket and combat boots, with her signature headphones around her neck. "Do you want to come with us?"

"Yes, but I can't," I say regretfully. "I should probably use the quiet to work before my tutoring session with Thierry. Bring me back something sweet?"

"As many chocolates as I can carry," Sophie says with a little chuckle.

When they leave, I turn on the study playlist Sophie made me and spread out on the floor with all my books. I tap my schedule with a pen. Fortunately, I have written a good draft of the play and only need to edit, so the schedule I made before I left the States still seems salvageable:

WHITNEY'S (UPDATED) RESEARCH AND REHEARSAL SCHEDULE FOR *THE LOVES OF JOSEPHINE BAKER*

Mondays, 7–9 p.m.: Reading/research, writing, and editing time.
Tuesdays, 7–9 p.m.: Blocking
Wednesdays, 9–10 p.m.: Monologue rehearsal
Thursdays, 7–9 p.m.: Reading/research, writing, and editing time.

Fridays: Rest day
Saturdays, 9–10:30 a.m.: Vocal and dance rehearsal
(reserve practice room in the annex)
Sundays, 8–11 a.m.: Full show rehearsal

Even though I can't perform all of my monologues, as they're not completely finished yet, I'm making sure to learn my songs and dances. Nora sometimes meets me after class in the theater annex in the evenings when she doesn't have her own dance rehearsals and helps me with my choreography, since the musical numbers are easier to put together at the moment. Sometimes we go over numbers in our room when Sophie's out, so we don't disturb her. All the additional reading materials that Monsieur Laurent has been steadily bringing to theater history class for me have been beefing up my project for sure, but it's still missing something. A personal touch. Something that'll make it clear that I deserve to be here, making art in the place my heroine loved.

I've been planning to make a pilgrimage to the Château des Milandes—Josephine Baker's French home—all semester, but the weekends have been sliding by me. I always write a study plan for my next week on Friday after my last class, but somehow something always comes up—an exhibit to explore, or a tour, or a new bookshop or café to try. And before I know it, it's Sunday night and I'm scrambling to finish my assignments, leaving very little additional time to work on the project I actually came here to do.

I can't say that I'm not distracted.

And as soon as the thought runs through my head, my phone lights up.

> **Thierry:** Hi. Where are you? Still coming to the café?

My scheduling-and-daydreaming session made the afternoon run away from me.

> Whitney: Yes!!!

I quickly collect a bunch of books, throw on my emerald double-breasted A-line coat, and fly down all six flights of stairs.

Thierry's waiting for me when I enter the cafeteria, and he's wearing a neat all-black ensemble, with a satin black bomber jacket over a black shirt and jeans. His sneakers are black with a few pops of white near the bottoms. I can't help but admire the ensemble; for someone who's not particularly fashion minded, Thierry knows how to make a good outfit.

He might also just be Parisian, which I think means that fashion sense is genetically transmitted.

"Are you free next weekend? Saturday?" Thierry asks me. I nod, leaning forward with interest. "My stepfather said it is okay for you to visit."

It takes me a moment to get that he is referring to the chocolate shop meet-up. I almost forgot that Thierry finally invited me to Chocolat Doré, and I'm suddenly vibrating with more excitement than my body knows what to do with. I wiggle in my seat.

"Oh. My. Gosh!" I squeal. "What do you wear to make chocolate?"

Thierry laughs. "Something you don't mind getting dirty. You will be working."

"Um, won't I have an apron?" I scoff. "That's kind of the point. If you wear an apron, you can still keep on your fashionable clothes."

Thierry scratches his neck. "I don't think that is the main reason you wear aprons."

I cock my head and stare at him.

"Okay, okay, wear what you want," Thierry says in surrender. "But if you ruin one of your pretty dresses, you cannot take more of my clothes."

A laugh escapes me and I steady myself on the table, one hand landing close to Thierry's. "You don't mind that I've stolen your clothes," I say before I can stop myself, a playful grin still on my face. I internally wince. *Flirting is not part of the plan to buckle down, Whitney!*

Usually, when Thierry and I get to talking, it's easy to make the noises of the cafeteria fade into the background. But when there are silences, like right now, it's like someone's turned the volume up on a TV. I hear the scraping of trays coming from the kitchen, the chatter of the few students around us grabbing afternoon snacks, and the squeak of the door opening and closing while I wait for Thierry to respond.

"No," he says finally. "I guess I do not."

Whatever reply I was planning catches in my throat as he brushes against me.

Okay, maybe Fatima has something to worry about after all.

<u>Pro/Con List: Thierry Magnon</u>

PROS

1. He seems to like me! Nora and Sophie think he
   likes me! So do Archi and Becca, and they don't
   even know him personally!
   a. He is so sweet, but I think he doesn't want
      anyone to actually know that.
2. How perfectly romantic to fall in love <u>in Paris</u>!
3. Thierry has exceptionally kissable lips. Not that I
   spend much time thinking about that . . .
4. . . . except I do actually spend a lot of time
   thinking about kissing Thierry, so maybe I
   could just ask him if he likes me so I can either
   <u>actually</u> spend time kissing him or get that time
   back entirely.
5. Even if nothing comes of this . . . he's the best
   part of studying abroad in Paris. He makes every
   day exciting. He keeps me on my toes. I never know
   where I am going when I'm with him, but I know I
   have to go along for the ride.

CONS

1. It's very possible that I, Whitney Curry, Duchess of
   Daydreams, have made up this entire thing in my
   head. He maybe isn't even thinking about me like
   that; I might have just imagined how it felt to
   dance with him at Halloween, and maybe the visit
   to the chocolate shop isn't a date at all.

2. Fairy tales end. The clock strikes twelve in about a month, and then it's back to real life for me. What good is it to fall hopelessly in love with a boy I'll never get to see again?
3. Furthermore, did I <u>not</u> come here for research? Yes, it <u>was</u> a lifelong dream to go to Paris and study abroad, but <u>mostly</u>, I wanted to write the best play any high schooler has ever written based on Josephine Baker. This whole thing is, frankly, distracting.
4. The "F" word: Fatima. I keep waiting for Thierry to tell me she messaged him . . . or to find a message from her to "keep away" in my own DMs. Who actually has the time to potentially be harassed by a French girl they don't even know? Sounds messy and far too much.

* Even with all these very real cons, I can't stop thinking about going to Chocolat Doré tomorrow. Maybe that's my answer. And if that's the case, I will need an outfit. . . .

SCENE SEVENTEEN

I PLAN TO LIVE IN A CHOCOLATE SHOP FOREVER

There's a simple, circular brown wooden sign jutting out from the building that reads CHOCOLAT DORÉ in gold letters when I turn onto the small, crooked street in Montmartre that Thierry gave me the name of. I breathe a sigh of relief. Before I left school, he texted me instructions for the best métro route, even though I had already searched for some myself, as well as really precise directions for how to get to the shop from the métro stop. He offered to meet me at the stop and walk me back to the chocolaterie, but I insisted I would be fine. I've only gotten turned around twice, which for me is a true victory.

I've been so busy worrying about getting over here okay that I haven't had time to be nervous about what will happen once I get to Chocolat Doré. Now, as I stand in front of the store, I run my hands down the front of my emerald-green coat, nervously regarding my reflection. Nora and Sophie meticulously helped me pick an outfit that is equal parts cute and comfortable. Underneath the coat, I sport a green plaid jumper and a tan turtleneck, and instead of an elaborately pinned braided updo, I just collected my braids into a high ponytail, leaving two braids out at the front to frame my face.

I'm reminding myself that I am confident, calm, cool, and collected, when movement beyond the glass catches my eye. I see a head peek out from a doorway near the back of the shop; then an entire body emerges. Thierry.

The painted green front door with the shop name lettered in gold on the glass opens, triggering the bell over it to tinkle merrily.

"Ah, super," Thierry says, "you made it. Please, come in."

As I ease into the shop, I have two thoughts: I'm once again struck by how unfair it is that boys can simply wear jeans and T-shirts and appear runway ready. His hair, I notice, though, looks marginally neater than the last time I saw him. His already manicured hair has new clean lines along the sides, and I guess—with satisfaction—that he likely got a haircut and fresh twists for this.

The second thought is about the heavenly smell that's overtaking me as Thierry gestures for me to leave my coat on the chair by the door. I pull it off and breathe in the scent of warm butter and sugar, all the while considering never leaving this shop.

I know I'm lingering near the doorway, which my mother says you should never do, but I'm taking it all in. The shop is beautiful. Chocolates that will keep—the boxed-up ones—are lined up in pretty golden bags on deep green shelves built into the wall on the right side. Overhead, there's a really elaborate golden chandelier with crystal-like gems hanging from it, and beneath us are old but nicely kept hardwood floors. There are a few tables in the middle of the floor with stands on them that, during the day, I presume hold chocolate displays. And on the left is a long counter with a wide stretch of a table between two cases, where chocolatiers must do some of their work for visitors. The cases are empty now, which is a little disappointing. But chocolate is on the way, I remember.

"Thierry, this shop is amazing," I tell him as I approach.

"You think so?" he asks. "I will share your praise with my stepfather."

It sounds like a good thing, but Thierry and I have spent too much time together over the last few weeks for me to take that statement at face value. Plus, there's a little tic in his jaw from overclenching.

"You don't like your stepfather?" I ask tentatively.

Thierry's eyes flash for a moment, but the anger is extinguished as quickly as it came.

"No," he says, and then, "No," again, but with less bite. "I mean, yes. He is a good man. He is good to my mother, and to us—my sisters and me." He tries to shrug the question away, but I stand still, waiting.

"He is just not my dad, you know?"

And before I get a chance to respond, Thierry gently takes me by the hand and ushers me through the doorway behind the counter, revealing a large white kitchen. There are a couple of ovens in one corner, a large stove against the far wall with stainless steel counters that extend on either side, and a huge island in the middle. The island already has some things set out on it, jars full of what I think are rounds of chocolate, flour, sugar, mixing bowls, whisks, everything we need to get started. There are also a few machines and tools around that I don't recognize and can't imagine a use for. I make a mental note to stay away from those in an effort to not destroy any part of his family's business.

I feel a wave of excitement wash over me. Who would ever have guessed that I'd get a private tour of a chocolate shop kitchen in Paris?

The space feels large despite being proportional to the front of the store, likely due to all the white paint. Thierry lingers by the door, tapping a finger on the counter nearest to him. His eyebrows are knitted together, and I know he's still thinking about what he said about his stepdad.

"Your stepdad doesn't have anything to do with Grumpy Thierry, does he?" I ask, slowly walking by a setup of utensils hanging on the wall.

"Grumpy Thierry?" he asks, coming out of his reverie, but just barely.

"Yeah, you know, you do that whole thing where your face scrunches up and you get all tense." I mimic his default expression, with a little artistic license that I'm sure makes me look like a dour old lady, and he laughs. "Actually, how do you do that all the time? This is super uncomfortable." I rub my shoulders as I unclench my muscles.

"I suppose I do make that face often," Thierry confesses. But then the storm cloud completely passes and he's offering a tiny smile. "I don't look like that, though."

"You absolutely do."

Thierry ignores me and grabs a couple of black aprons from the hook near the doorway and tosses one to me.

"Are you ready to make some chocolate?" he says,

gesturing to the island of ingredients with a flourish like he's the presenter on a game show. "Lucie has specified an assortment of truffles for her birthday. Truthfully, I'm glad to have the help."

"Oh, I was *born* ready," I say, hopping over to the island and immediately grabbing the jar of chocolate rounds, then posing with it next to my face.

Without even asking, Thierry pulls out his phone and snaps a quick picture of me. I know even before seeing it that it's about to be my profile picture on every social media platform.

After he informs me that the first thing we're doing is making ganache for his sister's truffles, I ask an obscene number of questions as we start melting chocolate.

"Do you roast your own chocolate here?"

"No, that is very hard to do in a shop. Most chocolatiers do not."

"This is, like, the rawest form of chocolate you can get to cook with?"

"Yes."

"Where do you get it from?"

"My stepfather gets his from a factory in South America. He has distant relatives that own it."

I stumble into the thorny parts of Thierry that I thought I had mostly managed to get past in the last few weeks. I follow him as he moves over to the stove but linger a little off to the side. We're both quiet until he stops his stirring and holds the spatula out to me.

"Do you want to stir?"

"Um, yes," I say, stepping up to the stove. Thierry's made a setup like I've seen on the Food Network, with a glass bowl filled with chocolate rounds melting over a pot of hot water, and I take the spatula to gently push the chocolate around. The chocolate is thick and still has very distinct clumps in it, though it's starting to smooth out.

"So your stepfather is South American? What country?" I'm focused on not burning the chocolate instead of ogling Thierry.

"His parents are from Colombia, but he is a little bit of everything. He has family that is West African, indigenous, and Spanish."

"Ah, that's cool," I say. I press on as the chocolate continues to melt. "When did your mother marry him?"

"When I was seven," Thierry tells me. "Not long after my father, and Célestine's, died."

There it is. La raison.

"I'm sorry," I say softly. He's quiet, and even though his arms are folded across his chest as he leans his hip against the counter next to the stove, he seems less like a grumpy young man and more like a sad boy. "I don't know what that's like . . . but I can tell it hurts."

Thierry gently reaches for the pot and bowl and shifts them over to the counter. Then he disappears into a huge refrigerator and comes out with a jar of cream in his hands.

"Maybe grief was difficult for me to understand when I was so small," he says. "But it felt like my mother wanted to fill the space my father left with anyone. I was so angry all the time. Nobody wanted to remember my father, it seemed, but me."

Now the pieces of his story begin to fall together. I can imagine a young Thierry, missing his father and trying to make sense of this new presence in his life, sitting on so much pain that he didn't have space for, and having it explode as anger.

"And even though you got used to things, like your mom's second husband, the anger just . . . stayed," I guess.

Thierry nods and touches the lid of the cream. My hand creeps forward along the counter just an inch. I want to cover his fingers with my own, but I know if I do, he may not say more. I lean forward but clasp my hands together.

"Sometimes I think I can control it. The anger," he continues, and I think about the fight on the soccer field before I even got here that led to this very moment. "Or I think I understand it. In life, there is loss. There is a new chapter. But then, sometimes, my frustration just . . . bursts out . . . and it shocks me because I didn't know it was still there. I suppose that is why Fatima and I broke up. . . . We fought all the time about my 'healing.'"

"I'm sorry." Then . . . "So . . . you and your ex-girlfriend . . . ," I say with expectation, hoping he'll catch the hint and fill in a few more blanks for me—and maybe clarify some of the concerns that have taken up residence in the back of my mind thanks to Nora.

"We fought. Past tense. That's not a concern anymore," Thierry replies, turning back to the cream and uncapping it, then passing it to me. "But you? You must have a boyfriend at home?"

"I have never had a boyfriend," I admit. There's more I could tell him: unrequited crushes and daydreams that come to nothing. I've always been too intense, too focused on one project or another, always at the theater, always at dance, and so when would I have the time? I might have the spirit of Josephine Baker on the stage, but my love life?

Much less spectacular. There were always boys, but no one who ever made me feel like a priority, nobody who inspired me to create space in my already full life. I've never felt that . . . until now. But all of it—what I've shared and what was left unsaid—feels too honest, so I cover up the moment with a bit of flair. "I've simply been too busy for such things."

"Your first boyfriend will be a lucky man," Thierry says gently. He gestures for me to pour a little of the cream into the chocolate. I do, slowly, and Thierry folds the chocolate over itself, enveloping the liquid. It looks simple, easy, but from the way the muscles in his arm flex, I can tell he's using a very precise amount of force. Not too rough, and not gentle either. The focus on his face is similar to what I saw the day I watched him play soccer.

"Can I try?" I ask. He nods, and we switch, and I take over the mixing. It is, in fact, harder than it appears to be. Bits of ganache fly up and hit my cheek at my erratic stirring.

Thierry smirks before rubbing his thumb under my cheekbone, lifting up the chocolate and then bringing it to his mouth to taste.

"Hm, you taste good."

My mouth falls open in shock, before I remember we had this exchange a couple of months ago, the day he rescued me in Montmartre. And then I laugh, a full-bodied laugh that has me doubled over.

"Thierry!" I gasp.

"What?" he asks, feigning innocence as he stares at me, making Bambi eyes. "You would rather I waste the chocolate? Here, try like this." And he stands behind me, placing a hand on mine to demonstrate the appropriate amount of force and technique for folding the chocolate with the spatula. I can feel his chest rising against my back, and I am very aware that if I can feel his breath, he can feel mine, and my breathing has suddenly gotten very fast.

"I spent all that time worried I'd been weird that day!" I say, craning my neck to glance back at him.

"Ah, no, it was very weird," he says, and I pinch my lips together. "But after I recovered, I decided it was also cute." Thierry releases me and puts the newly mixed chocolate on the island.

"So you initially thought that I was weird and cute?" I laugh again, but I'm genuinely interested in his response.

"Maybe not weird," he says, grabbing two spoons from nearby and dipping one into the ganache for another taste before handing the other to me. "When I met you that day in Madame Cécile Fromentin's office, I thought you were . . . passionate. And, yes, cute."

I lean forward, resting my elbows on the counter, and dip my spoon into the ganache.

"Vraiment?" I tease. "Do say more."

Thierry chuckles. "You are not satisfied?"

"Um, handsome French boy tells me he thinks I'm cute and *that's it*? Of course I'm not satisfied! I need details," I say, and taste the ganache. It's delicious, fresh and smooth, and melts on my tongue. I could bathe in this.

But now it's Thierry's turn to raise his eyebrows as he grabs a jar of what must be either raspberry or strawberry preserves from the kitchen island.

"You think I am handsome?" He spoons dollops of the preserves into the ganache, then hands me the spoon so I can taste that, too. The immediate tartness that hits my mouth along with the sweetness lets me know it's raspberry, and this is sinful. No matter how many French sweets I taste, nothing feels cloying with sugar the way American desserts do. Everything manages to be both decadently rich and light on the tongue.

"This is so good," I murmur, trying to keep the preserves in my mouth as I speak.

"The raspberry truffles are Lucie's favorites. I'll top them with cocoa powder when we are done," Thierry says, but then taps me on my shoulder to let me know I'm not getting off so easy. "I'm handsome?"

"I mean . . . well, yeah," I say finally. I can't stand the smug look on his face, so I throw a towel at him. "Don't tell me no one's ever told you that you've got a smile that should be illegal. Have you seen your dimples?"

Anything I've ever found pleasing about Thierry, I've more or less kept to myself up to this point. But the words tumble out of me, and though my face warms a little— *wow, did we leave the stove on?*—I don't want to take them back.

Thierry laughs sheepishly. "I promise, you are the only person who has ever told me that. Thank you."

"Okay, if we keep going at this rate, we'll never get anything done," I blurt out. I know we're having a moment, and I like it, but suddenly I feel like I need a time-out. I am not supposed to get sidetracked by Thierry!

Judging from the half step back Thierry takes from me, I think he agrees with the pause. We're focused for a little while as he coaches me to pour the ganache into a piping bag and then squeeze it into little square molds. When I'm done, he jiggles the tray, then picks it up and drops it a few times, presumably to get rid of any air bubbles.

Then he pulls over another bowl of melted chocolate and pours a little over the mold, dragging a scraper across it to even it all out. When he's done, he hands it to me, and I walk everything to the fridge.

"While we wait for that to set, do you want to make éclairs? Or a chocolate box?" Thierry asks me when I reemerge.

"A chocolate box?" I repeat with interest.

"Ouais, c'est une boîte de chocolat," Thierry says, making a vague cube shape with his hands. "I can make you a box made of chocolate. You can take some truffles and chocolates with you, and then you can also eat the box."

"You're absolutely just showing off now," I tell him, but I'm already back at the counter, ready for round two.

"Yes, I am," Thierry says, grabbing another jar of chocolate rounds and giving it a spin in the air before catching it again.

"If I didn't know any better, I'd think you were trying to impress me, Thierry Magnon." I try to sound haughty, but I can't muster up my usual front as I place my hands on my hips.

"Is it working?"

I bite my lip and busy myself with the ends of my apron ties to avoid making eye contact, but it doesn't work. I have to look up, and his earnest expression helps any residual knots of anxiety in my stomach untangle.

"A little," I say finally. Satisfied, Thierry goes to melt some more chocolate on the stove, and I follow. A few pictures on the far wall attract my attention, and I wander over as Thierry works. There aren't many. One shows a tall, brown-skinned man with curly hair in a chef's coat with his arms spread out in front Chocolat Doré. I think this must be Thierry's stepfather, because in the next picture, the same man hugs a dark-skinned woman with a chic pixie haircut as they sit on a bench somewhere along the Seine. This has to be Thierry's mother. She's gorgeous and has his flawless skin, expressive eyes, and dimples.

Under that is a photo of the same couple in wedding attire. Thierry's mother has on a stunning ivory mermaid gown with a veiled pillbox hat perched jauntily on her head. I'm admiring her impeccable fashion sense when I notice the two children standing in front of them. A tall girl in a tasteful, full-skirted pink dress throws a skinny arm around a tiny dark-skinned boy, who is stately, though dour, in his little fitted tuxedo. This is Thierry as a seven-year-old—I recognize him from the cloudy expression, his mouth fixed in a serious line.

"Yes, that's me," Thierry calls from the stove. He doesn't leave it for fear of burning the chocolate, but he knows I'm admiring the picture of the wedding. "Ce sont mes parents, et là, c'est Célestine. À droit, il y a une photo de Lucie. Ma petite sœur. Elle avait . . . cinq ans? Mignonne, n'est-ce pas?"

I turn my head to the right and see a photo of a little girl with brown skin and a mass of wild curly dark hair that almost overtakes her skinny little body. She grins wide, in spite of her missing front tooth, and her eyes crinkle beautifully at the corners. Like Thierry, she has the most adorable dimples.

"Oui," I say, almost under my breath. "Elle te ressemble.

Elle a . . ." I look to Thierry for help and gesture to my cheeks.

"Ah, les fossettes," Thierry says, supplying me with the word.

"Les fossettes," I repeat to myself.

"Ah, bon!" Thierry says, pulling the pot of melted chocolate off the stove. "We are conversing in French!"

I didn't even realize that we've slipped into easy French. No switch turned on in my head as I tried to process the shift. I just heard French and responded in it.

"Oh, my God! I did it!" I cheer, clapping my hands and skipping across the kitchen to him. He smiles as he pours the melted chocolate onto the table in a shining mass. "You're an excellent tutor."

I turn myself around to lean back against the island. I might be just a touch too close to Thierry. His hands, which have come to rest, are millimeters away from my own. I can see the nearly imperceptible rise and fall of his shoulders as he breathes. This close, I notice that under Thierry's long eyelashes he has a few small black beauty marks dotting his cheeks. He sees me seeing him, and his eyes drop to my lips. My stomach does cartwheels. Even though I like the feeling and want more of it, it's overwhelming.

"I should—" I start, ready to rack my brain for a reason to jump away from him once again. But Thierry's hand wraps around my wrist, stopping me. I stop and meet his gaze, his eyes shining.

"Whitney," he says, slipping his hand from my wrist and intertwining our fingers as he takes a step closer. "Please don't do that."

"Do what?"

"Try to change the subject when you know I would like to kiss you."

He waits patiently, running a thumb along the back of my hand.

"I didn't know for sure that's what was happening," I say softly.

Thierry snorts. "Yes, you did—"

He sounds like he's ready to argue with me, slipping into our usual routine, and the familiar tone is enough to make me close the remaining space between us and kiss him.

It's quick—a peck, really—and it surprises him. When I pull away, his eyes are wide, but they soften as he untangles his hand from mine to put it on my waist.

"I know you said you wanted to kiss me. But I wanted to kiss you first," I whisper.

And he laughs quietly before he leans in again for a deeper kiss. This time, I can taste the tartness of the raspberry preserves and the sweetness of the chocolate on his lips. I run my fingers along his jawline, on skin that's as soft as his lips. His hands are huge, covering a large part of my back as his tries to draw me closer. I expect my heart to still be beating wildly in my chest, but I settle: my heart beats against Thierry's, and I fit so neatly into his arms. I'm safe, warm, and comfortable, and when I breathe in, the delicious scent of heated sugar and Thierry's cologne greets me.

Soon, too soon, Thierry starts to pull back, but not before he drops several quick kisses on my lips. They feel tingly, electric, and after each kiss, I find myself still leaning forward, searching for another. Then he places his hands on the island on either side of me, enclosing me as I rest my hands on his shoulders.

"What are you thinking?" he murmurs, searching my face.

"I'm wondering how long you've been waiting to do that," I say, running my hands around the back of his neck and lacing my fingers together.

Thierry stops and thinks.

"I've wanted to since Montmartre," he tells me, his hands on my hips once more. "But when I heard you sing at Place Joséphine Baker, it became a top priority."

"Wow, and here I thought you hated me," I say, laughing. "What are you thinking?"

"I am thinking I want you to never think I hate you again," he says. "How do I make sure you know that?"

"Well, for starters . . ." I trail off, tugging gently at the collar of his shirt and pulling him to me again.

Thierry walks me back to the métro stop a couple of hours later, after we finish the chocolate box, taste the finished truffles for Lucie, and kiss (a lot) more. It's late, but still early enough for me to take the métro back to school, so we enjoy the chilly walk, fingers intertwined so securely that we have to stop and let people pass walking in the opposite direction. The streets feel smaller in Montmartre, narrower, with less sidewalk. They're built from brick, and zigzag, with colorful buildings blocking the view of the path a few yards ahead. As we leave the side street

Thierry's family shop is on and turn onto the main road to get to the stop, we pass a corner bistro that has fairy lights strung around the lampposts, illuminating the whole area. Paris during the daytime is spectacular, but evening Paris has a quiet beauty that I find myself falling in love with over and over again.

At the métro stop, Thierry hands me my brown Chocolate Doré bag, which he insisted he carry for me until now, and which is filled to the brim with my box, truffles, and any other treat he could find from the shop to give me.

When he starts to give me directions home, I surprise him by telling him I can take the Abyssess stop toward Mairie d'Issy, transfer at Sèvres-Babylone, take the M10 toward Gare d'Austerlitz, and get off at my usual stop. His eyes widen and his mouth opens, like he wants to say something—probably to tell me there's a faster way home—but then he changes his mind and kisses me on the cheek.

"Text me when you are back at the dormitory," Thierry calls after me as I descend the steps.

"Of course." I wave back. "Night."

"À plus."

The trip is painless, and I find myself wedged in a corner seat near the window, watching the dark walls pass. I try to read the posters and art I see on the bright station walls as we pull into them, but mostly I hug my chocolate bag to myself, as if trying to prevent a single moment that led to the making of its contents from floating away.

On the 10, I sit next to an older lady with a scarf pulled over her short white hair. She smiles at me, and I wonder if she can read my mind or if I'm smiling like a goofball.

Nora and Sophie are awake when I open the door to 5A just after eleven o'clock, and evidently waiting for me, as they accost me with squeals before I even have a chance to put down my bag.

"Well? How was it?" Nora says, jumping from her bed and grabbing my arm.

"It was really nice," I say, and then I hold up my bag. "He made me so much chocolate."

"Yes, but did you kiss?" Sophie asks impatiently. I know I have her full attention because she's snatched her headphones off and leaned forward, elbows on her legs. Even Nora holds her breath, waiting eagerly.

"Yes," I confirm, and brace myself as the room erupts with excited exclamations from my roommates. "You guys! Shh! People are sleeping!"

"You must tell us everything," Nora says, finally letting go of my arm so I'm able to shimmy out of my coat. "How was the kiss?"

I turn to face them with a smile, raising a couple of fingers to my lips, which still have the barest tingle to them. "Magical."

SCENE EIGHTEEN

GOLDEN HOUR

"What's the big surprise?" I ask as I try to prevent my tan pillbox hat from flying away in the gusts of wind that are hitting me. My hands are momentarily occupied, instead of wrapped in Thierry's large ones, as we walk, and considering I only have a month left in Paris, even these seconds feel wasted. We're headed to Shakespeare and Company, a famous bookshop I've been itching to get to for weeks, but Thierry asked if we could make a pit stop.

When I called an emergency group video call to tell Archi and Becca about my fairy-tale date at a Parisian chocolate shop the morning after, both of them whooped with excitement.

"Finally!" Archi screamed into the phone.

"Parisian boy's got game," Becca said approvingly, when I told her about Thierry's careful maneuvers to get close to me at the shop.

They both agreed that I deserve a great Parisian romance and that I should enjoy my time with this boy who clearly adores me and not worry about the rest.

"And you have to listen to us, Whit," Becca said. "We're your best friends. We know you better than anyone. This is so good for you."

As Thierry and I walk together, him periodically gazing down at me with a small smile, as if to check that I'm still here, and me squeezing his hand reassuringly, I can't help but believe they're right.

"It is just here," Thierry tells me now, pointing ahead, where I can see the street open up and the late-fall sun glisten on the Seine. His mouth quirks as he observes my struggle with the hat with a touch of mesh that falls over my forehead, which I'm trying to get to sit just so on my braids.

"You know, the chivalrous thing to do would be to assist a lady," I say huffily. I go diving into my clutch to find bobby pins, nearly running into an elderly couple with my inattention but saved by Thierry's quick reflexes.

"It is usually safer to assume you do not want assistance unless you ask," he replies, letting his hand drop from my elbow. "It is also chivalrous to heed the lady's wish, no?"

Even though we're almost at our destination, my cute hat is about to be lost to the streets of Paris, and there are people walking toward us from both directions on the sidewalk, I *have* to reach for both Thierry's hands and guide them around my waist. He softens when he realizes what I'm doing, and I put my hand through the wrist loop on my clutch so my hands are free to bring together behind his neck.

"And this is my wish," I tell him, smiling, tilting my head so I'm speaking centimeters from his mouth. When I glance up at him, he's looking at me through his thick eyelashes, mesmerized. Thierry tries to quickly steal a kiss and I lean back, grinning mischievously.

He groans at the missed opportunity but gently raises a hand to the side of my face to coax me forward again. This time, I let him kiss me.

What with Thierry Magnon's soft full lips traveling from mine to the spot just below my ear and his hands moving to grip my waist, I'm not doing much thinking. That said, it does briefly occur to me that I could root myself in this very moment for the rest of my life and die happy.

Thierry pulls back just far enough that I can see the whole of his beautiful face. The way his eyes dip down to my lips, I know he's considering another kiss, but a gruff voice behind us grunts, "Dégagez de là!" A squat middle-aged man with a very red face squeezes between us and the building to our right, staring daggers at us.

I try to choke back a laugh, and Thierry clears his throat loudly before gesturing for me to move closer to him under a tree.

"Come on, let's go," he says, nodding toward the river ahead.

"Or . . ."

"Whitney," Thierry laughs. Even though we've grown much closer, Thierry still doesn't laugh much, and I live for the moment when his short, rough laugh gets free of him. He always seems surprised when it does, as if he didn't mean to let it out, which makes me all the more eager to hear it. "You asked me if we were there yet every thirty seconds on the way here. Now you want to leave?"

I pout, but just a bit. I'm allowed to change my mind.

"Fine," I give in. "Allons-y."

Thierry and I hold hands as he leads me up the street. It's easy, a touch that took next to no time to establish, and familiar as home.

Soon we've crossed to the parallel street and the Seine stretches out on either side of us. There are railings on the quai, of course, but in front of them are tiny green stalls opened up like oysters, revealing rows and rows of books. When I compute what I'm seeing, my free hand reaches for Thierry's coat sleeve, my mouth falling open.

"You said you wanted to see Shakespeare and Company," Thierry begins to explain. "I thought you might want to see the bouquinistes along the Seine, too. We were going to be close, so . . ."

I break into a wide smile as I look from the stalls to Thierry, who's rocking nervously, as if he's worried I won't like his surprise. I quickly peck his cheek, which makes one side of his mouth tug up, then let go of his hand to turn fully to the books at hand.

The two of us spend close to an hour wandering along the seemingly endless green stalls of books and art. The area is clogged with book lovers, tourists and locals alike, dropping euros into the hands of sellers, who happily part with their wares. As I look through yellowing pages of antique and used books, I steal glances at Thierry. He's perusing the books so intently. He picks one up, opens to the first page and quickly skims the last, then pores over the cover before putting it back and picking up another that catches his attention. In his neat gray peacoat, fitted pants, and shined shoes, Thierry is exactly the kind of handsome that makes everyone notice.

Everyone including three girls a couple of stalls down, whispering to each other and eyeing him with interest. My hand floats above another set of books while I watch them.

I shake the thought away as I remember Thierry probably wouldn't even want their attention anyway and hand a bouquiniste two euros for the copy of *Madame Bovary* I've been holding, then add it to the small plastic bag of a few other thin paperbacks and a few postcards swinging from my wrist. I'm at Thierry's side in just a couple of steps, and the way he easily links his hand with mine and smiles at me deters the whispering girls. One tosses her long brown hair as she turns away, the other two following.

"Do you still want to go to Shakespeare and Company?" Thierry asks me as he pays for his book. The bouquiniste nods at Thierry, who doesn't wait for a bag but pockets the paperback with his free hand.

"Yes, please!"

Thierry grins. "I didn't know you liked books so much."

"Mais oui, generally books about art, music, fashion . . . same creative family, and I need to consume it *all*," I say. He replies with a sharp exhale that's almost a laugh.

Thierry tells me that Shakespeare and Company isn't far, so we walk there, barely paying attention to the world around us as we playfully bump each other. The last time I bump him, Thierry doesn't move away but pulls me close. He studies me with an intensity that tells me he's memorizing every single bit of this moment. My chest feels tight, a mixture of flattery and the sadness of knowing he's storing away these moments because we won't have many more.

But I don't want to think about that, so I don't. Instead, I kiss him. I'm considering abandoning my bookstore browsing plan, even though we've already made it to Shakespeare and Company, the deep-green sign visible in my periphery. I can see folks milling around, including a woman sitting outside the café next door who reminds me of my nana—

"Whitney?"

The woman who reminded me of Nana rises from her little table, extending to her full height of almost six feet, and I spring away from Thierry, putting a good foot of space between the two of us, because this woman, draped in an earth-toned shawl and gold statement earrings, is without a doubt my grandmother Diana Curry.

"Nana!" I say, trying to plaster a smile on my face as I walk over to her and her coffee companion. I hear Thierry murmur, "Nana?" but I keep going until I reach them. I hug Nana hard, drinking in her natural spicy scent mixed with the woodsy perfume she's been wearing my whole life, then kiss both cheeks of the other woman, who is about Nana's age but very different from her in appearance. This woman is small and has sharp features, with a tiny, well-groomed Afro, cat's-eye glasses, and a floral scarf tied around her neck over her black cashmere sweater. I don't have time to wonder who she is, because my grandmother is demanding all of my attention at the moment.

Nana is tall and full figured. Her light brown roller-set

hair cascades in waves around her face, which is enhanced with understated but elegant makeup, as if she is about to walk onto a stage any minute.

"What are you doing here?" I ask, both delighted to see my nana and somehow unsurprised to run across her spending a lazy afternoon in Paris, thousands of miles from home.

"Surely you don't think you're the only Curry allowed to gallivant across Europe?" Nana asks with a smile and a raised eyebrow. What she means is *Why do you think I have to ask anyone for permission to do what I want, little girl?* She doesn't say it, but her eyes do.

"Of course not, Nana," I reply, trying to course correct. "I only meant, did you travel here by yourself?"

"Yes, darling!" Nana replies, as if I've just asked the silliest question in the world. "I find traveling in groups exhausting. This is much more enjoyable. And if you would answer that little phone of yours, you would know I'm in town. I called you a couple of hours ago. . . . But I see now that you may have been preoccupied." She appraises Thierry for a moment, and I feel my cheeks heat before she turns her attention back to me. "If you must know, I'm only in Paris to pick up Théa, here"—she gestures grandly to the woman sitting at the table eyeing us over her coffee—"on our way to Berlin."

"Berlin?" I repeat blankly. "Nana, did you tell anyone—namely Mom—that you were off on a transatlantic jaunt?"

My grandmother waves the question away with both hands, which are adorned with all manner of golden bangles, and huffs in exasperation. Thierry, who has sidled up beside me now that he's assessed the situation, stifles a laugh.

"Well, I've told you!"

"Yes, but when I talked to you last, you only said you were *thinking* about coming to Europe, not that you *were* coming to Europe! And if you only called me a couple of hours ago, Mom is going to be worried!" I can feel a crease forming between my eyebrows, and I rub it as if to prevent it from becoming permanent.

"Whitney, my dear, your mother hasn't got as much imagination as *we* do, so I doubt she would have approved of my plan. That is why I didn't tell her." Nana shakes her head. "She's just the most lovable little thing on the planet, but her idea of *adventure* is running off and getting married to a businessman right out of undergraduate." She speaks with a bit of apology in her voice. "Nothing against your father, of course. He's a lovely man. I only hoped Yvette would wander a bit before settling down. And we see how that turned out."

I grimace, remembering the divorce, but then fight back a chuckle. Typical Nana.

"Now, is your program going well? I presume you are hard at work on your performance?"

"Yes, I am, Nana." I give her a quick summary of where I am now—with a full script and musical numbers that tell a story—but leave out the fact that something just isn't clicking. Then I chance a glance at Thierry. I've heard Nana's tirade about my mother's desire to be "settled" more times than I care to count, but I imagine Thierry might be somewhat taken aback. He gives Nana an expression of reserved interest, as if he wants to know more but is not keen to get too close.

When my gaze falls back on Nana, she is looking at me expectantly. She clearly hasn't missed my glance at Thierry, or our intimate moment just a few minutes ago. There's no playing this off, not with Diana Curry.

"Nana," I say, standing up straighter, "this is Thierry Magnon. . . . He's my . . . tutor."

Thierry nods stiffly. "Bonjour, madame."

Nana looks him up and down, then turns to me with disbelief written clear as day all over her face.

"Okay, fine, boyfriend. Thierry's my boyfriend," I blurt out, feeling heat blossom on my cheeks as I stare down at the ground, suddenly fascinated with some pebbles, to avoid both Nana's and Thierry's gazes. He and I have *not* discussed our relationship status yet, but it feels right to say. Even so, I can sense all my internal organs melting from stress and embarrassment, because what if I've been wrong about this in front of my *grandmother,* of all people . . . ?

Finally, I peek at Thierry, who seems to have had new life blown into him at my confession. He steps forward and kisses my nana on both cheeks, as well as her friend Théa, then launches into a quick but passionate speech to Nana in French about how nice it's been to get to know her granddaughter. His dark eyes have lit up, and I can see his dimples. I don't know whether my tutoring lessons are finally paying off or if I'm just used to the lilt of Thierry's words in both French and English, *or* if I'm understanding the emotion behind them, but nothing has sounded so clear to me since I landed at Charles de Gaulle in September. Whatever the case, I am astonished.

"Oh, no, dear, that's kind, but we won't have the time . . . ," I hear Nana saying as I check in on the conversation. Having zoned out, I try to backtrack to figure out what we're talking about, but Nana keeps going. "Yes, Théa and I have an early train out in the morning, and we've already made plans to see some of our old friends for dinner, but that's such a sweet offer."

My eyes widen: *Did this boy just offer to have a meal with my grandmother . . . who he just met?!*

Nana's electric brown butter–colored eyes land back on me, and I feel myself straighten.

"Whitney," she says firmly, "you have excellent taste in young men."

I exhale a little. I glance at Thierry, who gives me a tiny wink, and I smirk.

"Frankly, I was worried you'd take after your mother. So serious all the time," Nana continues, straightening her shawl, then centering the gold necklace so that the clasp spins to the back of her neck. I roll my eyes; Nana likes to pick at Mom, but it comes from a place of love. "I know you love things to be orderly, but it's reassuring that you can be flexible when the moment calls for it.

"Young man," she says, turning to Thierry, who perks up. "You will do right by my granddaughter, or you can rest assured I know people who will find you."

Thierry's eyes widen. I quickly step in.

"Nana, I'm sure you didn't mean to threaten Thierry," I warn.

"Oh, of course not," Nana says, waving me away again. "I am merely being emphatic."

"I'm sure," I say, skepticism dripping from my voice. "Bon, it has been such a delight to see you, Nana. We'll let you get back to your coffee with Madame Théa."

Théa, who has been watching the scene unfold with laughter dancing on her lips, merely gives us a small but warm smile.

"And will you *please* call Mom when you get to Berlin?" I press.

"You have my word," Nana says in a solemn voice that tells me she's lying. I laugh and lean in for another hug, folding myself into her tall frame and inhaling her soft rosewater scent, letting my worry float away, just as I did when I was little. The homesickness I've experienced so far has nothing on the ache I feel in my stomach now, knowing that even though home is here in my arms, she'll be gone again in mere moments.

I expect my homesickness and my desire to stay here in Paris to be warring, but the two feelings simply sit together, keeping each other company.

I let go of her as she says goodbye, then retakes her place across from Théa. Thierry nods toward Shakespeare and Company, and I smile and let him lead the way.

"Oh, Whitney," Nana calls after we take only a couple of steps. "Where did you get that coat? It's nice."

I laugh as I spin to show it off. It's an ecru-colored coat with a Peter Pan collar, two buttons at the chest, and a bit of brown faux fur at the wrists. "It's yours! I got it from your closet last winter."

Nana's loud bark of a laugh rends the air, and before Thierry and I finally leave, I hear her tell Madame Théa, "See? What did I tell you? *Taste.*"

The inside of Shakespeare and Company is smaller than I imagined, and filled to the brim with books. Between the books crowding the space and the tourists packed inside, it is warm, even with the front door open and the fall breeze coming in. I don't have time to really think about what section I want to find first; I simply have to move in, to let the couple trying to come in behind me pass.

I'm making a mental note never to come here in the summer, when I feel Thierry's arm gently bump my own.

"I understand why you are so animated now," he says. "You are very much like your grandmother."

"Well, I always did want to be just like Diana Curry," I reply, and before I turn to the books at hand, a question is on my mind. "What happened back there?"

Thierry's thick eyebrows furrow. "How do you mean?"

"You were like . . . all normal surly Thierry, and then all of sudden, you're dazzling my grandma?" I ask. He gets it now, and tugs at his earlobe.

"Ah. Bon . . . At first, you said I was your tutor. And . . . that is not so important, and I did not say anything. But then you said I was your boyfriend," Thierry says, not looking at me. "That was important to me. So I wanted your grandmother to like me."

When he finally meets my gaze, I can't think of a single thing to say in either English or French, so I give him a peck on the cheek, then intertwine my fingers with his as we turn to browse the shelves in front of us.

<u>Things I didn't expect to happen</u>
<u>while I was in Paris</u>

1. To have my French language skills do a complete 180. I'm not fluent, but I can absolutely make my way around a market without any help.
2. To have making friends take a while. But all good things come to those who wait. Nora and Sophie are amazing, and I'm glad I have them now.
3. To gain a small slice of fame among my classmates for an epic Halloween party.
4. To get a lot obsessed with falafel.
5. To have a somewhat overwhelming bout of homesickness.
6. To end up with a <u>very</u> cute Parisian boyfriend.

Who would've thunk it?

SCENE NINETEEN

THE UNIVERSAL BLACK GIRL STRUGGLE

The calendar, which now reads mid-November (and about a month until I'm scheduled to go home), is starting to feel like an enemy, and not just because of Thierry. I have next to no time to get my show to come together. I'm finished writing, but I keep editing the last act and adding little pieces from the things I learn in class and in my adventures around the city, because somehow it still doesn't feel right. The biggest parts now are just planning my blocking, designing my minimalist set, practicing my songs and the two dances I'm working on, planning my lighting, and figuring out costumes—all of which would be easier if I had a stage manager, a costume designer, and a lighting designer . . . and yet I'm convinced I can do it all myself. I brought much of what I plan to use with me, but inspiration strikes whenever I pass flea markets and thrift stores.

My dates with Thierry often include pauses during which I fish out my journal and pen to jot down a stray thought as we catch an exhibit at the Centre Pompidou, or visit la Pagode, or stop on the way to the cinema to check out the offerings at a vintage shop.

Presently, we're at the Pont des Arts, and I'm holding my Polaroid camera rather than a notebook. Neither of us mentions putting a lock on the bridge, but I do ask a passerby to take a photo of the two of us in front of the padlocks already there.

The woman agrees, and after a quick moment in which she figures out how to use the camera, she snaps a picture of us. By the time the photo starts to reveal itself, she's long gone, swallowed by the crowd of tourists and Parisians undeterred by the chilly air, so I can't thank her for what I suspect will be my favorite photo of Thierry and me to date. I stand in front of him, and he wraps his arms around my waist, resting his chin on my shoulder. If I had been taking the photo, I likely would have told him to smile bigger, but as I study it, I'm glad I have this reminder of the truth of us: his stormy intensity and my hopefulness, together in Paris.

"Oh, I need a second!" I say, quickly handing the photo to Thierry and swapping the camera for the journal from my purse. "Did you know Josephine Baker was married, like, four times? Several relationships. Seems like she really loved love, you know?'

Thierry makes a small sound of interest as he examines the photo. Then something seems to shake him out of his reverie.

"Why are you thinking about Josephine Baker being in love?" he asks. He leans forward and rests his forearms on the bridge railing.

"I'm always thinking about Josephine Baker," I joke, but Thierry raises his eyebrows at me. I press my back against the railing so that I'm facing him and scoot closer. "I was just wondering if different places make your feelings more intense. Like . . ."

He nods in understanding. "I am not sure location makes your feelings more intense . . . but I think Paris makes people braver. I feel people come here and allow themselves to fall in love."

Thierry flashes a smile, and I return one, before watching the couples on the bridge, letting myself process. Just a few feet away from us, two young men in their twenties kiss deeply before attaching a lock to the bridge. On the other side of the bridge, I see an older couple standing hand in hand watching boats float past on the Seine, the woman resting her gray head on the man's hunched shoulder. There are so many couples, so many different types of people, walking along this bridge. Many have their photos taken by professional photographers or, like us, nice passersby. I think of how all of these people demonstrated their bravery here, how they're willing to stand tall and proud in their love. And how brave Josephine Baker was to be all she was: a performer, a spy, a lover, a mother . . .

I flip past all the lists and notes in my journal to a blank page, thinking about how full Josephine's life must've been and how to showcase that in the set design, but I struggle to hold the journal against my thighs and write at the same time.

"Here," Thierry says, gesturing to his back and motioning for me to use him as an impromptu desk. The warmth of his body makes something click for me.

Josephine Baker's strength was her capacity to love. People, countries . . . it didn't matter to her. Her love made her art stronger. Love can make *my* art stronger. I suddenly know I need to weave more about Josephine's epic love stories into my performance; she isn't the legend without all her loves. I write against his shoulder for a few moments before I peer at the side of his face.

"What are you thinking?" I ask, closing the journal.

"That you are going to spend the rest of your time here on that project," Thierry says. "You need to be with people more."

I don't disagree, but even though I love Paris, my friends, and my new boyfriend, as November flies by, I'm starting to feel pangs of homesickness. Mom and Dad have already sent me texts in our group chat we all use once a year, asking for my thoughts on the Thanksgiving menu. One of my favorite parts of the year is helping my family decide what the meal will include and stepping into the kitchen to cook and bake. I can't stop the way my mouth twists when I think about the odd food combinations my dad will inevitably dream up with no one to stop him. Even though they're divorced, my mom still invites him for Thanksgiving.

"Honestly, I'm sort of missing home since it's almost Thanksgiving. The Currys always have a big to-do. . . . Everyone brings something. We like to gather and celebrate for literally any occasion. There's a lot of music, and it's really loud, and Nana and I usually sing something together . . . and my dad comes."

"You have told me about your mom, and I have obviously met your grandmother, but I don't know much

207

about your dad," Thierry notes gently. I know it's his way of pushing for information, but not so hard I'll shut down.

"Yeah, he and my mom are divorced," I tell him. "It was amicable. He was just never home. Traveling business-man, you know. Thanksgiving is one of the only times of the year I get to see him, when everyone is together and it feels like it used to when I was little."

Thierry nods. "Is that why you have been working so hard lately? You are trying to keep yourself busy so you will not miss home?"

"Maybe . . . ," I admit sheepishly. "You're great, my friends here are great, but I don't know, since I saw Nana the other day, it's like I've been walking around with an anchor in my stomach."

"We should do something about that," Thierry says, grabbing my hand and bringing it to his lips.

"What about another soirée?" I ask him. "We could have a Thanksgiving dinner party!"

"French people don't celebrate Thanksgiving," Thierry reminds me, but when my face falls, he quickly adds, "You will have to show us how it is done."

"It doesn't have to be a big thing," I continue quickly. "Just a few friends: Sophie, Nora . . . maybe Fabien and Amir?"

Thierry nods in agreement, then straightens up, stuff-ing his hands in his pockets. "Do you want to have it at my family's apartment? Lucie will be there, and my parents will be home, but . . ."

"Oh, my gosh, yes!" I say, already letting my mind get carried away with the preparations. I'm delighted at this opportunity to get to know Thierry even better. Every time I see him in a new situation, I learn about a new side of him. Sometimes I think I'll never know all of him, but I'm determined to try. "I would *love* to meet your family. You don't think they'll mind?"

Thierry shakes his head and laughs. "No. My stepfather loves an excuse to have a feast."

"Well, then it's settled," I reply, linking my arm through his and squeezing. My excitement must be shining on my face, because Thierry can't help but beam, too.

But then I raise a hand to my hairline, worry flooding me.

"Okay, I gotta go to a salon. I cannot meet your mother with my braids like this," I say, nervously fingering my roots, where I can feel entire coils of new growth. "I knew I would have to eventually, but now it's urgent." And as I'm spinning out and Thierry is trying to assure me that I look fine, I realize I'm going to have to figure out how to get my hair done not just in a strange city but in a whole other country. "Where do Black girls even get braids here?"

"I can ask Célestine for you, or maybe you can ask Mathilde?" Thierry suggests.

"Oh, those are great ideas," I say, the panic starting to subside. "I knew I was dating you for a reason."

Thierry snorts. "Interesting. I did not think that was one of them."

My eyes twinkle with laughter as I take Thierry by the hand and lead him off the bridge.

In a text message from Thierry, I learn that his sister Cé-lestine recommends I reach out to Mathilde's sister Élise. Apparently, Élise braids hair and has been doing Céles-tine's for years. Wanting to at least do my due diligence, I search a few natural hair salons in Paris, cross-referencing the websites with their social media accounts so I can see sample hairstyles. Unfortunately, most of the places I see are either booked solid or too expensive.

Eventually, I wander back to Célestine's social media to zoom in on all the pictures in which she has her hair braided, and I decide I'll take the chance. It's that or fig-ure out how to find a B-level salon that does Black hair in Paris and effectively communicate what kind of style I want with my less-than-stellar French.

Élise has Sunday afternoons off, so through Mathilde, she invites me to their home in the eleventh arrondisse-ment. I don't need to bring hair or anything, as she says she'll take care of that. I just need to pay her.

I trek through the city to find the apartment, trying to keep the rain off my freshly washed and blow-dried hair, which I twisted into lopsided braids on either side of my head. Just as Mathilde said, there is a tabac on this street next to a pharmacy; in between is the door to their apart-ment, its eggshell paint peeling. I ring the buzzer, and within a few moments of introducing myself, an unfamil-iar voice speaks back in French, telling me to come up.

Mathilde opens the door and greets me with a big hug and bisous, then ushers me into the living room. Her sis-ter is there, laying out hair and jars of oil and edge con-trol, with a few plastic combs beside her, next to a pillow in front of the TV. I take in the beige walls and small but warm living room with a sienna couch that has elaborate patterns on it. In fact, most of the things in here—the rugs, the pillows, a few small bowls I see laid out on surfaces—have intricate patterns, often in deep reds and blues. There's terra-cotta pottery on shelves in the corner near the television. It smells warm, the air filled with the faint aroma of chilis and saffron.

When Élise finally turns to me, I think that I wouldn't have assumed she and Mathilde were sisters if I didn't know beforehand. Where Mathilde looks vaguely wolfish, with her sharp yellowish eyes, light skin, and wild sandy curls, Élise is a deeper brown, with coily hair that she has collected into a puff on the top of her head. She wears a simple flowing dress but has wrapped herself in a woven shawl that's various shades of blue, turquoise, and gold. Behind her are photos of her and Mathilde at different ages throughout the years. They resembled each other more as preteens than they do now.

"This is the one who does not speak French, no?" Élise says, tutting. *The sarcasm must be hereditary,* I think with a grin. She gestures for me to take a seat on the pillow in front of her and immediately gets to work unraveling my lackluster braids.

"In my defense, I've gotten better!" I protest, and I hear Mathilde murmur a begrudging confirmation and Élise stifle a chuckle.

I expect Mathilde to hang around and chat a bit, but she soon retreats deeper into the apartment, leaving me and Élise to our appointment.

The silence is heavy between us, but the sound from the TV and the chatter that drifts up from the street keep it from being unbearable. Élise has already seen pictures of how I normally wear my box braids in our DM conversation, so she sets to work.

She draws a steel rattail comb against my scalp, parting my hair into sections, then uses it to take a swipe of oil from the open jar to her right. I can see that she's moved it from the comb to the back of her hand when she starts braiding down, her fingers flying. Her hands dance across my head in a rhythm that feels familiar despite my being thousands of miles away from home. The smell of the coconut oil reminds me of my mother. Élise grips the hair at my scalp firmly but not too tightly—I feel like all my brain cells are still intact by the time she makes it halfway up the back of my head—and only nudges my jaw with her knuckle when she wants me to turn to one side or the other.

When I start to feel myself sagging with fatigue after holding myself erect for a couple of hours, Élise puts her hand on my shoulder and tugs until my back rests against her knees and she can tackle the front left section. I let myself lean gratefully. She asks if I want water, but I raise my reusable bottle and say no.

At the end of the third hour, we both stand to stretch. I've got cramps in my legs from sitting, and Élise flexes her fingers and shakes them out before going to the kitchen for tea. She comes back with a second mug, and I cradle it with a smile. I avoid the mirror on the opposite wall from us, because Lord knows that tiny tuft of unbraided hair sitting on top of my head makes me look real silly and will actually be a couple dozen more braids to finish.

After our break, before getting back to my hair, she

turns the TV to a French movie I've never seen, and I wonder if I can figure out what it's about without English subtitles. I watch intently for about forty minutes—the whole rest of the film—but when the credits start to roll, I'm lost, and not just because I missed the beginning of the movie.

It seemed to be a romance: a guy and a girl bond over a quaint bookstore in the French countryside. They fall in love and have happy escapades, with several scenes of the two of them riding in a convertible on an open road, the girl's blond hair snapping behind her in the wind like rippling ribbons. In the end, the girl dies, and the guy goes back to the bookshop and renames it after her.

What the hell? Where's my happily-ever-after?

While Élise takes another break to find something else to turn to, I fish out my phone, which I've managed to ignore for the last few hours, and swipe past a few new messages from my mom and one from Archi. Somehow, this has been more relaxing than any hair appointment I've ever been to at home. Élise isn't much of a talker, but I've fallen straight into a comfortable silence with her and am grateful for the quiet.

I text Thierry and ask him about the movie.

> **Whitney:** Have you ever seen this movie? It's about a girl who falls in love with a guy who names a bookstore after her when she dies. Sorry, spoiler alert if you haven't.

> **Thierry:** I can't say I have heard of it. Do you know the name?

Whitney: Um, no.

Thierry: Who are the actors?

Whitney: This really blond woman with very large hazel eyes.

Thierry: Do you know her name? Did it say?

Whitney: No, but this is the worst love story I've ever seen.

Right after I hit send, Élise nudges me to hold my head up and back, and she finishes the very last small section of hair right on top. She murmurs, "Presque fini," and even though my phone buzzes against my thigh, I hold my head erect for these last few minutes. When she finally says "Voilà," I immediately hop up from my pillow and inspect my braids in the mirror.

I turn my head from left to right, admiring how neat Élise's parts are and how seamless the actual braids are, as she picks up my teacup from the floor.

"Oh, sorry!" I say. "Let me help!" But she smiles at me, then shakes her head and scurries into the kitchen.

"You like?" Élise calls from the next room. I hear running water, then the tap of a metal bottom on a stovetop.

"They're beautiful!" I assure her, rearranging the medium knotless braids that stop at the small of my back so that they cascade down the front of my body on either side of my neck. I move them to the side to admire the triangle parts and then pull them all over my left shoulder.

I try a few different arrangements, until I hear a door open and footsteps pad down the hallway.

"T'as fini?" Mathilde asks, coming to the front of the apartment. Her curly hair is tied in a bun, and small rectangular glasses sit on the bridge of her nose—a classic "I've got to get some serious work done" look. She fingers a couple of my braids and peers closely at my scalp. "Oh, c'est parfait, Élise."

"Merci," Élise responds, then tells me to sit at the table, where Mathilde joins me. I turn to her.

"What have you been up to?"

"I am helping our mother gain citizenship here," Mathilde replies with a sigh, rubbing her eyes underneath her glasses. "Not fun, but necessary."

"You're amazing to help like that," I tell her. Mathilde gives me a small smile and I wish there was something more I could do or say, but then Élise comes around the corner with a steaming pot of water, shooing her sister off. She quickly collects all my braids in a fist, then dips them in the water and swirls them around a bit.

Without being asked, Mathilde grabs a towel and pats my braids down as Élise lowers the pot, making for minimal drippage. The two of them work like a well-oiled machine. Amid the flurry of movement, I feel at peace. Everything in Paris feels heightened, each moment an exciting experience. But these last few hours have felt exceptionally ordinary, like I'm a living a normal life in a new city instead of acting as a long-term guest.

I ask Élise again if I can help clean up, but she refuses my offer again, instead choosing to press a banana and a granola bar into my hands. I juggle them as I fish in my wallet for a few twenty-euro bills to give to her, making sure I add a hefty tip.

Her eyes bulge and then she kisses both of my cheeks. "Merci, chérie," she says, and gives me another smile before turning her attention back to sweeping up the mix of synthetic and human hair that's fallen everywhere on the hardwood in the living room. Mathilde hops up from the kitchen table and walks me to the door.

"À plus," she calls as I take the steps back down to the street level. The door closes with a light pop, and I grab my phone to make sure I know how to get back to the school from here, but I get distracted by another message.

> **Thierry:** French people don't believe in the "happily ever after" love story. It's very American. There are so many other, better love stories.

I smile at his answer to my message about the weird French movie.

> **Whitney:** Like ours?

> **Thierry:** Oui, bien sûr.

I type back quickly before dropping my phone in my pocket and heading toward the nearest métro stop.

> **Whitney:** Well, good thing this American princess loves happily-ever-afters enough for the both of us.

SCENE TWENTY

GUESS WHO'S COMING TO DINNER?

Lucie, Thierry's little sister, greets me at the door when I arrive at the Magnons' apartment over their chocolate shop for the Thanksgiving dinner. She was already vibrant in the photos I've seen of her, but in person, she is like a tiny sun.

Her hair is pulled into two thick braids that trail down her back, making her dark eyes fully visible as they assess me. She crosses her thin arms over her soft-pink knitted sweater dress, and I suddenly panic that I am not going to impress this ten-year-old.

"Thierry!" Lucie calls. "Why did you not tell us Whitney was so pretty?"

As I laugh, half from amusement and half from relief, I hear loud footsteps coming from deeper in the apartment, until Thierry appears behind Lucie. He's wearing a simple tan sweater with the sleeves rolled up to the elbows that brings out the richness of his skin, with a pair of dark pants. Chic and hot. Classic Thierry.

"What did you think she would look like? A frog?" Thierry asks, blowing out his cheeks and crossing his eyes at his sister.

Lucie laughs, but then she gives him the same appraising once-over she gave me.

"She is too pretty for you," she says, and she turns on her heel, leaving us to it.

"Et alors?" Thierry shrugs, gesturing for me to come in with a quick kiss before calling after his sister to change into "real clothes" for dinner. I hear a muffled agreement and a door slamming.

"She speaks English?" I ask as Thierry takes the bags full of food I brought. I kind of overdid it this week in the tiny kitchenette on the first floor of LIA.

"French mostly, but she also understands Spanish because of her dad and learns English at school," Thierry tells me. "She goes to an international elementary school."

"Ah," I reply, then begin to take in my surroundings. I have been in France for almost three months, and this is only the second French home I've been in. Anywhere else I have gone has been tourist sites or adventures out with Thierry.

The Magnons have a cozy home, and it smells so inviting, likely due to residual baking aromas from the shop downstairs, but also there's the smell of cinnamon that clings to everything up here. The walls as I come in are painted a warm light brown, and they are covered with photos of the family. Thierry and his sisters are at the center of most of them—arms around each other at the Trevi Fountain in Rome, reclining on towels at a beach—but there are others that include his mother and stepfather, notably lots of wedding photos. There are who I presume are extended family members or friends, too, big gatherings in sprawling parks or in front of small houses on a lot of land that I'm fairly certain you can't get in Paris.

To my right, the space opens up into a living area furnished with a modern honey-colored couch and two white armchairs with golden embellishments woven into them in intricate patterns. There are two bookshelves along one wall that I wander toward. Closer inspection shows that they are full of dozens and dozens of cookbooks, with the odd nonfiction history book thrown in. The shelves aren't full all the way, and they also house a few odds and ends, trinkets that the Magnons might have gotten on vacations and holidays around the world.

As I turn to head toward the kitchen, I see stacks of cooking magazines on the coffee table, with an abandoned notepad and laptop set on top. The kitchen is on the opposite side of the space, small but cozy, with a gas range and a white refrigerator. There are a few colorful appliances on the brown-tiled counter: an espresso maker, a blue kettle, and a bright yellow toaster.

Thierry waits patiently as I take in the apartment, leaning against the refrigerator with his arms folded. There's a touch of anxiousness to his pose; he wants to know what I think of his home.

"I love it," I tell him. I take in the kitchen table, which has been extended with a card table and surrounded by some mismatched chairs clearly stolen from desks around the house and also a few folding chairs. It's covered with a long cloth, with colorful flowers and leaves embroidered on the edges.

He doesn't quite smile, but he does appear rather pleased by my response. I'm hoping he'll move toward me for a kiss, but before either of us takes a step, we hear the front door to the apartment open.

Three people come in speaking rapid French, leaving their shoes by the door and hanging coats on pegs. The first one to notice us is the girl in round glasses, who looks only a little older than us, and has her thick, coily hair braided in the front, then collected into a puff at the nape of her neck. She's the same shade of dark brown as Thierry, has skin with a natural glow to it, and wears a cropped sweater, baggy jeans, and platform sneakers.

"Oh, mais non," she says with her hand to her mouth. "Thierry, she is too cute for you!"

The couple by the door still settling in breaks into peals of laughter.

Thierry rolls his eyes, but it's good-natured. "In fact, you are not the first person to say this today," he tells her. "Whitney, this is my older sister, Célestine. Célestine, this is Whitney Curry."

I step forward with my hand extended, but Célestine leans forward with her hands on my elbows, air kissing both of my cheeks. Up close, I notice she has the same scattered beauty marks and long lashes that Thierry has, and a dark septum ring.

"Bonjour, Célestine, enchantée," I say. "Thierry didn't tell me you would be home! I didn't think I would get to meet you."

"Why would I not be home?" Célestine asks, confused.

"Oh, I thought you were at university," I continue.

"Célestine goes to university in the city, so she commutes," Thierry explains. "Many people go away to school in the United States, yes? Not so here."

"Got it! Well, I'm glad I get to meet you."

She smiles warmly at me before a tall woman moves forward. The woman has a different body shape and personal style than Célestine, but there's no mistaking that they are mother and daughter—they practically have the same face. Her simple, fitted ecru sweater and black slacks are the same sort of elegant I admired when I saw her wedding pictures at the shop. Thierry's mother's resting expression is rather sharp, but she smiles at me and leans in for air kisses as well.

"On m'a beaucoup parlé de vous," she says, and her hands come down to mine, giving me a little squeeze before letting go. "Bienvenue."

"Bonjour, merci," I say, returning her warm welcome.

"This is my mother, Adeline Magnon-Suarez," Thierry continues the introductions, and then turns to the last figure in the room. "And this—"

Before Thierry gets a chance to finish, his stepfather, a big man with brown skin the color of gingerbread and lots of wild, curly dark hair, wraps me in a huge hug. I want to laugh, but his stepfather is currently crushing the air out of me.

"I hear you like my shop!" he says, his voice bouncing with joy. His accent wobbles between French and Spanish, and I love how distinct it sounds. "Thierry is very good, very talented, yes, but you must come back and see how a master makes chocolate. And you will be able to visit our shops in America! We will have a store in Washington, DC, soon. You will visit, bien sûr!"

"I'd love that, Monsieur Suarez," I say. I can't help the grin on my face. Thierry's stepfather's energy is infectious and radiates out of his body so strongly you can almost see it. I know now where Lucie gets it from. Plus, my heart skips a beat when I hear that the shop will be expanding to my city . . . but I rein myself in. It's too much to let myself get carried away with the hope that perhaps Thierry and I won't have a late-December expiration date. "Thanks so much for letting us host a Thanksgiving dinner here!"

"When Thierry told us," Monsieur Suarez says, "I didn't quite understand, but I *do* understand delicious food and good company! We are glad to have you." He lets out a boisterous laugh.

"Avez-vous besoin d'aide?" Madame Magnon-Suarez asks quietly.

"Pas du tout," I assure her, and I point to the counter where Thierry has set up my bags. "I just need to warm everything up, but that's all!" I strategically spent much of my time over the last week—when not in class or rehearsing—making food.

"We brought flowers and wine, of course," Célestine says, rejoining us from the entryway, flourishing a bouquet wrapped in brown paper and a few bottles of wine in a smaller bag. "I can set them out." She busies herself searching for a vase in a cabinet near the doorway.

"And I hope you do not mind," Thierry says, "but I made some dessert." He opens the fridge to reveal a couple of round chocolate tortes.

"You are wonderful," I say, then kiss him on the cheek. His mother reacts very slightly, the barest of smiles. "Well, we should get started if we want everything ready by the time Nora, Sophie, Fabien, and Amir arrive."

Thierry's parents leave us to the kitchen, retreating deeper into the apartment, and after Célestine is satisfied with her flower arrangement, she grabs her coat and heads out again, promising to be back before we eat. The two of us settle into an easy rhythm as we unwrap my foiled food and stick it into the oven in dishes Thierry picks from the cabinets. He stops me from charring the food, reminding me that the oven temperature is in Celsius, and cranks it down. I have to tap the back of his hands as he tries to sample everything.

"I have never had American Thanksgiving food!" Thierry says in an appeal to me when I shoot him a glare as he tries to include a taste test with his inspection of my cranberry sauce. "How did you get here with all this?"

"I took a rideshare. And really, it's not that much . . . just some turkey breast, and gravy, of course, with greens, sweet potatoes, baked macaroni and cheese, and rolls. Oh, and the cranberry sauce I found at an American grocery store."

"I didn't know you could cook until you told me your idea for this party," Thierry says, unwrapping the macaroni and cheese. "And this isn't very much?" There are dishes and pans covering the length of the Magnons' kitchen countertop. I smile apologetically and shrug. At least I managed to make most everything in the communal kitchen in the dorm and just transport it over, rather than dirty every dish in the Magnon household.

"Well, I can do a great many things, Monsieur Magnon,"

I laugh, throwing the greens into the oven, too. "I like cooking. It's another way to tell a story." I pause and open the oven to gesture to the greens. "I can tell you about how my mother got the recipe for these greens by asking her mother-in-law for about ten years before she wore her down." Then I pick up the pan of macaroni and cheese. "Or how this macaroni and cheese is the only food Nana has ever contributed to any holiday gathering my entire life. She doesn't cook," I add when Thierry looks at me questioningly.

"The grandmother I met?" he asks. After I nod, he finishes with, "Okay, that makes sense."

"Do not be rude about Nana!" I say. I want to swat him, but I'm occupied with opening the oven door and sticking in the macaroni and cheese. "In her defense, this is probably the most delicious macaroni and cheese you'll ever eat, so it kind of evens out."

"You really like holidays," Thierry muses. It's not really a question, more of an observation, since I threw a Halloween party this semester, too.

"You don't?"

"Not as much as you. When I was small, Noël was always fun. My father would listen to the music for weeks, and he would always make so much food. . . ."

I stop moving as I begin to understand what Thierry doesn't say. My hands find his for a moment before I step into his arms and rest my head against his shoulder. He fits his chin on the top of my head, and we stay there for a moment, wrapped together, until we hear the buzz of the intercom.

Before either of us has a chance to move, a door opens deeper in the house, and Lucie flies past.

We hear the front door open and a bit of chatter from a couple of different people; then Lucie calls, "Thierry, your friends are here!"

"Ready to host a Thanksgiving dinner party?" I ask, pulling back from him to tilt my face up. He lays a quick kiss on my lips and nods before taking my hand and leading me to the door.

After Nora, Sophie, Amir, and Fabien arrive, it doesn't take Thierry and me long to finish getting everything together. The food is on the table less than an hour later, and we pass the time talking to our guests from the kitchen as they sit around in the living room. We gorge ourselves on salmon canapés that Sophie brought and immediately start pouring the wine Fabien left on the counter when he came in.

Sophie is soon drawn to Monsieur Suarez's record collection, which is housed in a wooden structure next to the bookcase nearest the window, and asks Thierry if she can play something. With his blessing, she pulls out a Duke Ellington record and starts up the player. Only a few bars play before it draws out Monsieur Suarez and Thierry's mother. Monsieur Suarez is moved by the music, but not for long.

"We need a little more *pow* for a party, no?" he asks, hunching over to scour his collection for something different. As he puts on a new record, Madame Magnon-Suarez pulls the coffee table to the side with Nora's help. Almost immediately, music with lots of horns, rhythmic drums, and Spanish lyrics comes blaring out of the sound system. "How about this?" And he and Madame Magnon-Suarez are dancing in the living room, with all of us clapping along. Lucie even comes out of her room to lean over the back of the couch and watch her parents step in sync as her father sings.

At the next song, Nora hops up and grabs Fabien and starts dancing, too, leaving Sophie and Amir to take videos on their phones as they applaud the dancers. Lucie wants to join, and she grabs Thierry by the hand, but not before he runs over to the record player. When an Afrobeat song thumps out of the player, everyone cheers, Thierry and Lucie taking center stage as they dance around each other.

As if summoned by the music, Célestine reappears in the entryway, and she shakes off the cold, joining her siblings in the living room. The three of them feed off each other, smiling broadly as they measure their steps and shimmy their shoulders to the rhythm. It may not be possible to tell from a picture, but as they dance, no one could doubt these three belong together.

Thierry makes his way over to me to check that I don't need anything else and also to try to pull me to the make-shift living room dance floor for a song, but I shake my head with a smile, pointing at the oven. The last thing I want is for anything to burn.

"I thought you didn't like to dance," I ask, remembering how I struggled to get him to dance with me at the Caveau de la Huchette and how reluctantly he gave in on Halloween.

"I like to dance, but not in front of just anybody," he says, and heads back to the living room with his sisters for another fast-paced song, leaving me to smile, knowing that I am now one of the select few people Thierry Magnon feels comfortable dancing in front of.

226

A couple of songs later, everyone is exhausted and either reclining on a chair or, in Lucie and Célestine's case, sprawled out on the floor. I clear my throat and gesture to the table, which I finished setting during the last two songs.

"Anyone hungry?" I ask.

"Ouais!" Fabien calls, hopping out of his chair so fast it's like he sat on a pin. "La princesse! Ça a l'air délicieux!" He eyes all the food, and I'm suddenly hoping I made enough.

Everyone slowly comes to the table, with murmurs of appreciation for the food, particularly from Monsieur Suarez. As everyone takes their seat, Nora asks, "Do we do something special before we eat?"

"Not really," I say, sitting down next to Thierry. "I mean, my family likes to go around and quickly say what they're thankful for . . ."

"Then we should do that," Thierry says decisively. "I can go first. I am thankful for my family, my friends, and a very surprising semester."

I raise my eyebrows at him. "I hope it was a good surprise."

He squeezes my hand under the table and winks. "Very good."

Fabien, who sits to Thierry's right, goes next. Everyone shares gratitude for a number of different things, but primarily for family and friends—"And delicious food," Lucie adds pointedly as she looks at me, the last to go, with the clear message of "Keep it snappy, sister."

"I am grateful for the best semester in the best city ever," I say, trying to keep my voice even, but it still wobbles with emotion. "For friends that have helped make Paris feel like home. I'm so glad to know you all." I smile around at these faces, then gesture to the food. "Dig in!"

"That was . . . so good," Fabien says, finally sitting back from his plate. Even with Fabien eating enough for a small family by himself, there was plenty of food to go around, and we'll even have some leftovers. The macaroni and cheese, however, was devoured, nothing left but a clay dish with residual cheese along the rim and an empty spoon. Much of that I attribute to Lucie, who, though small, packs away a lot of food.

We all are quiet and happy, that post-dinner haze settling in. I look over at the other end of the table, where Fabien and Célestine are sitting. I originally thought Fabien would be put out at not being able to sit with his friend, but judging by the way he leans over to speak low to Célestine, who's got a half-amused, half-exasperated expression on her face, I wager he's happy just where he is. I poke Thierry and surreptitiously point at them, and he only shakes his head with a deep but fond sigh, which lets me know this is comme d'habitude for Fabien.

"I agree," Monsieur Suarez says, throwing his napkin down. "Whitney, you are a very good chef!" The table agrees, Lucie even giving me a round of applause. On Lucie's other side, Nora and Sophie chat amicably with Amir. Monsieur Suarez throws an arm around Thierry's mother, who leans into his side, contentment on her face.

"Whitney is very talented," Thierry says, with, dare I say, a hint of pride in his voice. "She is an actress, but she also can sing and dance. And your French is much improved! You sound like a native speaker now."

"I wouldn't go that far," I say, holding up my hands to slow him down. "But any improvements are thanks to you. You're a great tutor." I reach for his hand with both of mine and squeeze.

"You are a good singer," Lucie agrees, breaking up the moment and holding up her phone to us. I see the video Thierry filmed of me at Place Joséphine Baker what feels like a lifetime again on a video-sharing app, and I smile.

"Lucie, how did you find that?" Thierry asks, reaching past me to swipe at his sister's phone.

"It was very easy," she replies, pocketing her phone before Thierry can steal it.

Monsieur Suarez is getting up from the table, announcing he'll make us all some coffee, when the intercom buzzes. Madame Magnon-Suarez pushes her seat away from the table to get the door.

"I am so sleepy," Lucie announces.

"Yeah, that can happen when you eat a lot of rich food," I tell her.

Lucie pouts. "That's not fair. If you eat well, you should be awake to enjoy it."

I'm about to heartily agree when Madame Magnon-Suarez returns, a frown on her face, followed by someone else.

The girl is as tall as Thierry's mother in her high-heeled boots and sports a long gray coat that comes down to her knees. It takes me a minute to realize that I've seen her before, with her long hair and dewy skin and full lips, just never in person. Her liquid black eyes are taking in the scene before her, and finally she says, "Qu'est-ce qu'il se passe?"

Thierry's frown matches his mother's when he finally addresses the girl.

"Fatima."

SCENE TWENTY-ONE

MAMA'S GIRL

Despite the apartment being full of ten—now eleven—people, it's quiet when Thierry pushes his chair back and stands to walk over to the entry. His mother steps out of his way with her wine-colored lips very gently pursed. She looks at me with what seems like apology in her eyes as Thierry walks over to Fatima.

I feel a little like the wind has gotten knocked out of me from the surprise of seeing Thierry's ex-girlfriend in his doorway, but when sensation returns to my extremities, a series of emotions chase each other around my stomach. The alarm bells that I ignored in prior conversations involving Fatima return full force while I cycle through sadness, frustration, and maybe a little anger. The specter of this girl has followed me all semester, and now she's here. I'm embarrassed by how small I feel in her presence.

I don't know what to do as Thierry and Fatima have a quick exchange, so I finger the edge of my napkin. My mind feels like it's full of TV static. It hasn't occurred to me how much Thierry slows down his French around me until now, when I hear him speaking with Fatima. Even after an entire semester of listening to him, at this pace, I'm only able to catch pieces of the conversation, which I mentally translate: "back from Senegal," "this girl," and "*my* boyfriend." (A loose translation; I'm pretty sure what she said was not actually very polite.) I see Célestine roll her eyes, but she keeps quiet and drinks her water as they go back and forth.

Even though Thierry is getting agitated, which I can tell by the way his jaw locks and tics, he keeps his voice even-keeled when he speaks to her, low, so that the whole room can't hear.

So that *I* can't hear. Even though she's still speaking, all I can hear is what I'm sure was "my boyfriend" in Fatima's voice ringing in my ears. I can't make it make sense. What Thierry has told me and his actions . . . they don't align with what Fatima is saying. But I remember the way he called Nora a "friend of a friend," hiding the fact that the two of them were linked by Fatima. I want there to be space for the truth to come out, and it might work out in my favor, but he has been hiding his connection with Fatima from me, whatever the reason may be.

I feel a prickle around my eyes, and I know that if I blink, water will spill over onto my cheeks.

Finally, Thierry convinces Fatima to talk to him outside, and she agrees, but not before locking eyes with me.

"I saw your videos. On social media," Fatima says in French, simpering. "They are adorable. It was so good of my boyfriend to help you with them. He's talented, and kind."

She said it again—"boyfriend"—and my head is swimming.

"Yeah, your ex has been super helpful," I manage with what is probably the last dash of sass left in my body. The static in my head is getting louder, and I'm wondering if I'm translating what she's saying correctly, given that nothing seems to be working inside my brain right now, but there can be no mistaking Fatima's tone.

And that's when I'm convinced that somehow, I've imagined all this. That he has just been biding his time until Fatima returned. That they weren't actually over, and I stepped into a mess that I should've known to avoid, given my work. I can't stop my mind from spinning out, making me feel like I've thrown my first big, important transcontinental adventure away on a boy. I should have trusted myself, should have prioritized what I said I was going to: *no distractions.* That flew out the window almost the first week, and now here I am, feeling the consequences of that distraction.

Around the table, Nora shifts in her chair, and Sophie purses her lips. Fabien scoffs but doesn't say anything as Fatima tosses her hair over her shoulder and walks out, Thierry trailing her. He doesn't glance at me before going, but in spite of everything, I want him to. I need him to be next to me, to reassure me that this doesn't mean anything, that I've imagined it. But the door closes with a light *pop,* and I'm left with my mind running three thousand miles an hour.

"Well," I say decisively, trying to put some control in my voice. "I'd better clean this up."

"No, I will do it," Madame Magnon-Suarez says, trying to wave me away. I'm already standing and collecting plates.

I try not to let my lower lip wobble as I turn to her. "No, please. Let me." I can't tell her that I need something to do, that if I sit here and wait for Thierry to come back, I won't be able to keep a nice, calm, stoic front, and I cannot start crying in this very nice French lady's home. Plus, as my mother says whenever my anxiety gets the better of me, "You don't even know if there's anything to cry about yet, Whitney." Not typically a helpful thought, but today it does what it needs to do.

Between that and the impeccable home training my mother imparted in me, I gather myself and head to the kitchen. Nora and Sophie join me in the kitchen, helping me pack up the few leftovers, then washing and drying the rest of the dishes. The steadiness of the motions and my hands in the water anchor me.

I'm just thinking I'll be all right when Lucie sidles up beside me while I'm peering into the refrigerator to make sure I didn't miss anything. Thierry's chocolate tortes are sitting at the bottom. The sight of them makes it difficult to swallow the enormous lump in my throat, like I've had three rolls and nothing to wash them down with.

"For what it's worth . . . I like you better, Whitney," the little girl says, and she quickly wraps her skinny arms around my waist for a hug.

"That's worth a lot to me, friend," I say, hugging her

back, a few tears finally escaping into the top of Lucie's curly black hair.

By the time Thierry returns—without Fatima—the apartment is clean. The leftover food and plates are re-packed in the Franprix bags I used to cart everything here, and Célestine wiped down the table, then put the extra chairs and card table back where they came from. I'm al-ready saying thank you and goodbye to Thierry's parents and sisters, all of whom embrace me warmly.

"I hope you will come back," Madame Magnon-Suarez says as she kisses me goodbye, but even as she says it, she knows that I won't.

I try to smile at her, but I know I look pitiful.

That's when Thierry walks in. I force myself to roll my shoulders back and take a deep breath. Even though the habits I've developed for confidence over the years help the air flow easier through my body, it doesn't stop the sinking feeling from taking over my stomach.

"Thierry, I'm going to go back to the school," I say sharply; I know he wants to talk, but I need a beat. I try my best to keep my voice level, but there's an agitated clip to it that I can't mask. There's more I want to say, but I can't be sure I won't cry if I do, so I push past him. Nora and Sophie follow.

I can hear Thierry calling me, but I don't stop as I make my way down the stairs to street level. It's already deep night, streetlights dotting the dark with spots of yellow.

I start to march toward the métro stop, Nora and So-phie trailing me, but there are other hurried footsteps be-hind us. A second later, Thierry is in front of me holding out his hands. He must have immediately come after us as we left, because he doesn't even have a coat on. I fight the urge to tell him to go back upstairs and get one, but that would imply I would stand out here in the cold while he did that and would still be here when he got back, when I realize there's nothing now, or in a few minutes, I want to say.

"Whitney," Thierry says. "Will you wait? Can we talk? Please?"

"For *what*?" I snap. "Talk about *what*? Talk about the fact that you had me cooking in your parents' house when Fatima *clearly* thinks you two are still together? What? Was I just someone to . . . fill time with until she got back? Were you two even broken up?"

Thierry's eyes widen, and he's stammering. "No, no, no, Whitney, we were—we *are*—broken up! She—"

"Then what was she *doing* here, Thierry?! Why did you go off with her? You didn't even check to see if I was okay, you just left." And now the tears that are coming aren't sad—they're angry tears, but it doesn't matter what the root is. Thierry Magnon isn't going to see them.

"I couldn't be two places at once. I was trying to resolve the situation. And you don't understand. Fatima . . . she is—"

"Nope," I say, cutting this whole thing off. "No. You don't get to pass this off as something your 'crazy ex-girlfriend' did. Thierry, you must have said or done something that made her think you were still together." I laugh derisively. "I absolutely fell for this. I did exactly what I was trying not to do when I came here—I let myself get distracted, and we see where it's gotten me. I'm so stupid."

"Whitney, you are not stupid! Will you just, please, let me explain? Fatima and I broke up before she even left for Senegal, and she found out I was dating you and got jealous. She was trying to goad you. We are not together, Whitney. I promise you." Thierry reaches for my hands, but they're full of the dishes and leftovers I'm toting.

I'm so angry I can barely make out Thierry through tears I refuse to let fall. I push past him and walk to the métro, not caring if Nora and Sophie are following.

But they appear next to me on the platform, and when the train comes they sit quietly across from me as we make our way back to the school.

It's not until we've transferred to the second train that I finally speak to them.

"Did you know Fatima was coming tonight?" I ask, not bothering to take my eyes off the spot I'm fixated on underneath the chair across from me. There's a stain there, dark brown, and I do my best not to think about what fluid made it.

"No," Nora says gently, and out of the corner of my eye, I see her stretch her hand out toward me, but she changes her mind halfway and brings it back to rest on her lap.

I really want to believe her, but an evil little voice in the back of my head says that she and Fatima have been together in this all along. That they've been laughing at me behind my back.

"Then you weren't telling her all about me and Thierry this whole time?"

Sophie looks at Nora with a hard expression on her face as the blond gazes at her knees, which are pressed together.

"Fatima is my friend, so at first, for a while, yes, I told her about you. I did stop, but I recently mentioned our plans for this evening. She seemed . . . interested. I told her not to come. . . . I didn't think she would . . . ," Nora confesses. "You've become my friend, too, Whitney, and I—"

"I can't," I say, a fresh wave of frustration flowing over me.

I turn away from Nora and rest my head against the window, watching the lights in the dark walls flash by as the train screams through the tunnels.

The quiet of 5A feels like it's squishing against the sides of my head, squeezing it like a lemon. I can't stand it, but I also can't do anything about it. If I try to talk to anyone, I'll have to explain why my heart feels so sore in my chest. And if I do that, I'll never stop crying. But maybe that's what I need.

When we got back to the dorms, Nora and Sophie checked to make sure I was all right once more before excusing themselves to watch TV in the common room. I didn't ask them what they will watch; I know they're only trying to give me some space.

Sophie gave me a small smile as she closed the door gently behind her. As soon as the last of her brown hair disappeared, I collapsed onto my bed and pulled my phone toward me.

Now I pull up a contact, and the phone only rings a few times before the connecting ping sounds.

"Hey, Whit!" Archi says with a smile, drawing out both words. "What's up—Whit?"

She sees my face and immediately shifts gears into concerned bestie mode. I tell her to hang on while I pull Becca onto the call. When they're both on the line, tiny pixelated faces staring back at me, I crack. All the tears I forced back at Thierry's find their way down my cheeks, and the story tumbles out.

They listen carefully and don't interrupt, other than to offer a sympathetic cluck of the tongue or to sadly murmur my name. When I'm done, we sit quietly; I need a second to catch my breath, and my girls need a moment to process.

Finally, Becca asks, "What would be helpful right now? You want us to kill him? You want advice? A pep talk? Say the word, and I'll be on the next flight to Paris. You just point him out, I'll take care of the rest."

Becca's offer makes me want to laugh, but the sound doesn't quite come out right—it's more of a hiccup.

"No, you don't need to kill him," I say gently. "Maybe I just want . . . Can I just be sad with you for a minute?"

"Of course, babe, as long as you need," Archi says.

And the three of us sit on the call, not speaking but still together, while my heart breaks.

After several minutes of comfortable silence, I manage to convince Becca and Archi that I'm okay. They ask me if there's anything I want to do or talk about, and I assure them everything will be fine. That I know what I want to do.

My friends seem hesitant but let me hang up, though not before lots of declarations of love and promises for more calls soon. Once they're gone, I take several deep breaths; then I call my mom.

The call connects almost immediately, and within seconds, my mom is there on the screen of my phone. Even though I can only see the top half of her face because she's holding her phone crooked at the moment, it's enough to make me want to run straight into her arms.

"Hey, my superstar," my mom says when she finally gets the phone set up right and I can see her entire face. She's sitting in the living room on the couch, probably having a lazy afternoon of magazine reading, if I know her.

"Hi, Mommy," I say, and my voice is so small I don't even recognize it as my own.

"Oh, baby girl, what's the matter?" she asks, fixing me with a gaze that penetrates me, even clear across the Atlantic Ocean.

"I . . . I know that the semester isn't over yet . . . but I . . . I'm homesick. Real bad. I want to come home," I lie. I don't want to leave Paris, but I can't walk the streets when everything reminds me of how I learned the city with Thierry. And when she smooths back her black hair streaked with strands of steely gray and sighs, I think that maybe I'm not totally lying. I wanted my space from her when I came, but after several months and thousands of miles, I need to breathe in her jasmine perfume to make me feel better, and have her fuss over me, asking me a million times if I am okay.

My mom is quiet for a little while, calmly waiting to see if I offer up anything else. When I don't, she says, "Whitney, does this have anything to do with a boy?"

I splutter in surprise, trying to say "No" and "Why

240

would you think that?" at the same time. Mom peers at me with her eyebrow raised.

"Well, one, I know it's been a while, but I have in fact been a teenage girl in love before," she says, "and two, Nana called me from Berlin, and she did nothing but rave about an upright young man you'd found yourself in Paris."

"Oh, Nana," I sigh, rubbing my temple with two fingers.

"Don't blame her. You were the one who told her to call me in the first place, if I heard her correctly," my mom says with a smile in her voice.

"Yes, but I didn't think she'd tell you *my* business!"

"Whit, when has your grandmother ever been able to hold water?"

I grimace. "Fair."

"Listen, I don't know what happened," Mom says, "and as much as I'd love to see you earlier than expected, I know you like to finish what you start. Plus, what about your project? You were so excited about that."

"I'm basically done," I tell her. "I wouldn't be able to perform it here, but the whole thing is drafted, with the performance bible complete. I was just going to edit and rehearse these last few weeks, but even more edits are overkill. I'm just being a perfectionist at this point. And if they really want the performance, I can always do it and record it when I get back home."

My mom is surveying me, and I know two halves of her are warring: the part that wants me back as close to her as possible and the part that wants what's best for me. I want her to know that this time, those two parts are the same. Being home is what's best for me.

"Whitney, I just want you to think about this," Mom

says. "I don't want you to do anything you'll regret. Because running away from hard things? That's not you. You've always run headfirst into adventure. I've never been like that, and it's been hard to let go and let you do your thing. But I see how much you've opened up in Paris, how much you love it. I would hate for you to let the story end here because it got hard."

Then she gives me a small smile. "If, in the morning, after you've slept, you still feel you need to come home, I will book you a flight."

"Promise?" I say, holding up my pinky to her like I used to do when I was little.

"Promise," she says, holding up hers in return. She curls her long finger as if it were closing around mine, and I do the same.

We don't talk for much longer, and I'm off the phone and freshly showered by the time Nora and Sophie come back into the room. I've turned to the side and pulled the blankets around myself and slowed my breathing to make it appear like I'm asleep so they don't bother me, and after about a half an hour of moving around, they settle and drift off. Only when I hear the soft exhales of Sophie's snoring do I unwrap myself from the tight blankets and let myself fall on my back to stare at the ceiling.

I don't know how long I've been lying here like that, but it seems like I blink, and the stars are replaced by the sun's rays and a pink sky.

To Leave Paris or to Stay:
That Is the Question
A Pro/Con List

STAY

1. It's <u>Paris.</u> Can I really leave this glorious city, with its open-air markets and freshly baked bread and sinful coffee and wide streets, three entire weeks early? I mean, there are still some sights left on my list. . . .
2. I have never run away from anything because it's hard before. Why should I stop now?
3. My play is finished, and I think I'll always regret it if I go home without performing in Paris like Josephine did. Hopefully, this won't be the only time I come to Paris . . . but there's nothing like the first time.

GO

1. I really am starting to get homesick— although, it's difficult to know if this is regular homesickness or "I need my mommy after I got my heart broken" homesickness.
2. I don't think I can walk the city with all the memories I have of Thierry. Every step will hurt. I should leave before my heartbreak taints everything I've built. Sure, it's colored blue now, but it won't always be. If I leave now, the sadness will fade before it has time to set in, and I'll be able to remember Paris for what it was to me.
3. If I don't leave now, I may never want to come back. I may let this moment convince me that I never belonged in Paris in the first place, when

Paris is in my blood, it's in my heart. It might become too hard to return, and I never want to feel that way about this city. Not while I have breath in my body.

NOTES
Whatever, this list doesn't even mean anything. There's nothing really left to do. I can email my play to Monsieur Laurent and still get full credit, and I'll make sure to send my review of Thierry's performance as a tutor to Cécile so he can go back to playing soccer. . . .

There's nothing holding me here.

I can go.

SCENE TWENTY-TWO

PARTING WITH SUCH SWEET SORROW

Because I am a woman of her word, I sleep on it like I told my mother I would. Well, kind of. I stayed up until dawn crying, but I did sleep much of the morning. By noon, however, nothing is different except my eyelids are tender and my nose is stuffed up from all the crying. Other than that, I'm still hell-bent on getting out of this city.

As she promised, when I grab my phone and text her that I still want to leave, my mom replies that she will get me a flight for tomorrow.

The sigh of relief I let out lasts approximately a second and a half—the time it takes for me to realize I have a bunch of notifications on my screen. Since last night, I've missed five calls from Thierry, three from yesterday and two more this morning. I have double the number of texts from him, plus a flurry of messages from my friends, checking in on me after last night.

I leave all of them unread and flop face-first into my pillow.

Then, eventually, I sit back up because I remember Nora and Sophie are probably watching me be a weirdo, but their areas of the room are clear. I don't know what I expected from them after last night, but avoiding me like the plague was the not the tack I would have taken.

Feelings of frustration and abandonment roll off me in waves. The energy propels me out of bed until I'm standing in front of the closet, pulling down all my dresses and sweaters and stuffing them haphazardly into my trunk and suitcases.

Putting over three months of my life in France in bags hurts more than I expected it to. Now, the clothes I unpacked in September are the dress I wore on the first day I met Thierry or the jumper I wore to Chocolat Doré, where we kissed for the first time. They're not just clothes, they're memories I can wear. It doesn't take me long to put my clothes away—I simply stuff dirty laundry into trash bags—so I move on to the walls, where I remove fairy lights, posters, and the Polaroids I've accumulated.

My fingers linger on the photos. The first pictures I took, from Monsieur Polignac's car, of the Pont Alexandre III and the Eiffel Tower. The ones of 5A in the early days before Sophie and Nora and I became a team, and a few of us hanging out in the room together after. I see Halloween party pictures and stills from the Black Americans in Paris tour I took on my first weekend. And even though my heart aches when I see them, knowing this is what I'm leaving, it's worse when I see the ones of Thierry: our adventures, our dates, at soccer. I even have photos of the chocolates he sent me home with from our first date, the ones that were almost too pretty to eat.

With a deep exhale, I stick all the photos in a plastic bag and stuff them down into the trunk between the side and my clothes. My area of the room isn't blank, but it's starting to seem like Whitney Curry in Paris never existed; this space, without my pictures and posters and trinkets, could've belonged to anyone.

My throat feels like it's closing up, so I decide to get dressed and go for a walk. I want to leave my phone in the dorm, but I've managed to go mostly my entire trip without making mindless decisions, and I'd hate to start the day before I go home. Instead, after I slip into a pair of high-waisted jeans, a camel turtleneck sweater under my green coat, and ballet flats, I turn it on silent, drop it into my bag, and head out. Before I leave the campus, I stop at the administrative building and let myself in.

Henri is not at his desk, but Cécile is in her office on the phone when I pop my head in. She waves me to come in, and after I explain to her that I'm leaving the program, her eyebrows rise mere millimeters in what I presume to be surprise. But she gives me all the paperwork I need to sign and tells me I can drop it off on my way out in the morning.

I already have one form that is complete, and that I desperately need to be rid of. Cécile takes the sheet when I hand it to her, quickly glancing at the "Tutoring Review" heading and nodding at me, making it disappear into one of her many color-coded folders beside her computer monitor. I pause at how fast the paper disappears, almost like me and Thierry, here and then gone in a flash. . . . I give her a small smile, then leave the building and head toward the street.

I walk by Monsieur Laurent's office and slide a copy of my play script under the door. I titled it *The Loves of Josephine Baker*. I know a semester isn't exactly enough time to write your magnum opus, but I've certainly put everything I have into these pages over the last few months. Even if the play will never be performed, I still want someone to read it. To know that fifty years after her death, Josephine Baker is still lighting up the lives of young performers like me. It was a labor of love, and love is meant to be shared.

I don't know where I'm going, but my feet carry me toward the river. Everyone around me seems to be having a better day: the cold doesn't bother the teens who walk in packs like wolves or deter families with small children. Older people still amble along the streets to the best of their abilities. But even people-watching, one of my favorite things to do in any city, doesn't lift the heaviness in my heart.

When the Seine and the skeleton of Notre Dame on its island are in view, I figure there's not much I want to do other than walk along the river for a while. My feet find one of the smaller footbridges by memory, not because I lead them there, and I cross over onto the Left Bank, stopping frequently to watch boats pass and birds swoop overhead. I even wave to a few people standing on the decks of them, a tiny grin on my face, as they call back excitedly in various languages.

I keep walking until I find myself in front of the Louvre. It's not too crowded for the middle of the day on a Friday, so I decide to join the people in the line in the building's courtyard. In spite of my mood, my breath still catches when I see the glass pyramids. I make sure to take a few selfies; only I'll know that my enthusiasm is fake.

Inside, I grab a map from a nice lady at the visitor center and then start to wander. The Greco-Roman section is the first I end up in, and I wander among faultless statues, intricately designed vases, and various artifacts: coins, spearheads, and other quotidian items. There are paintings lining the walls as well, but fewer of them than there are in other sections. I could spend the whole day in this section alone, but since I'm here, I check the map and head toward the Mona Lisa.

There's always a crowd around the small painting, but today it's easier to see than the first time I visited the Louvre in September. I take a selfie with my phone instead of my camera so I can use the photo online later. Afterward, I walk up as close as the red velvet rope will allow and whisper goodbye to the portrait, as if she were alive and knows who I am and will miss me.

Hunger pains eventually register in my stomach, and I leave the castlelike institution and walk back in the general direction of the school. I consider having a croissant and coffee, like I did on my first morning in Paris, but I smell something buttery before I see a tiny crêperie up ahead, and I offer the teenager behind the counter a five-euro note in exchange for a crêpe packed with ham and melted cheese.

I munch on it, pigeons waddling around me on the sidewalks like pedestrians as I weave through crowds of Parisians and tourists, taking in the colorful shops filled with the best food and flowers and wine and produce. My heart breaks twice, once for Thierry, and once because I know I will never love another place like I love Paris.

SCENE TWENTY-THREE

I ATTEMPT TO FLEE

It's foggy when I wake up the next morning, and I'm miserable about it because the least the weather could do is be agreeable for my last few hours in my favorite city.

Nora and Sophie are both crestfallen when I start to pull my trunk and valises toward the door of our room with every intention of hauling it down six flights of stairs to the lobby, where I'll wait for my rideshare.

"Whitney, you don't have to go," Sophie says, taking half a step forward.

I manage a wobbly smile that I wish were cheekier, but even I can't act my way through this heartbreak. As if it weren't enough that Thierry and I are on the outs, having to say goodbye to my new friends shatters me all over again.

Nora stays to the side, though she has her hands clasped together and her mouth puckered like words want to slip through her lips.

Finally, she speaks.

"I know it wasn't right to talk to Fatima about you, and I'm sorry," Nora says. "I promise I didn't know she would come to Thanksgiving. When you and I became friends . . . all the time we spent planning the party, your rehearsals . . . I realized I didn't want to share anything more with her about you, but I had already shared too much. I'm sorry, Whitney."

As she speaks, more of the truth settles in me. I can hear how earnest Nora sounds. But the hurt still burns.

"I forgive you," I tell her, reaching over to squeeze one of her hands. "And I get it . . . but it's still time for me to go home."

Nora nods like she's accepted that there's nothing she can say that will make me stay.

"Let us at least help you downstairs," Sophie says.

I agree, and the three of us carry my bags, which have accumulated a significant amount of heft since I arrived in September, down the stairs and to the lobby of the building.

I'm debating whether to check my phone to see how long until my rideshare arrives or go ahead and do my last goodbyes with Nora and Sophie, when someone barrels through the front doors of the school.

Thierry Magnon is in front of me, chest heaving, with some folded paper clutched in one hand and a small bag in the other.

Out of the corner of my eye, I see Nora and Sophie exchange glances, then slowly back away from us to give us a bit of space.

That's when I notice that Thierry has sweat on his forehead and I blurt out, "Thierry, did you run here?"

"Ah," he says, straightening up with his hands on his hips to catch his breath. "From the métro stop, yes. I was worried I would miss you."

"Were you really that concerned? You could've showed up any time yesterday," I say, not bothering to leave the hurt out of my voice. I realize that if Thierry had found his way to the dorms yesterday, I would have talked to him.

"Yes, but you could have also answered my calls," Thierry replies, as if ready for any verbal volley I may toss his way. "And anyway, when I was not calling you, I was making this yesterday."

He puts the bag down on the floor in front of him and unfolds the paper. It's a map of Paris . . . but with a whole story on it. There are dozens of Post-it notes and stickers, as well as things written directly on the map in colorful permanent marker. There are even a few pictures paper-clipped to the edges. Some places in the city, like the Latin Quarter, have a lot of stickers and notes. Montmartre, I notice, has a glittery heart sticker.

"That's a lot of glitter," I say, trying to make it seem more like an observation than something I'm impressed by.

"I had some help from Lucie," Thierry admits nervously. "When she found out you wanted to leave . . . well, she didn't want you to leave."

"That's nice of Lucie, I guess," I snap. I love his sister, but she's not the one I need to hear didn't want me to leave.

"There's something else . . . ," he tells me. He motions for someone I didn't realize was hanging back to come forward.

Fatima is here. She's dressed down in jeans and a turtle-neck with a nice coat and no makeup, but she's still stunningly pretty. We stare at each other for a moment before Fatima manages a small smile.

"I am sorry for how I behaved the other night," she begins, and she clasps her thin hands together in a nervous gesture that feels out of place on a confident girl like her. "Thierry and I . . . we have known each other a long time, so even though I knew he was seeing you, I was a little shocked to see you together in person, and I acted out. . . ."

Fatima steps closer to me still and reaches for my hand. I can smell Chanel's Coco Mademoiselle on her and see the natural glow of her skin.

"I want him to be happy, and it seems like you help with that," she says earnestly. "Don't punish Thierry for something I did. I am sorry."

I nod, words stuck in my throat, and pull away from her, turning to Nora and Sophie to fill in the blanks.

"I talked to her after dinner," Nora tells me. "I wanted to know why she did what she did. And when Sophie and I heard you were leaving, we had to do something. We hoped you might accept her apology—and mine."

"You knew I was leaving?" I asked her. She nodded, shooting a glance at Sophie.

"We heard you speaking to your mother," Sophie chimed in, guilt that she eavesdropped written on her face. "So we called Fatima and made sure Thierry hurried. He was already on the way. We're sorry. We only wanted you to stay."

Everything is starting to make more sense, but I still feel unmoored, and I need something to anchor me.

My heart double-times when Thierry finally steps toward me, holding the map in his hand and glancing at it nervously as he speaks. My throat starts to close again, and I will myself not to cry no matter what he says. I resolve to stare at a spot on the floor.

"Every day since I have met you has been an adventure," Thierry starts. "I wake up, and the first thing I think is 'How can I spend time with Whitney today?' All I want to do is explore Paris with you. I have lived here my whole life, but when we go places together, everything feels new. It is exciting." I finally look up and see that Thierry's eyes are shining. I know what he means. Paris is an adventure all by itself, but with Thierry, it shines brighter.

He takes a breath, then keeps going. "I know our story is not over, but I will not ask you to stay for me, even though I would miss you so much if you go home now. You should stay because you want to. Because there is still more for you here. Because you want to perform your show." Behind him, Nora and Sophie nod enthusiastically. After all the time I've spent with them rehearsing, I would think they'd be tired of my performance.

"But please." Thierry pockets the sheet and reaches for my hand. "I hope you will stay, Whitney," he says, squeezing my hand ever so slightly.

I *want* to believe him, hang on to this shred of hope that he could still be my favorite part of Paris.

I see the furrow between Thierry's eyebrows as he tries to figure out what to do next. It's at that moment I turn back to the map.

A photo sticks up from the paper, and I can see that it's Thierry and me at Chocolat Doré standing next to a counter full of truffles. It was taken after we had our first kiss; I can tell because his arm is around my waist, and I've got my hands resting on one of his shoulders as he reaches out his other long arm to take a selfie.

Thierry sees me touching that picture, reaches for the bag he left to the side when his impromptu performance started, and hands it to me.

I reach inside to find a chocolate box, wrapped in chocolate with a red chocolate heart on the top, similar to the one he gave me on our first date.

"Chocolate really does solve anything, doesn't it?" I ask. The box starts to shake in my hands as I start to realize what a gigantic mess *I've* made, and when I look up at Thierry, his outline is blurry.

"Why are you crying?" Thierry asks me. His hand rises slightly at his side, as if he wants to reach for me but doesn't quite know if it's safe. Then I really cry because *I* caused that hesitation. *I* am why Thierry isn't sure of himself around me in the moment.

"Thierry . . . I've made a mess," I hiccup, tears streaming down my face. "I always joke about being a disaster, and it's supposed to be *cute* and . . . endearing, but I *ruined* this."

Thierry's signature brow furrow appears again. "Ruined what?"

"*This*," I say. There are teardrops on the top of my chocolate box now, and all I can think of is how I've also messed up this perfect thing this wonderful boy has made me. "I should've just talked to you. I should never have run off and pretended nothing we had was real. That was easier than admitting everything hurt because it *was.* Real." I gulp air like a fish out of water. "All of this . . . If I'd answered your calls . . . we could have had even more time together. I tried to cut our love story short because I jumped to conclusions. Fatima wasn't the problem. I had this unexpected, grand love story, one for the ages, and maybe I thought because it was going to end anyway, I might as well go out with a bang."

I finally focus in on him and see that Thierry is watching me intently, quietly, letting me get all these mixed-up words out, but there are just a few left I still have to say.

"I am *so* sorry," I say. "Please say you'll forgive me."

Thierry takes that as his cue to step into the space between us and hug me.

"There's nothing to forgive. And you haven't made a mess. Nothing that we cannot fix together," he says into my hair. Then he pulls back, and his dark eyes round with hope meet mine. "Will you stay?"

I fold myself into him again, nod against his neck and exhale.

"I will stay."

SCENE TWENTY-FOUR

I GIVE THE PERFORMANCE
OF MY (HOPEFULLY LONG) LIFE

The LIA's one small auditorium is just big enough to fit the students of my school—about one hundred and fifty people—and I can hear the chatter of my classmates as they take their seats in the audience.

I want to peek around the curtain and see if I can spot Thierry, but I turn to check my makeup in the tiny mirror I brought with me from my dorm. I prop my phone up so that the light shines on my face, illuminating the heavy black liner around my eyes and the glittery blue eye shadow. I pucker my glossy red lips for the full effect. When I stand back and admire my figure in the black gown with the low neckline, I smile with approval. Maybe I'm not a dead ringer for Madame Josephine, but this is an impressive homage, even for me.

I double-check the box that's just hidden from the audience's view by the curtain to ensure all my props are there: a skirt of artificial bananas, a long beaded necklace, a stuffed cheetah, several loose pages of sheet music. Earlier, Henri rolled an old upright piano to stage right, and a microphone down center stage. A stool stands behind the microphone.

It will be one of my more stripped-down performances—there was no time for elaborate set designs. But the more I thought about it, the more appropriate it seemed. Yes, Josephine Baker was known for her elaborate costuming, but people came to see *her*. *She* is the star of the story I'm telling. All I have to do is let myself be as big and flashy as I want to be.

I take one quick peek into the crowd. I can see Sophie sitting in the back at a table with large machines that operate the sound and lights. Then, Monsieur Laurent walks onstage from the opposite side toward the mic, to gentle applause from my classmates.

"Bonjour, bonjour," he says, his neon orange socks capturing my attention more than the enthusiasm of his voice. "Today we will have a treat! Whitney Curry will present her senior thesis project to us. It is a thirty-minute vaudeville-inspired performance based on the life and loves of the Black American singer and dancer Josephine Baker, which she has written and directed herself. After, she will give a short statement about her work and answer any questions. It has been a delight to read her work this semester, and I know you will all enjoy her performance! Thank you!"

Monsieur Laurent bobs his head toward the crowd and glances over at me in the wings, beaming.

As the applause fades, the lights go with it, leaving us all in a suspended darkness.

Nora appears next to me, clad in black, with her big binder in her hands and a headset over her blond hair, which is all that I can see clearly of her at the moment.

"Okay, Whitney, allons-y," she whispers. I grip her hand and squeeze.

Then, with quick, determined steps, I walk onto the stage, hearing the clack of my heels against the wood until I land directly in front of the mic.

I stand there, one hand on a hip popped out to the side and the other cradling the mic. My heart is thudding directly up against my ears, but it's the most thrilling anticipation. I break into a wide smile as the lights come up, a spotlight on me, and I imagine how the rhinestone jewelry I'm wearing must sparkle to the now shapeless audience.

"You ain't never heard a story like this!" I say, letting my voice push out from my diaphragm so it fills the entire auditorium, even without the microphone. A jazzy number starts to spill out of the speakers and when I start to sing "Dis-Moi Joséphine," I'm gone.

Because it's just me onstage, with no breaks and no one there to catch me if I falter, it's one of the most taxing performances I've ever put on. When the first song ends and I'm greeted with applause, energy courses through my veins, and I find the strength to start my story. I tell the audience about Josephine from St. Louis, the girl who was so deeply called by another country, whose soul was made of art.

I am so glad I decided to incorporate song and dance performances, because no tribute to Josephine Baker would be complete without both. I weave short snippets of songs between monologues I wrote and rewrote over the course of the semester. I recall telling Thierry outside the Panthéon earlier in the semester that I don't always have the words for the sensations I feel, but there's always a song for them. The recollection makes my heart swell as I sing "Paris, Paris," feeling carried away by the happy lilt of the music.

Though I planned for a thirty-minute performance total, between needing to take water breaks, costume changes, and the thunderous applause at the end of each number, I'm inching closer to thirty-five. I go back onstage for my second act clad in a trench coat and sunglasses, to tell the story of Baker's time as a spy for the French Resistance, clutching sheet music that I drew with hidden messages in the lines. The audience responds to the story with satisfying gasps that give me energy as I carry on.

For the last act, the part of the performance that took me the longest to write and be satisfied with, I speak of Baker's loves. I tell the audience of her love of art, her love of chosen country, and her many partners and children.

Somewhere in the middle of that monologue, a truth hits me like a ton of bricks: Love was never a distraction for my idol. She not only embraced it, she ran into it headfirst. It made her a stronger artist, and a beautifully complicated human. There was enough space in her heart for so much of it, too. Love was only a wondrous addition to her already full and vibrant life.

Before I realize it's happening, I say as much to the crowd, departing a little from my script and finding that a couple of tears have trickled down my cheeks. I can't make out anyone in the crowd with the lights blinding me, but I feel my stomach settle, knowing that the person I want to lock eyes with is there, cheering me on.

When I finally make it to my last song of the show, "J'ai Deux Amours," I feel it in my core. It radiates through my feet and to the top of my head. The first time I sang this song in Paris, I hadn't yet opened myself up to nearly enough experiences to truly internalize how much it meant to me. Trying to run from Paris and Thierry was my attempt to flee from how afraid I was of such big emotions. But now, with my arms open wide toward the crowd, I have finally made space for both the love I expected—Paris—and the one I tried to deny all semester.

The lights go down, and as the audience cheers, I can't help but feel like I've made a lot of people proud—most importantly, myself.

My heart is still racing when I rush from backstage to the auditorium's small atrium. When I round the corner and nearly barrel into a huge crowd of my classmates, they break into applause again. The standing ovation was overwhelming, and tears ran down my face in spite of myself when I saw Thierry and Nora in the front row clapping and calling "Brava!"

"Whitney, that was wonderful," a girl—Hyunyoung—from my literature class says, barely able to make her soft voice heard over the applause.

Others follow suit, coming up to me to offer their congratulations and praise. My cheeks ache from all the smiling, but I can't stop.

Eventually Monsieur Laurent makes his way over, his pride clear on his face.

"That was very, very good!" he says, nodding so hard his glasses slide down his nose and his bun of curly hair bobbles on his head. "I am so glad you are feeling better and decided to stay. We would have missed such a fantastic performance if you had left early."

"Merci, Monsieur Laurent, c'est très gentil," I say, beaming up at him. "Did I pass?"

Monsieur Laurent appears baffled for a moment; then, as what I am asking clicks, he breaks into a boisterous laugh that makes a few of the students standing behind him turn.

"Did you really think you would fail?" he asks.

"I don't know," I say, shrugging. "I didn't want to be presumptuous!"

"An A plus," Monsieur Laurent assures me. I think my heart might burst from the satisfaction.

"You are definitely my favorite teacher," I tell him. "Thanks for everything."

Monsieur Laurent scratches the bridge of his nose, a spot that makes me think he might be trying to discreetly wipe away a tear. A few seconds pass before he gathers himself.

"Merci," he says finally. "You will send me the final copy of your project—the script—tomorrow, yes?"

"Oui, oui, bien sûr," I tell him, and he claps me on the shoulder one time before moving on. As soon as he leaves, I'm attacked by a flash of blond hair, and I'm pulled into a massive hug.

"You were so good!" Nora tells me, pulling back and grasping both of my shoulders. "I don't understand, you are always good, but today it was so different!"

I know what she means. It's the audience. I feed off the energy of the crowd. When I get responses from the audience, I find ways to dig deeper and pull more out. I've been like that since I was little.

Sophie appears next to Nora, and I quickly embrace her, too, thanking her for running my board.

"You were amazing!" Nora continues to gush, her blue eyes electric as she remembers the performance. "I laughed and cried and held my breath. You are so talented, ma chérie."

"Oui, elle est très douée." Another voice joins the fray over Nora's left shoulder, and I see Thierry, who has apparently been patiently waiting his turn to talk to me. The folks around me part, and it's like stage curtains opening to reveal the best of my life, which is not staged at all. He's carting his gym bag over his shoulder, so I know he's on his way to soccer practice. His coaches reinstated him shortly after receiving my review, and I've been spending chilly afternoons out by the field waiting for his breaks to get a few kisses. I consider trying to hurry this process up so he can get to practice, but the only thing Thierry seems impatient about giving me is whatever he's hiding behind his back.

With a flourish, he produces a bouquet of red roses wrapped in butcher paper and holds it out to me with a sly grin.

"Pour ma princesse," he jokes. I accept the bouquet but whack him lightly with it. Who would have known la princesse américaine would end up like this?

"Do you have time for a quick walk with me before practice?" I ask, lacing my free fingers with Thierry's.

"Always," he replies, bringing my hand to his lips to kiss it gently.

We wave goodbye to everyone as we leave the theater and then head off on a small circuit around the campus, heading toward the large path with loose gravel that has the dormitory building on one end and the main boulevard on the other.

I smile, but it's tinged with sadness.

"Or until the end of next week . . . ," I say. I peek over at him, not enough to see his whole face, just his mouth, which is sealed shut in a line, and his neck as he swallows. "I mean . . . did we do all this just for me to leave next week?"

Thierry finally stops walking, the gravel no longer crunching under his feet, and he gently pulls my hand so I'll stop and face him.

"Did you know Célestine is planning to study abroad in Baltimore this spring?" Thierry asks me, his brown eyes on me.

"I did not, but I'm not seeing how this is relevant, Your Honor," I reply in my best DC lawyer voice.

"It is relevant because with the shop, my parents will not be able to get away much to go visit her . . . ," he says, letting his voice trail off. I'm starting to make the connection, but I won't allow my heart to fill with hopefulness yet. Baltimore is only a short train ride from DC. . . .

"They're sending you in their stead?" I ask tentatively, and when Thierry nods, I cover my mouth.

"At least a couple of times," Thierry says. "And one time will be for at least two weeks, as my dad wants me to look at a few locations for an expansion of Chocolat Doré there and take some pictures for him."

"Ooh, so you'll be like a chocolate spy in America?" I ask, leaning toward him. "Josephine Baker would approve." But then something else catches my attention. The pride in his voice when he talks about the business trip his stepfather will be sending him on . . . the way he said "Dad."

"'Dad'?" I ask with an inquisitive smile.

"I decided to take a page from your book and be brave and just talk to him. We had a good chat recently," Thierry tells me with a small, sheepish smile. "So good, in fact, that he said I can have a summer job when we open the DC location . . . if I want."

This is the moment I explode with excitement.

"I hope you said YES!" I squeal, losing my flowers and throwing my arms around him, causing him to drop his gym bag off his shoulder and nearly lose his balance.

"Of course I did," Thierry says with a laugh, a vibration that I feel in my heart because our chests are close together. The golden early-evening sunlight hits his skin and makes it glow in a way that makes me want to touch it, but unlike the first time I noticed it, this time I actually can. I run my fingers along his jaw and smile. "You will have to show me DC the way I showed you Paris."

"I want nothing more," I say, planting a kiss on his lips. Even though I'm caught in an embrace, I push gently against his chest. "We can absolutely do this. A whole summer together, visits this spring, and we have video chats and texting for in between."

Thierry adjusts his arms around me—as if I'd dream of

leaving this moment. "And something tells me you may also like love letters."

"A form matched only by the pro-con list," I laugh. "Actually, don't tell my lists, but I think love letters might be superior."

I think back to how this all started—before my friends, my school, my performances . . . Thierry—when Monsieur Polignac asked incredulously if I planned to see Paris by list. How I laughed.

But he was right all along.

The only way to do Paris is not by list, but by love.

How I, Whitney Curry, Did Paris Like a Pro

1. Worked on my French every day. Talked to people in French when I went out. Didn't get discouraged if they spoke back to me in English. Practice makes progress.
2. Made some friends, even though it took a while. Forgave them when necessary; they forgave me, too.
3. Leaned into my adventurous spirit. Wandered. Went off the beaten path. Saw things that aren't in the tourist guides.
4. Found a way to preserve my memories in a photo album filled with Polaroids.
5. Bought an extra suitcase for all the various trinkets I amassed. (And for all the excellent clothes.)
6. Danced at every occasion.

7. Found an excuse to have a good party and bring people together.
8. Let people help me. When I was lost, or homesick, or really needed someone to do my hair or help run my one-woman show, I let them.
9. Delighted in the many unexpected, unplanned moments I had. You never know who you may meet on the streets of Paris.
10. Learned to be open to falling in love—with the city, with the food . . . even with a grumpy someone who I didn't see coming.

ACKNOWLEDGMENTS

Glory and honor to God for every blessing, especially my favorite one: giving me to the best parents anyone could ever ask for. Eric and Faye Stringfield, y'all are my favorite people in the entire world. Thank you for everything you have done—all the encouragement, all the experiences, all the support you have given me over my life. None of this would be possible without you. To my favorite writing assistant, Genghis Khan, who often reminds me that you do in fact need to leave the computer sometimes for treats: you are the best boy.

Leah Pierre, my agent and my friend, I appreciate you for being my biggest cheerleader and advocate. I couldn't ask for a better person to navigate publishing with. Dhonielle Clayton, I'm grateful you saw something in my words and wanted to create something with me. To the Cake Creative/Electric Postcard Entertainment Team—Clay, Haneen, and Carlyn—thank you for all the support. To Connolly Bottum, I appreciate you for always seeing and honoring Whitney with your edits. To the Joy Revolution team, David and Nicola Yoon and Bria Ragin, thank you for your editorial time and attention, and for taking on this series. Thanks to Wendy Loggia, Beverly Horowitz, and Barbara Marcus, who ultimately gave *Love Requires Chocolate* and the rest of the Love in Translation series a shot. And of course, thank you to all the various hands in production and design who made this book possible: Liz Dresner, Kenneth Crossland, Hannah Hill, Shameiza Ally, and Colleen Fellingham.

I cannot write a book that is effectively a love letter to Francophile Black girls without shouting out to those who fostered that love in me over the years. Thank you to Madame Vinet, who introduced me to French. Thank you to Madame Moyer and Madame Seavey, my high school French teachers, who encouraged my creativity.

So much of my deep love for the French language and culture is a direct result of my experiences with the University of Virginia French Department and my time living in La Maison Française (The French House) from 2013 to 2016, with a number of my friends, but especially Khanh, Radobice, Linda, Jacqueline, and Caroline. Thank you to the professors—Professeurs Tsien, Dramé, Lyons, Kreuger, and McGrady—who left quite an impression on me. Professeur Horne, thank you for your kindness to me on our study abroad to Lyon. Last, but certainly not least, to Professeur Ari Blatt: thank you for teaching me in at least three classes, for being the person to tell me I could actually study comic books, for directing my undergraduate thesis and being a great advisor, and, of course, for accepting me on my first study-abroad trip to Paris.

To the sister circle—Micah Ariel Watson, Kelsey Watkins, Chardé Reid, Leah Franklin, and Alexis Richardson Pagnia—I love y'all for making space for my every dream, and for catching me when I faltered and setting me back on my path. Thank you for never being more than a text away.

To the TV Twitter Team—I truly do not know where I would be without y'all. Can't wait for our next *Avatar: The Last Airbender* watch. To my writer friends—especially H. D. Hunter and Taylor Harris—thanks for letting me bug you with all manner of questions about the publishing process. To my UVA/William & Mary/University of Richmond folks—Professor Harold, Dean Gregory, and Ms. Cathy; Chris, Cameron, and Ellie; Jennifer; Jessica; Khanh; Dr. Losh; Justin and Sam; Tim; Robin—thank you all for always believing in me.

To the many fantastic teachers from whom I have been blessed to learn, and the students with whom I have had the honor of building community: you all are my motivation. But I am nothing without the love and support of so many friends and family members, who I won't list, only out of fear of missing someone, as I inevitably will, but know I love you deeply.

ABOUT THE AUTHOR

Ravynn K. Stringfield is a writer and professor originally from Suffolk, Virginia. Her creative nonfiction has appeared in publications such as *Shondaland, ZORA,* and *Catapult Magazine. Love Requires Chocolate* is her debut novel. She can often be found haunting coffee shops in search of the perfect hazelnut latte, knee-deep in art supplies, or curled up with her dog, Genghis, telling him about her Lois Lane obsession.

ravynnkstringfield.com